CONATION

Open your eyes...

Rick Johnson

Copyright © 2020 Rick Johnson

All rights reserved

The characters and events portrayed in this book are fictitious. Any similarity to real persons, living or dead, is coincidental and not intended by the author.

No part of this book may be reproduced, or stored in a retrieval system, or transmitted in any form or by any means, electronic, mechanical, photocopying, recording, or otherwise, without express written permission of the publisher.

ISBN-13: 9798614396848

Cover design by: Art Painter
Library of Congress Control Number: 2018675309
Printed in the United States of America

CONTENTS

Title Page	1
Copyright	2
PROLOGUE	7
CHAPTER ONE	10
CHAPTER TWO	16
CHAPTER THREE	23
CHAPTER FOUR	31
CHAPTER FIVE	38
CHAPTER SIX	44
CHAPTER SEVEN	53
CHAPTER EIGHT	59
CHAPTER NINE	68
CHAPTER TEN	78
CHAPTER ELEVEN	84
CHAPTER TWELVE	93
CHAPTER THIRTEEN	100
CHAPTER FOURTEEN	106
CHAPTER FIFTEEN	112
CHAPTER SIXTEEN	120
CHAPTER SEVENTEEN	125
CHAPTER EIGHTEEN	134

CHAPTER NINETEEN	140
CHAPTER TWENTY	149
CHAPTER TWENTY-ONE	158
CHAPTER TWENTY-TWO	166
CHAPTER TWENTY-THREE	176
CHAPTER TWENTY-FOUR	185
CHAPTER TWENTY-FIVE	189
CHAPTER TWENTY-SIX	195
CHAPTER TWENTY-SEVEN	202
CHAPTER TWENTY-EIGHT	208
CHAPTER TWENTY-NINE	213
CHAPTER THIRTY	219
CHAPTER THIRTY-ONE	227
CHAPTER THIRTY-TWO	236
DISCUSSION TOPICS	244
Acknowledgement	249
Books By This Author	251
About The Author	253

PROLOGUE

High above a clearing, a black raven circles the misty forest treeline, and then cries out. A short, stocky woman with braided salt and pepper hair, and a brown, wizened face, stops digging in the earth to glance up at the grey-white sky. The raven flaps its glossy wings and cries out again—this time, it sounds almost like a human baby. Startled, Itzamna rocks back on her heels and drops the trowel from her hands. Rich, dark soil trickles through her calloused fingers, as she squints her amber eyes and peers at the raven orbiting overhead.

The wind begins to whistle in Itzamna's ears, and then gradually morphs into the familiar sounds of her Ancestors chanting and singing. Their voices reverberate in her head—louder, louder, and louder, until her body begins to shake with the power of the rhythmic energy. Itzamna's soil-stained fingers pull her woolen wrap tightly across her collarbones. She closes her eyes, raises her thumb to touch her forehead, and then suddenly falls to the ground—flat on her back, still as stone. The raven cries out again.

◆ ◆ ◆

Itzamna opens her eyes. She is floating in the shadows above a white, medical operating room, witnessing a scene unfolding below. The chanting of her Ancestors hushes, continuing as a soft whisper in her ears. Itzamna watches as a swaddled, crying newborn is lain face down and strapped to a surgical table.

The baby's flushed face rests in an opening in the table,

which allows her to breathe freely while the back of her tiny neck is exposed. The operating room nurse swabs the porcelain skin below the downy hairline, sterilizing it. Then, she lifts a small syringe and injects it into the back of the baby's neck. The newborn shrieks her distress.

The doors to the operating room swing open and two doctors enter—an older man and a young woman. They are both wearing pale blue scrubs with an *IP* logo and surgical masks and are holding their freshly sterilized hands high in the air. The older doctor, with bushy, gray eyebrows, nods to the nurse. She gloves the two doctors, and then hands the older doctor a scalpel.

"You injected the numbing solution, yes?" he asks, gruffly.

The nurse nods. "Yes, Doctor."

The older doctor turns to the younger one. "As you know, the infant must be awake during implantation and fusion. The numbing solution takes most of the pain away—not all, but most. Don't worry, she won't remember any of it."

As if on cue, the baby wails even louder, and the younger doctor winces. The older one shakes his head. "Can you believe parents used to have to listen to this stressful racket all the time? Thank The Order for biochemical technology and neuroprocessor chips. No more crime, no more social or economic instability, no more... *this*," he says, gesturing to the distressed infant. "Just clear purpose and emotionally contained citizens. Of course, we don't discuss *that* particular aspect of neuroprocessor technology outside of the Implantation Program." He gives the nurse and younger doctor a stern look. Both nod vigorously in agreement.

The older doctor begins to chuckle. "When I first started with the program, it took a full year for the neuroprocessor chips to fuse with the brain."

The younger doctor's eyes widen. "An entire year?"

The older one nods, still chuckling, "I know, I know, can you imagine? Now it only takes a few hours. Technology—it's amazing!" He gently pats the crying baby's back. "Relief is coming. You'll be serene soon enough, little one. What's her name?"

The nurse responds, "Ren. Ren Sterling."

"Ren, soon, you'll be another citizen ready to contribute to The Order." He lowers the scalpel and cuts into the infant's neck. She screams.

◆ ◆ ◆

The raven screams from its perch on a tree-top branch. Itzamna's eyes open. The chanting in her ears has stopped, leaving only the sound of wind rustling through the evergreens. Itzamna rises from the damp ground just in time to see the raven take flight toward Caracol, the Naturals' village. Gripping her woolen wrap in her wrinkled, brown hand, Itzamna strides quickly away from her garden, across the clearing, and through the woods—following the raven's path.

◆ ◆ ◆

The dim sun is higher in the sky now and is slowly burning off the grey mist. Two women are sitting on a decaying log. The elder, Chimalis—a tall, lanky woman with smooth, light brown skin and graying hair—chews on a leaf as she tends to the dwindling fire. She sets another log on, and then stoops low to the earth, blowing on the embers. The younger woman, Sora—with a strong, angular face and muscular build—coos to the month-old baby in her arms, nursing her under the warmth of a woolen poncho. In the distance sits a cluster of sturdy, small huts built mostly from earth and wood.

Itzamna emerges from the trees. "Sisters," she says. Chimalis and Sora look up at Itzamna expectantly. "The Prophecy has begun. The One that will lead the non-Naturals to freedom has been born."

CHAPTER ONE

It's night and it's raining. I'm standing in the middle of a street in Capitol City, only it's a street I don't recognize. There's chaos all around me—people are screaming, running, and breaking store front windows. Black smoke billows from several buildings, and just a few feet away from me a vehicle is on fire. My throat and eyes begin burning from the acrid smoke. I can't see more than a few feet in front of me.

    I wake up, gasping for breath, and sit straight up in bed. Raising a hand to my pounding chest, I can feel that my pink flannel PJ's are wet. I'm soaked with sweat. I blink my eyes to make sure my bedroom is real. "I'm home, I'm safe, I'm okay, it was just a bad dream," I tell myself, and begin rubbing the back of my neck with slow, calming circles.

    Piper, my fluffy, white Maltese dog, wags his tail at me sleepily from the foot of my bed and yawns. I take a deep breath and slowly exhale. Eventually, my heart stops pounding. The white sheets beneath me are also soaked with sweat. Gross. I slide off my bed onto the dark wood floor.

    "Piper, get down," I command. Piper just wags at me, but I nudge him until he hops down, and then I strip off my sheets—piling them by my bedroom door. I pad barefooted to my bathroom, which I painted my favorite color, apple green, two years ago, when we first moved into this house. My neuroprocessor is still turned off, so I flip on the light manually, and then turn on the shower. Climbing out of my damp pajamas, I stare at the dark circles under my indigo eyes in the steamy mirror. I'm not used to looking so tired.

    I pull back my long, light brown hair into a ponytail,

step into the hot water, and then position myself and my hair so that it can pound on my tense shoulders without getting my hair wet. I drop my chin to my chest and I close my eyes. I'm exhausted from not getting enough sleep.

I'd never even heard of nightmares before I started having them several months ago, and now I have them almost every night. Dad says not to worry—that it's just my fluctuating hormones affecting my neuroprocessor, and everything will settle down eventually, but until then ... lucky me, I guess. I turn off the water, grab a fluffy green towel, and then wrap myself up tight. A little chilled, I sprint across the wood floor, jump on my bed, and then dive under my downy, white comforter as fast as I can. Piper thinks we're playing a game, so he runs and jumps on the bed too. He licks at the water beaded on my arms, making me giggle. Piper always makes me feel better. He burrows into the comforter, flips onto his back, and snuggles against me.

As I rub Piper's little pink belly for a few moments, a strange sensation begins on the back of my neck where my neuroprocessor is implanted. It... starts to burn. I try stretching my neck to ease the discomfort, but the burning becomes even more painful. In the center of my forehead, another sensation begins. It feels like pressure, as if someone is trying to push my head backward, *hard*. So hard, in fact, I can't fight it. At the same time, I hear a whistling sound. It's faint at first, but it becomes louder and starts to sound like... chanting... singing? Overwhelmed, I fall back on my bed and close my eyes.

◆ ◆ ◆

I'm running on a soccer field with my best friend, Noelle Gracely. It's night, and it's not a field I've seen before. The sky is clear and the air is chilly. I can see my breath as we're practicing drills. Noelle's curly, dark brown ponytail bounces as she passes me the ball. I kick, but the ball shoots past me, and Noelle and I start giggling. The ball keeps rolling, so I chase after it as fast as I can. Suddenly, a sound of a massive explosion erupts in the distance. The ground shakes and a huge fireball launches across the starry night sky above us. I hit the turf chin first, skidding several feet.

Bruised, with the wind knocked out of me, I glance up. My dad is standing before me, covered in ashes from head to toe. "Dad?! Are you okay?" I ask. He smiles sadly, and then turns and walks away. "Dad! DAD!" I call after him, but he disappears into the haze of smoke enveloping the field.

◆ ◆ ◆

My eyes open, and I'm staring at my bedroom ceiling again—not a night sky, not a soccer field. It's quiet. I no longer hear the chanting. The pressure on my forehead is gone, and the burning at the back of my neck is dissipating. What was *that*? Did I fall back asleep and not know it? I glance over at Piper. He's still in the same position with his belly up, watching me and wagging his tail. I don't *think* I was asleep.

How long have I been lying here? With a quick, deliberate movement of my eyes, I activate my neuroprocessor. Up pops the time, date, and interior temperature—**6:50 AM, October 10, 2117, 69 degrees**. My neuroprocessor seems to be working just fine. As usual, my schedule for the day also appears in the top left corner of my vision. I drag it to the center of my sight, and then enlarge it. **First period: Study Hall**.

Thank The Order I have Study Hall first today! Noelle and I take it together, and she has a way of making me feel calm and normal when I'm having a hard time. I really wish these nightmares would stop already. Although, I don't know what you'd call the thing I just had, since I wasn't asleep. A *daymare,* maybe?

With a thought and a blink, I send a message to Noelle: **"Hey. You up yet? I had really crazy dreams again last night."**

Her reply flashes in my eye. **"From Noelle: I'm up! Sorry about the dreams. Shake them off. We have a soccer game to-**

night. Get ready to kick some ass!"

As I laugh at Noelle's reply, her words flicker and dim. How strange. Until recently, my neuroprocessor has always worked perfectly. It's the third time this week it has flickered. I shake my head involuntarily, as if that will help. So annoying—there must be something wrong with it. I hope Dad has time to run some diagnostics on my processor before he leaves for work.

"From Noelle: What are you going to wear today?"
"Clothes." I reply.
"From Noelle: Ha Ha, very funny."

I jump off my bed and hurry to my closet, staring at my options. I wonder if I'll see Zian today. I hope so. Officially, he's just a friend, but secretly I have a serious crush on him. Zian usually joins Noelle and me for lunch, but lately he's been extra moody and distant. A message appears in my eyes and snaps me out of my ruminations.

"From Mom: Are you up, Ren? Breakfast is ready."
I send a message back: **"Coming!"**

I quickly slip on my favorite pair of jeans, a t-shirt, a sweater, and leather boots. October in the northern part of Cascadia can be chilly. As soon as I'm dressed, I sprint downstairs. Piper follows me, bouncing down each step. I rush into our white, modern kitchen, and then plunk myself down on a bar stool at the grey granite island. A bowl of steaming, hot oatmeal is waiting for me. There's one next to me for Tia, my younger sister, but Dad's place mat is empty.

"Is Dad sleeping in?" I ask my mom, hopefully, who is standing at the sink, rinsing dishes.

"He worked late at the Lab, then slept on the couch in his office," Mom replies as she unties the apron around her waist and dries her hands.

"Oh." I say, deflated.

Hearing the disappointment in my voice, Mom turns to me with a reassuring smile. "Your father is doing very important work for The Order, Ren. We have this beautiful house and comfortable lifestyle because of it." I nod my head—she's right, of course. My father is a Senior Researcher at Ash-Tech, and for the past two years he's been leading the latest government-sponsored neuroprocessor project. Under Dad's supervision, the processor continues to get smaller, faster, and better, while the applications become increasingly advanced. I'm so proud of how hard Dad works for The Order, I could burst, but I miss seeing him more.

I sigh. Mom rests her hand on my shoulder. "He'll be home for dinner tonight. You can talk to him after your game, okay? I'm going downstairs to work for a few minutes." She gives my shoulder a gentle squeeze, before heading down to her art studio in our basement.

Tia trudges down the stairs, grumbling, "Morning." She flops onto the bar stool next to me, and moans at the sight of oatmeal. "Again?" She sighs dramatically, leaning her fourteen-year-old face into her chin. Her face is made-up perfectly, and her long, blonde, sleek hair is pinned back with a headband. My younger sister is determined to become the most popular girl in the ninth grade. Tia's clothes—she has about twice as many as I do because she's always begging Mom to take her shopping—are more fashionable than comfortable or practical. Dad likes to joke that Tia should have been born into a Financier family, the segment of The Order that has the most money, because she's so good at spending it.

"You're wearing high-heeled boots to school? Really, Tia? You're only in ninth grade, who are you trying to impress?" I ask, rolling my eyes. I can't resist.

"What?!" Tia retorts huffily, just like I knew she would. "Not everybody can become Student Body President like you, Ren."

Fair enough. Although, it's not like there were a lot of people who could run—only the sixteen Foundation Team members can run for student government. Noelle is the one who convinced me to run for President. I didn't think I'd win, but.... I did.

A group communication from Mom interrupts us: **"From Mom: Hurry up! Clean your breakfast dishes. We leave in five."**

I rush to the sink, rinse my bowl, and then bound up the stairs two at a time, leaving grouchy Tia in my wake. I grab my backpack, quickly brush my teeth, and hurriedly apply some mascara and lip-gloss. I sprint back downstairs, pat Piper on the head goodbye, and then bolt out the front door.

Mom's got the car running in the driveway, but there's no sign of Tia yet. Typical of Tia—she's always late. I slide into the front passenger seat, and we wait. Frustrated, Mom finally honks the horn. Tia runs out the front door, and then trips on one of her high heels. She limps to our car, and tosses herself in, sighing.

"Nice boots," I say, snidely. I can't help it.

"Shut up," Tia snaps, giving me a dirty look. She tosses her long, blonde hair and stares out her window.

"Ren." Mom's voice has enough warning in it for me to know when to be quiet. I shut my mouth and stare out my window too. As we drive through our neighborhood, we pass all the other massive houses with perfectly manicured lawns. Too perfect, I always think, when we get to this point in the drive.

We live in a big, gated community exclusively for the Financiers and the Intelligencia. Our housing development's motto is *"Extraordinary houses flowing thoughtfully with nature,"* which, unlike Mom and Tia, I find oddly annoying. Houses can't "flow." Mom is *very* proud of the neighborhood, as is Tia. Honestly, I could care less about the fancy houses, I just like all the parks and hiking trails.

My family is part of the Intelligencia, the segment of The Order composed of people like my dad—academics, engineers, and researchers, mostly in the areas of technology and medicine. We moved in when Dad started working at Ash-Tech. I don't know why my neighborhood makes me feel uneasy—it's beautiful—but for some reason, it does. Then, just as quickly as it comes, the unsettled feeling dissipates, and I relax the rest of the ride to school.

CHAPTER TWO

Mom pulls our car up to the drop-off zone in front of Pittock High School. "Have a great day, girls," she chirps cheerfully. Tia nods, and wobbles a little as she climbs out of the car. She slams the door and walks away as quickly as she can in those towering boots, disappearing into the mass of bodies entering Pittock. I lean over and give Mom a gentle squeeze on her shoulder.

"Thanks for the ride, Mom," I say, as I open my door and grab my backpack.

"Be nice to your sister... and have a great game!" Mom calls out, getting in her last bit of mothering as I close the door.

"Okay!" I shout, as I sling my backpack over my shoulder and join the throng entering the school. Pittock High sits right next to the Ash-Tech campus on a large hill overlooking downtown Capitol City. I love that I'm so close to where my dad works. I know it's silly, but sometimes I stare over at the Ash-Tech buildings to see if I can catch a glimpse of him. I haven't seen him yet.

Although most of the school was built only about forty years ago, Pittock High appears much older, with its distinguished grey slate roof and red brick exterior, partly covered in ivy. I can't lie, I have school pride. Pittock is Capital City's best high school, named after Pittock Mansion, the original building for the school. We have the brightest, most dedicated teachers in the City, and the most advanced tech available in our classrooms. The only downside to Pittock is that there's a lot of academic pressure. Students are expected to take as many advanced placement classes as possible, receive excellent grades, and then continue their studies at the best colleges in Cascadia.

Financier and Intelligencia teenagers living in Capitol City attend Pittock High. Financier kids are recognizable by their expensive, flashy clothes and cars, as well as their crazy hairstyles—the bigger, the better as far as they're concerned. Financiers are also super competitive in both academics and sports—cut-throat even. I'm glad I'm not a Financier; it's too much pressure. Intelligencia kids tend to dress more modestly than the Financiers. Most of us— excluding Tia—aren't as interested in material things like the latest fashion in clothes, because we come from families that value ideas more than money.

As I trot up the stone front steps of the school and through the open doors with the rest of the masses, I easily spot tall, curly-haired Noelle wearing black athletic pants and a black and white zip-up jacket. Like me, Noelle's hair is always pulled back into a ponytail. Neither of us can stand having hair in our faces. "Hey, what's up?" I ask.

"Not much. I'm just pumped about our soccer game tonight. Rawr!" Noelle growls as she flexes her muscular arms. I give her bicep a squeeze.

"Rock solid!" I laugh, and then sigh. "I'm excited too, but I'm tired. I had another nightmare, well... two, and then, get this —my processor flickered again this morning! Annoying, right? I want to stop by Tech Lab during study period to get it checked."

"Sorry about the nightmares, Ren," Noelle replies. "I slept great!" she confesses, with an apologetic laugh.

"I hate you," I say sarcastically.

Noelle laughs. "Maybe your processor is malfunctioning? Want me to come with you to Tech Lab? I've finished my homework—no need for Study Hall."

"Yea sure, I just need to stop by my locker first."

"Me too," Noelle replies, as we stroll down the hall together. We both send messages to our Study Hall teacher, Mrs. Dunn, letting her know that we need to go to Tech Lab to speak with Mr. Johns about my neuroprocessor.

"**No problem,**" Mrs. Dunn responds immediately.

I reach the row of shiny metal lockers, and then use my

neuroprocessor to enter my security code. My locker door releases with a click. As I slide my backpack inside, I spy a small piece of white paper taped to the top shelf. It has one word written on it, 'Conation', and some sort of symbol... a wide-open eye. I lift the paper, and stare at it. How strange. Is this some sort of prank? I direct my neuroprocessor to search for the definition of *Conation*. **"Conation: An inclination or impulse to act purposefully and intentionally; volition. Pronounced: kō-nā-shən"** appears in the center of my vision. Suddenly, it feels like my stomach has dropped to my toes, only I don't know why. I wince and put my hand on my belly.

Noelle rushes across the hallway. "Are you okay, Ren?" she asks.

I always tell Noelle everything, but for some odd reason I feel like I really shouldn't tell anyone about this. I stuff the paper into my pocket and lie. "I'm okay, Noelle, just tired. Let's go to Tech Lab."

Noelle wraps her arm around my shoulder. "You look pale. Are you sure?" she asks.

"It's okay, I'm fine," I reply, and smile—trying to be as convincing as possible.

My thoughts are rapid-fire as Noelle and I stride down the hall toward Tech Lab. Who put the paper in my locker? Why does it say 'Conation'? *An inclination or impulse to act purposefully and intentionally...* What does *that* mean? What does the symbol represent? How did someone get into my locker? Is this a joke, a prank for the new Student Body President? I feel uneasy, and my stomach is twisting in a way it never has before. I quickly scan the hallway, but I don't see anyone watching me and laughing.

The door to the Lab is wide open, and Mr. Johns, our balding Tech Lab teacher, is the only person there. He's sitting at his big wooden desk, engrossed in reading something on his neuroprocessor. Noelle clears her throat and Mr. Johns glances up, startled. "What can I do for you, girls?" asks Mr. Johns, adjusting his bow tie. "You're here awfully early this morning."

Suddenly, I feel better. Calm. I don't know what's happening to me—one minute I'm uncomfortable and the next, I'm fine. I stand, awkwardly, not quite knowing what to say. For a moment, I don't even remember why we're here. Noelle peers at me curiously, and then turns to Mr. Johns, replying matter-of-factly, "Ren's neuroprocessor flickered this morning. That's not supposed to happen, right?"

Okay, now I remember. I clear my throat, "Yes, it's happened three times this week."

The warm, inviting look on Mr. Johns' doughy face disappears, and is replaced with confusion, worry, and then, suspicion. "Tell me what you mean by *flickered*," he replies, squinting through his small, round glasses as he stares at my face.

Hesitantly, I answer, "Um... I was communicating with Noelle when it just... flickered. The words from her communication dimmed for just a few seconds, then everything brightened back to normal. It's probably nothing, but--"

"When did this happen, exactly?" Mr. Johns interrupts.

"I had just woken up."

My response seems to increase his concern. "Did anything happen before the flickering?" he asks, squinting his eyes even more.

I hesitate to respond at first. I have a strange feeling that I shouldn't say anything more... but then—just like before—I begin to feel calm again, so, I tell Mr. Johns the truth. "Yes, I had a nightmare. Would you scan my neuroprocessor to make sure it's still working properly?"

"NIGHTMARE?! No one has nightmares anymore, Ren!" Mr. Johns flushes, his voice rising. He stands and begins pacing, seeming almost... angry. Noelle turns to me, wide-eyed. Neither of us expected this reaction from Mr. Johns. Sheesh, if I tell him about the 'daymare', he'll probably have a heart attack. I guess I should have kept the nightmare thing to myself.

"Um, my dad says it's just my hormones affecting my neuroprocessor, and that eventually things will even out..." I sputter in reply, wishing I could just run out of the room. Mr.

Johns hurriedly pulls a neuroprocessor scanner from his desk, rushes over to me and holds the scanner to the back of my neck.

He mutters suspiciously, "What are the odds that Peter Sterling's daughter would be having *nightmares*?" The twisting feeling in the pit of my stomach returns. I really wish I hadn't said anything. He holds the small device over the back of my neck where the chip is implanted for about thirty seconds.

"All the metrics are normal. It's operating perfectly," Mr. Johns announces finally, smiling. I know he's trying to reassure me, but his face looks oddly tight. "I'm sure it was just some anomaly. You two better go ahead and get to your next class."

As Noelle and I head out into the hall, I glance back at Mr. Johns. He's still watching me with a pinched look on his face. I can tell that he's already communicating with someone on his neuroprocessor. He closes his classroom door abruptly with a bang, and I flinch.

"Are you sure you're okay?" Noelle asks.

Um… no, but whatever… "Yes… yes. Let's just go to class," I say.

❖ ❖ ❖

I desperately want to forget about Mr. Johns' odd reaction, but I can't. I find it nearly impossible to focus in Advanced Physics, or in Advanced Calculus class. Partially, because I'm distracted by the wild hairstyle of the Financier girl in front of me in Calculus. She has a myriad of bright colors swirling around her hair—teal blue, peach, royal blue, and neon green—pulled up into an intricate, multicolored bun on top of her head. The bun is mesmerizing to look at, but that's beside the point. I can't stop thinking about what happened this morning. Why did Mr. Johns react so strangely when he heard about my neuroprocessor flickering? Why was he so interested in my nightmare? Beyond worried, he seemed… angry… accusatory, even. That's the first time he's ever let on that he knows who my father is, which is odd. Also, who was he communicating with as soon as we left his office? Around and around, the same questions loop in my thoughts.

"Are you just gonna sit there, lazy?" Noelle asks. I look up to see Noelle standing over me, grinning. All the other students have filed out of the room. Embarrassed, I snap back to reality.

"Sorry!" I say, and quickly stand. I try to chat with Noelle as if everything is normal, but my thoughts are still racing as we walk into the lunchroom and sit down at the end of our usual table filled with senior-class Intelligencia. Just as I open my lunch bag, tall, broad-shouldered, dark-haired, blue-eyed Zian plunks down right next to me. My heart always beats a bit faster whenever I see him. I smile, but he just takes out a sandwich and starts eating. He's sullen and withdrawn—typical Zian.

"Hey. What's up, Zian?" asks Noelle as she nudges him under the table with her foot.

Zian shrugs and gives a strained smile. "Not much," he replies.

Zian Reddington—widely considered to be the hottest guy in school—is a bit of a mystery, really. He's a great athlete but doesn't play any sports. He could date almost any girl he wants but shows no interest. Except for hanging out with Noelle and me, he's mostly a loner and keeps to himself. He even keeps his neuroprocessor turned off most of the time, which is unusual—not only for the kids at school—but for absolutely everyone I know. It makes communicating with him impossible most of the time.

Like the other kids at our table, Zian's family is part of the Intelligencia. His father was a scientist and researcher at Ash-Tech until he died in a boating accident about five years ago, when Zian was in eighth grade. It was a sudden tragedy—one that's left a mark on him. He's careful never to get too close to anyone. Even though Noelle and I are his closest friends, Zian always seems to be holding back from us. We've learned to just give him space and not to expect too much from him.

"I need a refill of my drink. Anyone else need anything?" asks Noelle, as she hops up from the table.

"No thanks," I reply.

Zian shakes his head. He turns away and pops a piece of gum in his mouth. Just as I'm about to jump into the conversation about AP Physics occurring between Tonya Ferris and Pati Simms, two other Senior girls at our table, Zian gently touches my arm. An electric shock shoots through me. I turn toward him. His pale blue eyes peer deeply into mine. There's tenderness in his gaze. My heart beats even faster and I open my mouth to speak, but nothing comes out.

As soon as Noelle returns, Zian quickly removes his hand and looks away. I can feel my cheeks getting hot, flushing red. Noelle and I catch each other's eyes, and she gives me an inquisitive look. She knows that something just happened, but neither of us say anything.

"Did *you* understand what Mr. Rueben was saying in Physics this morning?" Pati leans across the table toward me, tucking her red curls behind her ears. Noelle replies, fielding Pati's question. Zian stands up from the table. He touches me softly on my shoulder and gazes at me again, making my entire body tingle. My cheeks become even hotter and redder. Ugh, stop, cheeks, before I look like a beet.

Zian leans over and whispers in my ear, "Stay strong, Ren. You need to stay strong." He quickly straightens up, grabs the remains of his lunch, and tosses it in the trash.

Wait, what? What did he mean by that? How does he know I've been having a hard time...? I open my mouth to ask, but he strides quickly across the lunchroom and disappears out the cafeteria door. Zian is as mysterious as always.

Noelle leans forward. "What was *that* about?" she asks quietly, so the others don't hear.

Puzzled, I shake my head. "I don't know."

CHAPTER THREE

"Why does The Order operate so efficiently?" Ms. Eyke, our inspirational Foundation Team teacher and Student Government mentor asks rhetorically, with her hands hooked into the pockets of her burgundy corduroy jacket. She smiles, flashing her dimples. "*Clear purpose.* It's clear purpose that The Order provides, which has made the greatest improvement to our nation—causing all crime and confusion to be virtually eliminated. Who can tell me about the Modern Dark Age, and the rise of The Order?" My hand shoots up instantly, almost robotically.

"Ren." Ms. Eyke calls on me.

"A hundred years ago the former United States of America was experiencing massive amounts of social change and unrest due to individual selfishness and a corrupt, ineffective government. The Modern Dark Age began right after the start of the Civil War II, in 2036, when several terrorist organizations detonated nuclear weapons, obliterating all the major cities on the East Coast as well as southern California, killing millions of people and destroying the habitability of much of the country.

In 2047, The Order was officially formed in what had been the Pacific Northwest of the United States. The former city of Portland, Oregon was declared the Capitol City of our new nation, Cascadia, which encompasses the habitable zone from what was Northern California to the Canadian border. The Founders of The Order envisioned our society returning to traditional family and social values and being built on the Four Pillars of its People: The Financiers, the Intelligencia, the Providers, and the Producers."

"Bravo, Miss Student Body President and Foundation

Team Captain, Ren! Yes! Precisely." Ms. Eyke's straight blonde hair bobs as she nods her head, and her dimples deepen even more.

I smile back. Ms. Eyke's smile is infectious. I love how she goes out of her way to praise and encourage all her students, and I love being on the Foundation Team. I feel lucky to be one of the sixteen students selected from Pittock to compete against other High School students across Cascadia about our knowledge of the founding of The Order!

"Of course, you all know about the Financiers and Intelligencia," Ms. Eyke continues, "but who can tell me what makes the third segment of The Order, the Providers, so important?"

Ms. Eyke scans the room and calls on Pati Simms, who is waving her hand. Patti is decidedly more confident in Foundation Team than Physics.

"It's because they're the most diverse segment—economically and racially—and they provide a multitude of services to us all." Pati answers, tucking her red curls behind her ear as she speaks.

"Well-said!" Ms. Eyke exclaims as Pati grins. "Yes. Providers are health care workers, lawyers, schoolteachers..." Ms. Eyke takes a quick bow before continuing. "Electricians, plumbers, small business owners, construction workers, artists... really any kind of service worker you can imagine. How well would The Order function without Providers? Not well at all!"

We all nod appreciatively. The end-of-class bell rings. Ms. Eyke holds up her hand to stop us from leaving immediately. "Your homework is to memorize your written responses to the competition questions. Next class, we'll break into four groups so you can focus on your assigned segment. Have a great rest of your day! I'm proud of you," she says.

Inspired and happy, I bounce out of class with my fellow teammates, but as soon as I enter the hallway, I suddenly remember the events of the morning—the daymare, my processor flickering, the piece of paper with Conation on it, Mr. Johns' angry reaction, and Zian's strange but encouraging words. My palms start to sweat, and my stomach begins to twist. Then, calm sets in once more. This is awful. Why am I so uncomfortable one minute, and then relaxed the next? It can't be just hormones. I'm beginning to think I'm losing my grip on reality.

◆ ◆ ◆

Finally, closing bell rings. I meet Noelle at the front entrance of the school, so we can walk to the shops close by and get something to eat while we work on homework. We always power up before soccer games. I order my usual vegetarian burrito, and Noelle chows down on her favorite—a chicken and rice bowl. Once our homework is complete and our stomachs are full, we hurry back to Pittock, and rush to the gym to get ready for the game.

Okay, I say "gym," but really, I should say "state-of-the-art stadium," with the best equipment and amenities of all the High Schools in Cascadia. Wealthy boosters fund our team. They also expect us to compete for the City and National Championships every year and win. No pressure, right?

Noelle and I hit the locker room, which is abuzz with excitement, and quickly change into our metallic blue and gold soccer uniforms with the Pittock High School (PHS) logo. Our uniforms are made from a downright amazing material that synchs with our neuroprocessors—giving our coaches, and us, real-time information about our heart rates, blood pressure, and hydration and energy levels. They look pretty bad ass, too.

A whistle blows and the locker room falls instantly silent. We all direct our attention to the front of the room, where our head coach is standing. Coach Cari is about to start her pregame speech, and she doesn't tolerate anything less than complete focus from every single one of us. She's not someone you'd ever want to cross. Muscular, with dirty blonde hair, Coach Cari paces slowly around the locker room while chomping on a piece of gum. She's always chewing gum.

"Now that I have everyone's attention, we can get down to business," she half-shouts. "Do I need to remind you ladies how important the game is today? Do I need to remind you of what's at stake?" She pauses dramatically for a moment before continuing, "This is the game that will either end our season or send us to the league championship game. I, for one, do not want this magical season to end. We've come too far to stop now. We know what we're capable of. We're ready for this game. Each one of you must contribute tonight, and you must do your best. That's the only way we'll win... Now, I've decided to make a few changes to the lineup, based on what I've been seeing in practice this week. Jen Duggins, I'm starting you as goalie. Noelle Gracely, I'm moving you from defense to midfield. Ren Sterling, I'm moving you into the starting lineup as a striker. I have a good feeling about this, Sterling. Tonight's your night."

The whole team turns and stares at me. I haven't been named as a starter in a game the entire season. I'm decent, and get playing time each game, but no one sees me as one of the most talented players on the team! My cheeks start to burn. I detest how easily I blush. It's so embarrassing.

"The complete lineup is posted on the wall," Coach Cari continues. "Play this game with the most focus and intensity you've ever had." Then Coach Cari pivots and looks directly into my eyes. "Make it the best game you've ever played. Now get out there and kick some ass!"

The locker room echoes with cheers and yells of excitement. Most of my teammates run over to check the lineup posted on the wall. In the middle of the chaos, Donna Royce and two other Financiers approach me. Donna's father is the President of the largest bank in Cascadia, and her family is extraordinarily wealthy. She's also one of the best players on the team. Donna leans over into my face and sneers, "You better not screw this up, Sterling." The other two Financier girls glare at me.

"Back off, Royce!" growls Noelle. She stands toe-to-toe with Donna, who shakes her blonde head dismissively and then slinks away with her two puppets trailing behind her.

"Don't let them intimidate you, Ren. You're a great player. Just do your best," Noelle says reassuringly, as she pats my upper arm.

I nod nervously. "Thanks for always having my back, Noelle."

She grins. "What are friends for?"

I smile back, and try to look confident, but my stomach feels fluttery and twisty again. We're about to play the best team in the Provider division. Their school is attended by working-class Providers, who are known for being very aggressive competitors. We all think they play dirty. I can't believe Coach Cari chose me to be a starter in such an important game. What is she thinking? Can this day get much weirder?

◆ ◆ ◆

The game is in Pittock High's stadium, which can hold up to 15,000 people. My heart is pounding as we sprint onto the field. The air is cool, but dry. I feel dizzy when I look up into the stands packed with screaming fans, and wince from the bright lights when I look out at the field. I don't know if I can handle this. "Don't screw up, Ren, just don't screw up," I tell myself.

Each one of our home games brings a sold-out crowd. This game, however, has added excitement because of the rivalry between our two schools and what's at stake. We've been told that government officials are going to be in attendance, in the exclusive luxury suites—which is just one more thing to worry about.

Noelle stands to the right of me as we stare at the packed stadium, taking it all in. "I hear that the President might be up there," she says.

Gah. Just what I need—more pressure. I can only manage to nod my head, because my mouth is too dry to speak. The referees blow their whistles, indicating that the game is about to begin. We rush together and form a huddle around Coach Cari on the sidelines. She shouts, "Okay ladies, I shouldn't have to remind you: Make sure your advanced soccer functions on your neuroprocessors are turned ON! Now, I want complete focus. Be aligned with your processors and with one another. No distractions. Hands in."

We huddle close. Coach Cari raises her voice even more. "I want focus. Smart play. Aggressive play. Be alert out there. The ball should be in their end of the field all night. Win—on three. One, two, three!" she shouts.

We all scream together, "Win! Win! Win!"

The game begins. I'm so nervous I feel like I might vomit. The constant yelling of the crowd and the bright stadium lights are so disorienting that I don't even know what's happening in the first few minutes of the game. Then suddenly, I'm calm and focused. Next thing I know, I'm running for the ball on the other team's side of the field. It's my chance to score. I'm running as fast as I can, side-by-side with a Provider player who is elbowing me as we run. I've got to get to the ball first.

I adjust my angle when my neuroprocessor sends me data about the distance and speed of the ball. My heart is pounding as I go to kick with all my strength. Just as my cleat touches the ball, though, the ground suddenly buckles beneath me, and the whole stadium shudders. BOOM! There is a deafening noise—an explosion. I'm knocked to the ground. I glance up, stunned, as a huge fireball shoots up into the air over the top of the stadium.

I try to stand, but suddenly another ear-piercing BOOM rocks the stadium, and another fireball shoots into the night sky. I clutch the turf with my fingers, ears ringing. I'm terrified! I don't know if I should run or stay put. The explosions, the fireballs—I've seen this before... I saw it happen in my "daymare"! I feel like I should know what to do, but I don't.

The referees blow their whistles to stop the game. Panic breaks out in the stands and on the field. Terrified people are trying to get out of the stadium, pushing down the aisles. Players are running around the field while others are sitting dazed on the turf. It's utter chaos, pandemonium.

"Do not leave your seats," the announcer orders over the loudspeaker. "Remain calm. The stadium is not damaged. Stay in your seats. We don't know what happened, but you are safer here. We will provide more information as soon as it becomes available. We repeat, remain in your seats." The crowd begins to calm somewhat. People stop pushing and return to their seats. The noise level begins to drop, though the ringing in my ears continues.

A government-sponsored news alert comes through our neuroprocessors. **"From Govt: An anti-government terrorist organization has just bombed the Ash-Tech corporate headquarters."**

What does that mean? Why would terrorists bomb Ash-Tech? Is my Dad okay? I run toward Noelle on the field, panicked. "What in The Order is going on?" I shout.

"I don't know! This is crazy!" Noelle shouts back.

Just then, another message flashes in my eyes. **"From Govt: Two bombs were detonated. One bomb targeted the main Ash-Tech building, while another blew up a transport vehicle."**

Everyone receives this information at the exact same time. There is a loud, collective gasp, followed by hushed voices. Then, the sound of mass questions and excited, worried talking fills the stadium. Noelle and I stand huddled together, with our arms linked. If this is just like the "daymare", my Dad should be appearing now, covered in ashes, but safe. I scan the soccer field. Where is he?

Then, a third communication appears. **"From Govt: Witnesses report the bombs detonated when a lead scientist at Ash-Tech entered his transport vehicle. Dr. Peter Sterling is missing and presumed dead, the sole apparent victim of a terrorist assassination."**

My knees buckle. Noelle tries to catch me, but I fall. I can't breathe. My chest feels like it's caving in as my heart is being ripped right out of it. The ringing in my ears is drowned out by a wail that bursts out from deep within in my gut, throat, and torn-out heart. "NO, NO, NO. PLEASE, NOT MY DAD!" I howl. Then, the world turns sideways and goes dark.

CHAPTER FOUR

My eyes open. I'm lying on my left side, and the turf is pressing into my cheek. I don't know how long I've been here. Everything around me seems to be moving in slow motion, as if I'm underwater. I look up into a sea of faces staring down at me. The lights of the stadium are blinding. Shrieking emergency sirens pierce the air. I can't think. I'm having trouble catching my breath. Then I remember, and my heart feels like it's been pulled straight out of my chest, and then ripped in two: Dad is dead.

Suddenly, I'm being pulled to my feet by two sets of strong hands. It's Noelle and Coach Cari. They swing my arms over their shoulders, pushing their way through my teammates, who have crowded around me. "Give us room!" yells Coach Cari. My legs are so wobbly, I can barely walk. Noelle and Coach Cari carry me from the field through the chaos. This feels like one of my nightmares.

"Please wake up. Wake up." I mutter to myself.

As Noelle and Coach Cari guide me outside the stadium, I hear someone shout, "The ambulance is here. Does she need medical treatment?"

Coach Cari hesitates as she receives a message on her neuroprocessor, and then hollers back, "No! She's not hurt. I'm bringing her to her mother right now!"

A man dressed in a crisp, black Government uniform appears and motions for us to follow him. Coach Cari and Noelle help me toward a glossy, black Government vehicle. The Government agent swings open the backdoor of the car as we approach. Coach and Noelle help slide me into the backseat, where my mother and sister are clinging to each other and crying. I lunge for them and we become a mass of wailing bodies as the vehicle speeds away.

"Why would anyone want to hurt Dad?" Tia cries, clinging to Mom.

Mom appears haggard—older than I've ever seen her, as if she just aged ten years in a day. "Who in the world would do this? How could terrorists detonate bombs? This makes no sense. Isn't The Order supposed to protect us from terrorists?" Mom's voice breaks as she questions no one in particular.

Dropping my head into my hands, all I can think about is how much I wish I could wake up from this nightmare. Eventually, when I look up again, I can see that we've been driven into our gated community, and news reporters line both sides of our driveway. As soon as we park, the two Government agents who drove us home exit the vehicle and open both rear doors. Mom, Tia and I climb out. The agents hurriedly escort us up our front stairs and into the house while reporters snap pictures.

"Officials will be here shortly to meet with you," one of the agents says gruffly. The other agent adds, a little more gently, "Don't worry, we'll be standing guard on your front porch." They close our front door on their way out, leaving us in a dark and silent house, except for the lights from the reporters' vehicles, which are streaming in through our windows. Neither Tia or Mom move a muscle, so I flip on a few lights in the house with my neuroprocessor, and then guide them to the kitchen. The three of us slowly sit at our white kitchen table, staring at each other, in shock.

"What are we supposed to do now?" Tia asks in a hoarse voice.

"Wait, I guess," I manage to reply. "Someone from the Government will be coming to speak with us." Piper bounds into the kitchen through his doggie door, wagging his tail. He licks my leg hello. I rest my hand on his head, grateful for his comfort.

"What are they going to tell us? That Dad is dead? I don't want to hear that!" Tia angrily exclaims. Mom is silent. Tears slide down her cheeks, and her shoulders shake. Tia continues shrilly, her voice rising. "What happened? Who did this? What's going to happen to us? Will we still get to live in this house? Is Dad really dead? Do you think they made a mistake? Maybe they're wrong, maybe Dad is still alive!"

Mom covers her ears, shouting, "Tia, stop it, WE DON'T KNOW! We don't know what happened!" Mom drops her face in her hands and sobs. Still agitated, Tia stands and paces. My neuroprocessor begins to light up with communications from family and friends expressing their support or wanting to know what happened. I just want it all to stop, for everything to be quiet, for this entire night to be just one of my bad dreams. Overwhelmed, I turn off my processor, and rest my head across my arms, on the table.

Piper suddenly growls, and then barks as three men enter our kitchen. Two are dressed in black government uniforms with the logo, *SED*, on them. A third man is wearing a long, black, leather trench coat. "Shhh, Piper be quiet! Sit," I command. Piper gives one last bark, and then sits obediently at my feet.

The tall, bald, muscular man in the leather trench coat steps forward and offers his hand to Mom. "My name is Special Agent John Rudy. I'm the Director of the Subversion Eradication Division. I'm sorry for your loss," he mumbles, with a flat affect. Mom nods, unable to look at him or speak. Tia sits down and stares at the table—mute.

I stand and offer my hand. "Please tell us what happened." I say, trying to keep my voice from cracking. I offer Agent Rudy the last empty chair at the kitchen table—my dad's chair. I stare as he sits, remembering the thousands of times Dad sat there, wishing with all my heart this bald man in the black coat was my father instead. I wrestle my thoughts back to the present moment and sit down, too.

Special Agent Rudy turns to Mom, who still can't look at him, and so, he pivots to me. "I can tell you what we know so far. At 5:37 P.M. this evening, two bombs were detonated at the Ash-

Tech corporate headquarters. One bomb destroyed the surveillance center, knocking out all electronic recordings of the front of the building and parking areas. The second bomb destroyed your father's car. We believe your father was in the vehicle," Agent Rudy reports, matter-of-factly.

Mom spontaneously releases an anguished sob, and then clasps her hands to her mouth. "No!" cries Tia and buries her face into Mom's shoulder.

Special Agent Rudy recoils slightly at the display of emotion, and then continues. "We don't have confirmation, however, because of the power of the blasts." Tia and Mom glance up, suddenly hopeful. I feel hopeful too. Could Dad still be alive?

"What do you mean you don't have confirmation? You mean, he might not have been in the explosion?" I quickly ask.

Special Agent Rudy gives a curt shake of his bald head. "The first blast destroyed the visual recording equipment. The second bomb incinerated the car into pieces of dust. Dr. Sterling was seen entering his vehicle by co-workers just before the explosions, but we won't know with 100% certainty until the dust fragments can be thoroughly tested. We'll compare the fragments to your husband's DNA," he says, with a faint shrug to his shoulders.

Mom, Tia, and I gasp in horror, our hopes dashed. A sob escapes from my mouth—I can't help it. Finally, when Mom speaks, her voice is hoarse and hollow. "How can this happen? Who would do such a thing?" she asks.

Agent Rudy stares at Mom for a moment, with his cold, gray eyes, and then asks, "Have you ever heard of *Conation*, Mrs. Sterling?"

A chill runs through me. My mom and sister slowly shake their heads from side to side. "No. What does it have to do with my husband?" Mom asks, puzzled.

"I have," my voice trembles as I reply. Agent Rudy says nothing—instead he turns to me, and stares right through me. My hands begin shaking and I feel like I'm going to be sick. "I'm not sure if this is important, but... there was a piece of paper taped inside my locker this morning. It had the word "Conation" on it. I just thought it was a prank or something," I mumble, hardly able to get the words out. "Did... did that paper have something to do with my dad's murder?" I ask, my voice barely a whisper.

Surprise, and then suspicion registers on Special Agent Rudy's face. He leans across the table. I can see he has a faint scar just above his right eye. He hasn't shaved in a few days, and I can smell stale coffee on his breath. "Did you see who put it in there? Do you know how it got there?" he spits the questions angrily into my face.

Taken aback by his anger, I shake my head. "No! It was just there when I opened my locker!"

He stands. "Think. This is VERY important! Did you see anything else? What else do you remember?"

"I opened my locker and the paper was there. That's it." I reply, raising my hands in a helpless gesture. My answer doesn't seem to appease him. Agent Rudy leans across the table further, and stares icily into my eyes.

"Have you heard the word 'Conation' before seeing it in your locker today?" Is he asking or accusing? It's difficult to tell by his tone.

I shake my head again, my voice trembling as I reply, "I've never heard of it before, Sir. I'm sorry. I truly don't know anything." Special Agent Rudy's upper lip curls in a sneer. He spins away from me abruptly, and nods to one of the other men wearing a black SED uniform, who steps forward.

"My name is Agent Greene. I've been working on the Conation file for some time now. Let me give you a bit of background. Conation is the name of a terrorist organization focused on subverting government technological advances. They presumably targeted your husband because of his position at Ash-Tech and his work on neuroprocessor technology. We've been tracking them for several years, although we still don't know very much about them. Anything you can tell us would be extremely useful." Agent Greene presses his thin lips together and gives a curt nod.

"Terrorists? That makes no sense. Why would anyone want to subvert our technology?" Mom asks, bewildered, as she raises her trembling hand to her mouth. "Are *we* safe?" she asks, gesturing to Tia and me.

As Agent Greene nods, his auburn hair flops around his forehead. "We believe your husband was the only target at this time," he replies, as he shoves his hands into the pockets of his black uniform. There's a weighted silence as we try to digest all that's been said.

Finally, Special Agent Rudy begins buttoning up his coat. "We should go and let you folks get some rest. We'll continue this discussion as soon we know more," he says briskly. Agent Greene and the other man turn and leave immediately. Special Agent Rudy pauses, grabbing my arm. "If you remember any details, Ren, let me know. The terrorists will strike again." His words send a send a chill down my spine.

I recoil from his touch. I can't help it. He lets go of my arm and finishes buttoning his trench coat. "Contact me if you can remember anything, no matter how small or seemingly insignificant. I've sent my contact information to your neuroprocessor." I nod my head in agreement, and he exits the kitchen. I immediately receive Agent Rudy's communication and add his information to my processor contact list.

Mom asks me with a trembling voice, "Ren Sterling, what else do you know? How could that piece of paper possibly get into your locked locker? Are some of your friends involved in this?"

Seriously? I shake my head. "Mom, I don't know anything! I'm telling you the truth. If I knew anything, of course I would tell you and the SED agents." I don't know why she's doubting me. We sit in silence for a long time. Eventually I get up and make some coffee, and then pour a cup for Mom. She sips the coffee and stares out the kitchen window.

Tia rests her head on the table and rakes her nails across

her legs. Tears stream down her cheeks—pain and fear racking her thin body. She looks over at Mom and whispers, "What are we going to do?" Mom doesn't respond. I think she might be in shock. I lean over and gently caress Tia's head. She sits up and collapses into my arms. We hold each other, rocking gently while we cry. Eventually, when I can't cry anymore, I stand, kiss Mom's soft cheek, and wrap my arm around Tia. I walk her to her room, tuck her into bed, and rub her back until she falls asleep—like I used to do when she was little.

I tiptoe out, leaving Tia's door open slightly, and head down the hall to my bedroom, leaving my door open slightly, too—just in case she calls out for me. Was it just this morning that I was in my bedroom last? My dirty sheets are still on the floor, my bathroom light is still on, but it feels like this morning was a lifetime ago. I'm too tired to put on fresh sheets, so I curl up under my comforter on the bed, grabbing a green throw pillow and squeezing it to my aching chest. I'm more tired than I've ever been in my entire life. Piper jumps up on the bed, then rolls over onto his back and offers me his pink belly. I rub his tummy until he curls up and falls asleep.

It has started to rain outside. The pitter-patter, which usually sounds so comforting, sounds oddly hollow. He's gone. My smart, funny, loving, wise Dad, is gone. Suddenly, the dam inside me breaks, and the sobs come hard and fast until I finally cry myself to sleep.

CHAPTER FIVE

When my eyes open, it's still dark outside, but the rain has stopped. I don't know what time it is, and I don't want to see all the communications on my neuroprocessor, so I leave it turned off. The center of my chest aches. I can't believe Dad is dead. I slide off my bed and tiptoe in the dark, over to my window. Opening it, I take a deep breath of fresh, night air. The fog has rolled in, and I can barely see the giant fir tree on the edge of our property. Suddenly, I see a shadowy figure underneath the tree. Tall, with broad-shoulders and dark hair—it's Zian!

  I wave. He waves back, motioning for me to join him. I quickly slip my socks and boots on, and then tiptoe downstairs. I open the back door and step outside. The cool, damp air on my skin makes me shiver. I should have grabbed a sweater. The fog is thicker now than it was just a few minutes ago, and I can barely see a few feet in front of me as I cross the backyard.

  Suddenly, two strong hands gently grab my shoulders. I let out a frightened yelp but stop when I realize it's just Zian. He lifts a hand from my shoulder and raises a finger up to his lips. His hair is curly from the damp night air, and clings to his forehead as he whispers, "Shhhh."

  Zian takes my hand and guides me into the green space bordering our property, near one of the trails. My heart is pounding. At least it's dark so he can't see that I'm blushing. Zian stops, and then turns around and pulls me close. I can feel his heart beating. He leans down. My stomach flutters—is he going to kiss me?! His lips brush my cheek and he whispers in my ear, "Stay strong, Ren. I'm here for you."

  Suddenly, I hear a voice behind me, my dad's voice. "Ren,

it's time for you to trust yourself. It's time for you to *open your eyes*."

I spin around, calling out "Dad?!"—but there's no one there, just pine trees and fog. I turn back to Zian, but he's vanished as well.

My eyes pop open. I sit straight up in bed—heart pounding, palms sweaty. The back of my neck is burning. It's still raining outside, and Piper hasn't moved. It was just a dream. It was just a stupid dream. I shake my head. "That sucks," I say to Piper as I rest my head on my knees, hug my arms around my shins, and squeeze. I could use a real hug from Zian right now. My entire body aches. I feel like I have the flu, only I know I'm not sick.

After a few moments, I feel a bit calmer, and flip on my neuroprocessor to see what time it is. It's **5:37 A.M.**, and I have **63 unread communications**. Wow. No use trying to sleep. I wrap myself up in my fluffy white bathrobe and head downstairs. To my surprise, Mom is still seated at the kitchen table, with the same coffee cup in front of her. She looks like she hasn't moved all night. I gently place my hand on her shoulder. "Mom?"

Mom gazes up at me with vacant eyes, shakes her head slightly, and then whispers, "I couldn't sleep in the bed without him." She stares down at her paint-stained fingers. "I don't know what we're going to do." I quickly wrap my arm around her trying to comfort her.

"We'll figure it out together, Mom."

She shakes her head slightly. "I received a government communication this morning. They found human tissue in the samples they ran from the transport blast sight. They ran DNA tests." Mom's voice cracks, and tears start streaming down her cheeks, dripping onto the kitchen table. "The samples are a match, Ren. Your father is gone."

"NO!" I hear a guttural scream. I turn around—Tia is standing in the doorway of the kitchen. Sobbing, she turns and flees back upstairs to her bedroom, slamming the door behind her. I wish I could do the same. My eyes burn, but no tears come. I feel like my lungs are being crushed by a heavy weight. I open my mouth, but nothing comes out.

Suddenly, there's a commotion on our front porch and I hear raised voices. I leave Mom in the kitchen, and sprint through the living room to our front door. Outside, I hear a man's voice, "We'll have to scan your neuroprocessor if you don't have another form of identification." The government agents must have guarded our house all night.

"Back off! I'm family! Get out of my way and let me inside!" a woman's voice shouts. I'd know that voice anywhere. I quickly open the front door, surprising the two government men guarding it.

"Let her in. She's family," I say. A short, blonde, flurry of energy catapults herself into our living room, and then shuts the front door behind her. "Aunt Bliss!" I exclaim, before her strong arms wrap around me, squeezing me tight.

Aunt Bliss is my mom's older sister. While Mom married Dad, and became part of Intelligencia, Aunt Bliss remained a Provider. She's a hair stylist, and she's married to my Uncle Ray, who is also a Provider. He owns a small carpet cleaning business. I've always adored Aunt Bliss. She's feisty—physically and emotionally—unlike Mom, who has always seemed a little fragile. Fun loving, yet always dependable, Aunt Bliss is the perfect Auntie, in my opinion.

Aunt Bliss kisses my forehead. "I'm so, so sorry about your dad, sweetie," she whispers. The dam inside me breaks again. I bury my face in Aunt Bliss's shoulder and sob, while she rocks me gently in her arms.

◆ ◆ ◆

Eventually, with Aunt Bliss's arm wrapped around me, I walk back to the kitchen where my Mom is still sitting with a vacant look on her face. Seeing Aunt Bliss seems to snap Mom out of her daze a bit. She stands up, and they hug for a long time, both crying. Eventually, Aunt Bliss sits Mom back down, and then disappears upstairs. I heat up coffee for Mom and me, and we sit sipping the comforting, hot liquid for several moments until Aunt Bliss reappears with Tia in tow.

Aunt Bliss sits Tia down at the kitchen table. Tia's eyes are practically swollen shut from crying. Aunt Bliss grabs a cup of coffee for herself, and then sits down as well. She tucks her blonde hair behind her ears, takes a sip, and then starts talking. "There will be many people trying to contact you—friends, family, even reporters. I know it's tough to talk about, but we need to plan a small service. We should go ahead and have it this weekend," Aunt Bliss says, gently but firmly. I nod hesitantly in agreement, Tia does too. Mom doesn't respond. I'm so relieved Aunt Bliss is here to help! I know everything will get done that needs to get done, now that she's here.

"I think we should have people come here," Aunt Bliss continues. "We'll need to send out neuroprocessor invites, contact caterers, and rent extra chairs. I'll get to work on all of that this morning." Aunt Bliss turns to Mom, and gently places her hand on her arm. "Brooke, go take a bath and crawl into bed. You'll need your strength for the service. Ren, why don't you take your mom upstairs?"

I nod and help Mom up. She feels delicate in my arms, as if one wrong move could break her. I keep my arm around Mom's slender waist as we slowly make our way upstairs, guiding her down the hallway to the Master bedroom. I flip on the light with my neuroprocessor, and then walk Mom straight into the bathroom. I sit her down on the edge of the tub and turn on the water.

Mom watches silently, with her shoulders slumped, while the tub fills. She looks like an old woman, and a small child, at the same time. I wish there was something I could say to help her, but I can't think of anything. I test the water a few times to make sure it's not too hot.

"Do you need me to stay, Mom?" I ask.

Mom shakes her head. "No. Thank you, Ren," she quietly replies.

As soon as the tub is full, I turn the water off and then slip back out into my parents' bedroom, closing the bathroom door gently behind me. My dad is literally everywhere I look. There are pictures of him on the walls, his books on the shelves, and even his dirty clothes still lie in a heap on the floor. I half-laugh, half-cry when I see his clothes on the floor. Dad was always lost in his thoughts and was never that great at picking up after himself.

I gather his clothes up, and open the door to the walk-in closet, so I can drop them in the laundry basket. A sob catches in my throat, though, and instead of dropping Dad's blue and green plaid button-down flannel shirt in the basket, I lift it up and hug it to me. It smells like him—like shaving cream and coffee. I wait a few moments, but I can't seem to let Dad's shirt go, so I take my bathrobe off and slip Dad's shirt on over my pajamas. I just want to feel close to him.

Carrying my robe, I leave the closet and turn down the big, peach-colored, down duvet on my parents' bed. Then, I close the blinds, and flip off the light with my neuroprocessor. Hopefully, after her bath, Mom will climb straight into bed and fall asleep.

◆ ◆ ◆

I spend the rest of the day in my room responding to communications on my neuroprocessor, and in the kitchen, planning Dad's memorial service with Aunt Bliss. We're keeping the service small, due to the terror threat—only family, close friends, and Dad's closest colleagues at Ash-Tech are invited. The Order frowns upon all forms of religious practice, and considers them misguided superstitions, so memorial services generally consist of friends, family, and colleagues giving short speeches about the significance of a person's life and their contributions to the betterment of The Order. Intelligencia funeral services, however, usually include intellectual discussions on themes such as loss, connection, and meaning. Since we're Intelligencia, we'll be including a time for this open sharing of feelings and ideas at the end of Dad's service.

Honestly, I'm dreading the whole thing. I'm glad Aunt Bliss made us set Dad's memorial service for tomorrow. I just want to get it over with.

CHAPTER SIX

I awaken on top of my unmade bed, still wearing Dad's green and blue flannel shirt. I don't even remember falling asleep last night, I was so tired. Thank The Order I didn't have any nightmares last night—one night of reprieve, at least. I flip my neuroprocessor on, but it flickers so much that I just turn it back off. Whatever. I don't have the patience to deal with it today. It's the day of Dad's memorial service.

I peek out my window. The sky is clear, and the rising sun makes the red and gold leaves of the trees in our backyard look like they're on fire. I slip on my green, fuzzy slippers and head downstairs. Aunt Bliss is in her bright pink P.J.'s cooking breakfast in the kitchen while communicating on her neuroprocessor. She smiles when she sees me. "Good morning! Guests will be arriving at two o'clock, Ren," Aunt Bliss raises her voice above the sizzle of potatoes and eggs frying.

"Is there anything I can do to help you right now?" I ask, as I fill a glass with water.

"I think I've got all the details worked out," Aunt Bliss replies, "but after breakfast I want you to clean the living room. Remove any unnecessary furniture to make room for the rental chairs. You can relax until a few minutes before two o'clock, and then I want you at the front door to greet guests as they arrive. Direct them to the living room to be seated. Tell the guests the service will begin around two-thirty, and food will be served immediately after. It's fine to ask Noelle to be a greeter with you, for emotional support." I must look a little overwhelmed, because Aunt Bliss sets down the spatula and turns to give me a quick hug. "I know it's a lot to ask of you, Ren. Do you think you can handle it, honey?"

I honestly don't know if I can handle it, but I say, "Yes. I'll do my best, Aunt Bliss."

She smiles. "I know you will, sweetie. Have some breakfast. You'll need your strength today."

The potatoes and eggs smell delicious, but my stomach turns at the thought of eating. I shake my head. "I'm so sorry Aunt Bliss, but I think my stomach is too upset to eat anything." She nods empathetically and gives me another quick squeeze.

◆ ◆ ◆

The morning races by as Aunt Bliss, Tia and I frantically clean and prepare for guests. Tia is surprisingly easy to deal with. Mom mostly stays in her art studio in our basement. She says that painting and making pottery calm her down better than anything else.

Flower deliveries from people sending their condolences begin streaming in, the rental chairs are delivered by late morning, and the caterers arrive shortly after noon. Once the caterers appear, I excuse myself to shower and get dressed.

Piper is curled up, napping on my bed, avoiding the mayhem downstairs. I unbutton Dad's shirt, but still can't bring myself to toss it in my laundry basket, so I leave it on my bed. I turn on my shower, and climb in.

The last time I took a shower, Dad was still alive. The past few days seem so surreal—like one of my nightmares. When I close my eyes, I can see Dad—his greying hair, his dimples. He's so close I could touch him, but when I open my eyes, he's still gone. How is it even possible that he's gone forever? Why can't time move backwards? Why can't it be Friday morning again, when my Dad was still alive, and I can warn him about the bombs... I lean my head against the shower tiles and sob while the hot water pounds on my shoulders.

Finally, I shut the water off, and wrap myself up in my

fluffy, white bathrobe. I pause in front of the mirror above my dresser. My eyes are red from crying. I start to brush my wet hair, but then something catches my eye in my open jewelry box. The box is small—I don't wear much jewelry—and made from mahogany. I dip my hand inside and lift up a gold chain necklace with a gold, spiraling seashell pendant on it—a Nautilus.

Dad gave it to me several months ago because one of our favorite topics of discussion is the Fibonacci sequence and how it is repeated in nature—in leaves, in Nautilus shells, and even the stars. Dad said he saw the necklace and bought it because it reminded him of me. I fasten the necklace around my neck so that the gold shell rests in the hollow between my collarbones. Today, I'm going to wear it to remind me of him.

Realizing I took longer in the shower than I should have, I hurry to my closet and slip on my dark navy sweater dress. I don't have a black dress, so navy will do—and my favorite brown boots. I rush back into my bathroom to blow dry my wet hair. I don't bother putting any eye make-up on. Why set myself up for mascara streaks on my cheeks? I leave my hair down, so I can cover my face if I start crying, and then sprint downstairs to wait for Noelle.

◆ ◆ ◆

Noelle arrives just a few moments later, wearing a black skirt and a black blouse. I hug her tight. It's so good to see her! I really need her today. My whole world has been turned sideways but being with Noelle makes everything feel a little more normal. She even teases me about wearing navy instead of black and gets me to crack a smile for the first time in days.

Just before two o'clock, Noelle and I position ourselves by the front door. The doorbell starts ringing right away. We greet the hushed, solemn guests as they enter the house, shaking hands, and thanking them for taking the time to celebrate Dad's life. Most of the guests are Ash-Tech and government colleagues of my dad. Honestly, it's exhausting to engage with people I don't really know. Each one tells me they're sorry for my loss. "I'm sorry for your loss too," I reply.

Once all the guests have arrived, Mom, Tia, and I sit down in the living room, and the service begins. It's short and emotional. Mom and Tia weep quietly throughout the entire service. Aunt Bliss is the only person from our family to speak. I don't think I could even get two words out without crying. Several of Dad's close colleagues do break down crying and excuse themselves from the room. Most of the guests seem too upset to speak for long. We don't even end up having the philosophical discussion typically held at the end of Intelligencia services. I think everyone is still in shock. I know I am.

◆ ◆ ◆

There's a collective relief when the service is over. Our guests flock to the fantastic spread laid out by the caterers in the dining room and kitchen. I'm so glad Aunt Bliss thought to hire them—good food seems to make everyone feel better. People begin to talk and eat. There is even an occasional laugh here and there, which is a little shocking to hear at first, after hearing only crying for the past two days.

Now that the stress of the service is out of the way, I'm starving. It's been almost two days since I could eat. Noelle and I wait until the crowd thins in the dining room, and then scoot in to survey the platters of sandwiches and bowls of salads. There's so much food! We'll have leftovers for days. As Noelle and I pick up plates, I notice that Uncle Patterson, Dad's younger brother, is at the other end of the dining room table, spooning pasta salad into a bowl. I've always loved kind, soft-spoken Uncle Patterson, although I don't see him that often. He's a psychology professor at Capitol University, where he teaches and conducts research. Like us, Uncle Patterson is part of the Intelligencia. I never realized how much he looks like Dad until now.

"Hi Uncle," I say, as I pick up a particularly tasty-looking mozzarella, tomato, and basil sandwich. "How did you get in without me seeing you?"

"I snuck in through the back door, kiddo," he replies with a wink. Then Uncle Patterson sets down his spoon. A deep sadness settles over his demeanor. "I'm so sorry, Ren. I can only imagine how hard this is for you." Noelle gently squeezes my arm, and then slips out of the dining room into the kitchen, where most the guests are, to give us a moment of privacy.

Uncle Patterson gently wraps his arm around my shoulder. His black wool sweater smells like books and aftershave. He kisses me on my forehead. "Your father loved you so much, Ren." I nod, unable to speak—tears flooding my eyes. "How are you holding up, dear?" Uncle Patterson asks.

I wish I could describe the horrific pain that shoots through my heart whenever I remember Dad is dead, but a lump is lodged in the back of my throat and I can't talk. I take several deep breaths, and finally say, "It hurts."

He nods and gives my shoulder a gentle squeeze. "Let me know if there's anything I can do to help. I'm here for you, Ren. You're not alone."

I nod. "Thank you. How are *you* holding up, Uncle?"

"I miss my brother." Uncle Patterson's voice breaks. He stops talking for a moment, then swallows and continues. "Your father was an incredible man, Ren. This is very hard—very unnecessary. His death didn't have to happen." There is an undertone of anger in his voice.

"What do you mean, 'his death didn't have to happen'?" I ask. Before Uncle Patterson can answer, though, Noelle steps back into the dining room, carrying two glasses of fruit punch —so I introduce them. "Uncle Patterson, this is my best friend Noelle. Noelle, this is my Uncle Patterson," I say.

"Nice to meet you." Noelle says. Her brown curls bob as she sets down the punch and holds out her hand.

"Pleased to meet you, Noelle." Uncle Patterson reaches out to shake Noelle's hand, and suddenly I spy a ring on his pinky finger with the symbol of an open eye on it—just like the note I found in my locker! I can't help myself, I gasp.

"Uncle Patterson, where did you get that ring?! What is that symbol?" I ask.

Uncle Patterson quickly pulls his hand away and shoves it into his pants' pocket. Just then, two government men dressed in black SED uniforms enter the dining room. One of them is Special Agent Rudy. He casts a suspicious glance at Uncle Patterson and me as they pass by us and continue into the kitchen. I don't know when they got here—they certainly weren't invited to Dad's service.

Uncle Patterson hurriedly sets down his bowl and napkin, turns his back to the agents, and avoids looking in their direction. He's noticeably upset. Quickly wrapping his arm around me, he whispers into my ear, "I have to go now. Stay open to what's happening to you, Ren. Pay attention to your dreams. Learn from them. Trust yourself... I love you." Uncle Patterson kisses me on my forehead again, gently, and then flees the dining room in the opposite direction of the agents.

How bizarre! My heart is pounding, and my brain is buzzing. Why did Uncle Patterson run out like that? Why is he wearing a ring with the Conation eye symbol? How did he know about my dreams? Did Dad tell him? What can I possibly learn from *nightmares*? As if on cue, Agent Rudy and his sidekick re-enter the dining room. Their faces appear neutral, yet their bodies are tense, on edge. Agent Rudy steps forward and holds out his beefy hand to me. I shake it, politely. It's sweaty. Ugh.

"Thank you for coming," I say, not meaning it at all.

"Again, I'm sorry for your loss, Ms. Sterling. This is such a tragedy. The government is committed to finding these criminals," he says. Why does his voice sound hollow to me?

"Thank you," I reply, politely.

There is an awkward silence for a moment, and then Agent Rudy continues. "I hope you can assist us with our investigation, Ms. Sterling. Any details you provide may help us solve this crime and bring the terrorists who murdered your father to justice. I need you, your mother, and your sister to come to the Central Government Building tomorrow morning at 9 A.M. I'll send a car to pick you up at eight-thirty. Please be ready."

Wait, what? Seriously?! The day after my dad's service? I blurt out, "But Agent Rudy, I have school tomorrow!"

Agent Rudy's upper lip curls. "Young lady, this is far more important than school," he replies, his voice dripping with condescension. "I'll write you an official Government excuse note if you need."

I feel sudden dread at the thought of meeting with Agent Rudy tomorrow. I scan my brain for another way out of the meeting. "Have you asked my mom? Why can't just she meet with you?" I ask.

"Because *you* are the person we need to speak with the most," he retorts.

Hearing this, my stomach sinks, and my heart races. "I don't understand. Why me?" I ask, trying to keep my voice from rising.

Agent Rudy scowls. "Just be ready in the morning. Hopefully, everything will get cleared up tomorrow," he says gruffly. Agent Rudy and the other SED agent stride out of the dining room, into the living room—the same direction Uncle Patterson fled. *What* will get cleared up tomorrow? What is Agent Rudy talking about?

"What was that about?!" asks Noelle, shaking her head in bewilderment.

I shake my head, too. "I have no idea Noelle, but that Agent Rudy guy seriously gives me the creeps."

Noelle nods, her dark curls bouncing. "Yeah, me too!" she exclaims.

Noelle and I pick up our plates and sit down next to several guests on a couch in the living room. I try to eat but I've lost my appetite again, so I set my plate aside. Questions loop through my mind. Why does Agent Rudy need to speak with me so urgently? What could I possibly tell him that could help catch Dad's killers? Why was Uncle Patterson so nervous when he saw the government agents? Why was he wearing that ring with the eye on it? Could he possibly have something to do with Conation? And what do my dreams have to do with anything?

A tap on the window above my head startles me, snapping me out of my thoughts. I swear, if it is that Agent Rudy creep interrupting Dad's memorial service again, I'm going to give him a piece of my mind. I jump up, turn around, and peer through the window. A pair of pale blue eyes framed by dark hair stare right back into mine. It's Zian—standing on our back deck! My heart skips a beat.

Zian lifts his hand out of his navy down coat pocket, waves hello to Noelle, and then gestures for me to join him outside. I glance over at Noelle. "Go. Go! I'll hold down the fort here," she says encouragingly, placing her hand on my back and nudging me forward. My palms start to sweat, and my legs wobble a bit as I walk to the door. I open it, and then step outside. The air is crisp and cool.

Zian immediately pulls me into his arms and holds me tight. He's never hugged me this close before! I can feel the strength in his broad, muscular shoulders. His hug is both tender and protective. He smells so good, like sandalwood. I can't help but blush. The energy between our bodies is electric.

Zian steps back, takes my hands in his, and stares deeply into my eyes. His blue eyes remind me of the color of cornflowers. "I'm so sorry about your dad, Ren. I know how much it hurts..." Zian's voice falters, and suddenly I remember that Zian, of all people, knows how painful it is to lose a father. "If you're okay with missing the rest of the reception, come with me, Ren. I have something important to show you."

I feel tingly all over, and light-headed. At this moment, I'd go anywhere with Zian. All I want is to be in his arms again.

I nod, breathless. "Okay, let's go."

"Follow me."

"Let me grab my coat, first." I say. "I'll meet you on the front porch."

Zian nods. "Of course," he replies, and shoves his hands

back into his pockets. I quickly open the door to my house, and then make a beeline for the coat closet. Noelle rushes over to me.

"What does Zian want?!" Noelle asks, practically bursting with curiosity.

"He wants to show me something." I open the coat closet and grab my down coat.

"When will you be back?" asks Noelle.

"I don't know," I say, and then glance around the living room. "If any of the guests need anything…"

Noelle grins and flips her hand. "Pff, I've got you covered. Go have some fun, girl. You deserve it."

"Thank you, Noelle. You're the best." I give Noelle a quick hug, slip on my coat and zip it up. When I open the front door, and rejoin Zian on the porch, he holds out his big, strong, warm hand, and I take it. My heart flutters. This is the first time we've ever held hands.

Holding tightly to Zian's hand, I follow him as he makes his way along the side of my house and through our backyard. I can see Aunt Bliss, Mom, and Tia through the kitchen window talking with several guests. Suddenly, I feel a stabbing pang of guilt. I know I should probably be responsible and tell them where I'm going, but since Dad died, all I've been is responsible. Matter of fact, I'm always the responsible one. I need a break. Besides, Noelle will cover for me.

Zian gently squeezes my hand as we stroll through the green space near the trail at the edge of our property, in the exact spot where I saw Zian in my dream. What an odd coincidence that I dreamt of being here with him! We follow the trail through the woods, until it ends at a sidewalk and the street. As we step out onto the sidewalk, I see Zian's small, silver car parked a few yards away. I'm tingly with anticipation—I have a feeling that my world is about to change, forever.

CHAPTER SEVEN

As I jump into his car, Zian flashes me a mischievous smile. It's so unlike Zian's typical sullen countenance that my heart literally skips a beat. What's gotten into him? I'm certainly intrigued. Where he's taking me? I was so excited to be with him and get out of the house that I didn't even ask.

"What happens when you look around here, Ren?" Zian asks, waving his hand in the air.

I shake my head, confused. "I don't know what you mean," holding my hands up to the heat vents.

Zian pulls the car away from the curb and begins to slowly drive through my neighborhood. "Do you ever pay attention to the feelings deep inside of you, Ren, to your intuition?" he asks.

I give Zian a puzzled, sideways glance. What's he talking about? "Isn't intuition just another misguided superstition, like religion?" I ask.

Zian shakes his dark head emphatically. "No! Not at all. Try using it now, Ren. What do you see right now? Even more importantly, what do you feel?" he asks.

Well, I *feel* like kissing Zian... but I glance over at him, and he isn't flirting—he's serious. Something deep inside of me knows what he's asking. I gaze at my neighborhood, and then close my eyes and try to *feel* as we drive. Here goes nothing.

"Empty," I say, opening my eyes again. "Everything looks beautiful and safe, but it feels empty, like something is missing. Honestly, Zian, I *always* have this feeling in my neighborhood, but I've never described it to anyone else before. I thought it might sound crazy to say that my neighborhood doesn't feel *real* to me."

I glance over at Zian to gauge his reaction. He gives me a warm, understanding smile. He's so gorgeous when he smiles. "And what happens inside of you when you have that feeling, Ren?"

"Well... sometimes it makes me feel uneasy," I say, touching my stomach unconsciously. "Other times I feel excited about what else might be possible, I guess."

Zian nods vigorously in agreement, as if he understands exactly what I'm saying. "And how often have you been outside the usual places where you hang out—your house, school, and certain parts of downtown, Ren?" he asks. I feel surprised by his question, and then slightly irritated, as if I need to defend myself. Why would Zian ask me that? I've been all over Capital City... haven't I? I scan my brain for memories of experiences outside of the places that typically make up my life. The strange thing is, I can only come up with a few.

Zian watches my face intently. "You spend all your time in your *zones of comfort*, don't you?" he asks, with just a hint of judgement.

"Well, yes," I admit begrudgingly. "But there's no reason to go anywhere else." I'm struck by a thought. "Wait. Is that why I constantly feel like I'm missing something?" Zian flashes me another smile, and my heart flutters.

"Wanna see some new things today, Ren?"

"With you? Definitely." My cheeks flush at my boldness.

"First, shut off your neuroprocessor."

"Why?" I ask, curious.

"Just for a little while, so you can focus on your intuition without distractions," Zian replies. "Do you trust me?"

I nod. "Yes, of course. But first, I need to tell my Mom I'm leaving, so she doesn't worry."

"Absolutely," Zian nods in agreement.

I send a group message to Mom, Aunt Bliss, and Tia. **"I'm taking a short break from the reception to get some air with Zian. I'll be back soon."** Before I can receive any responses, I shut off my neuroprocessor.

Zian turns his little, silver car toward the exit of my neighborhood. We pull up to the gate by the guard station and stop. Zian lowers his window.

"Hi Tom," I say to the muscular, balding man who works the guard station on the weekend.

"Hi Ren, where ya headed today?" he asks.

"We're just going for a drive," Zian answers quickly. I nod in agreement. Tom looks suspiciously at Zian, and then back at me.

"I'm taking a break from my Dad's memorial service to get some air. It's such a beautiful afternoon. We'll be back soon." I say, reassuringly. Tom shrugs and pushes the button to open the gate.

"Have a nice drive, Ren," Tom says, giving a little wave. I wave back, and Zian raises the window.

"Ever wonder why the guard always asks where you're going?" Zian asks, as he drives the car forward through the gate.

"I've honestly never thought about it before," I reply. "But you're right, it's weird. Why would he need to know where I'm going?"

"Right—why *would* he need to know?" Zian asks. His blue eyes meet mine. I don't know, I don't have an answer. Something doesn't feel right. Suddenly, my stomach twists, and my heart beats faster.

"I have that weird feeling again," I tell Zian.

"Good—it's part of your intuition. Try to pay attention to how you feel when we travel into different areas, Okay?"

"Okay," I reply, a bit disconcerted. The car is toasty warm, now. I take a deep breath, sit back, and watch the afternoon sunlight dancing on the tree leaves as we drive down the road from my neighborhood. Zian turns his car into another housing development that isn't gated.

As we roll slowly through the development, Zian says, "This is a middle-class Provider neighborhood. Kids that live here go to a different school than we do."

I nod. "Yeah, I know. My Aunt Bliss and Uncle Ray are Providers, and live close by. It's kind of like my neighborhood, except the houses are smaller, and there are no hiking trails." That weird feeling occurs inside me again. I've never really stopped to think about why Providers have less than Intelligencia.

Zian drives us out of the neighborhood, and we travel down the main road again. The houses and yards become even smaller, but they're still nice. "Working-class Providers live here," Zian says. We continue driving. After about thirty minutes, the neighborhoods really start to change. Some of the houses and buildings are falling apart. The streets and sidewalks are not well-maintained. There's trash in the street. The cars are old and in poor condition. "This is where some of the Producers live," Zian says.

My insides feel heavy. "I wouldn't want to live here," I tell Zian quietly. "It's depressing."

He nods solemnly. "I know. Just wait, there's more."

Zian directs his car back toward our part of town, and then continues onto another road. We pass a sign that says, 'Gladstone Farms.'

"Wait!" I exclaim. "I remember this place! I've been here before."

Zian quickly pulls his car into the mostly empty parking lot next to the farm's Visitor Center. "Yup, it's the model farm that all second and fourth graders visit," he replies.

We get out, stretch our legs, and stand by the front of the car. From our vantage point, I can see the perfectly maintained, whitewashed barns and buildings. As I survey the idyllic view of the afternoon sun shining on the lush pastures, the farm animals, and the beautiful surrounding hills, I feel a sense of contentment.

"It's beautiful!" I exclaim.

Zian nods slowly in agreement. Then he asks, "Do you want to see where the food we eat is *really* produced?"

That weird feeling in my stomach returns. "What do you mean, Zian?"

Zian pivots to face me. His cornflower blue eyes stare directly into mine with a gaze so intense, it almost hurts. "I don't have to show you anymore, Ren. I can take you home right now."

"Why wouldn't I want to see more?" I ask, puzzled by his seriousness.

Zian shakes his head, and sighs. "Because, it will change how you see things, Ren. It will change everything. It will be difficult for you to return to your normal life. It might even be dangerous. The government doesn't want you to see what I can show you."

I can feel the blood rise to my face as my heart beats faster. "You're freaking me out, Zian! What are you talking about?"

He looks away. "Forget it. I should just take you home."

"NO!" my voice rises, as my heart beats even faster. "Tell me what you're talking about."

Zian shoves his hands in his coat pockets as he stares off into the hills. "Have you ever asked yourself where all of our food and other goods come from? Have you ever asked yourself how The Order is maintained? What if it's not what you think, Ren?"

More questions? I asked for answers. "ZIAN! I LEFT MY DAD'S MEMORIAL SERVICE TO COME OUT HERE WITH YOU!" I shout, suddenly losing all patience. "SERIOUSLY, WHAT ARE YOU TALKING ABOUT?"

Zian quietly replies, "Life isn't fair for all segments of The Order, despite what the government tells us and what we learn in school. Although none of the citizens of The Order are truly free, some have many more opportunities while others experience a lot more oppression."

I step back, aghast. "Oppression?"

Zian nods. "To truly understand what I'm saying, you need to see it for yourself, Ren. Either you can return to your normal life now, and forget I ever said anything, or I can show you more, and your life will never be the same. It'll be easier for you if you don't know the truth."

I rock back on my heels. My head is spinning. I'm quiet

for a few minutes as I try to sort through all that Zian has said. Then, something stirs deep inside me, and I have instant clarity. Without saying a word, I walk back to the car and get in. Zian quickly follows and climbs into the driver side. I turn to him and say, "Let's go. I need to see whatever it is you wish to show me. I don't want to go back to my 'normal life.' It's not normal anymore anyway, since my dad was blown up by terrorists."

Zian winces, and then reaches out and squeezes my hand. "Okay, Ren," he says softly.

I try to look straight ahead so I don't make eye contact and start crying. Zian starts the car, and we pull out of Gladstone Farm's parking lot. I wonder—what am I getting myself into?

CHAPTER EIGHT

Zian drives past the end of Gladstone Farms, and then continues driving down a road that runs parallel to apple orchards and rolling fields of root vegetables almost ready for fall harvest. I lower my window a bit to smell the fresh air. I can see that we are heading east, toward Mount Hood, the largest of the mountains east of Capital City.

Zian lowers his window, too. "Have you ever wondered why you've never been to the east side of the mountains, Ren?" he asks.

"No, not really. I guess I assumed the habitable zone ends at the mountains." I reply. "And I'm just so busy with school and soccer... and everything I need is not far from my house. Why, have you?"

"The habitable zone goes much further east of the mountains, although our government doesn't publicize that. It's true that all the cities and bigger towns in Cascadia are on the west side, along the corridor between the western coast range and the central mountains; so are the farms that the government allows us to see," Zian replies, avoiding my question.

"Wait, what do you mean, 'allows us to see'?" I ask, confused.

"I'm taking you to an area where we'll be able to see some things the government doesn't want any of us to know about—almost to the Indigenous settlement." Zian says, as we turn down another road.

So, he *has* been further east. "Cool! We learned about the Indigenous people living in the mountains in history class last year." This will be fun.

59

"Yeah... But it's not at all like what they teach us in school, Ren," Zian says, grimly.

The weird feeling in my stomach returns. Maybe this *won't* be fun. "What do you mean? What's it... like?" I ask, hesitantly.

Before Zian can answer, we come upon a sign next to the road that reads: Restricted Area – No Entry. Whoa. I don't think we should be here. I glance over at Zian to see his reaction. He looks worried, too.

I flip on my neuroprocessor and do a quick search for "restricted area," but can't find any information. Zian slows his car as we drive around a bend. A gate blocking the road appears, with a small, beige building that looks like a guardhouse alongside. A black government vehicle is parked next to the building.

"Damn! That isn't supposed to be here! They must have moved it up a few miles," exclaims Zian.

"What is it? What's happening?" I ask, anxiously. My heart starts to race.

"It's a security checkpoint. We can't turn around now. They've seen us. Damn, damn!" Zian stares down at his hands nervously, and then takes a deep breath. "Okay, follow my lead, Ren," he says. I swallow the sudden lump in my throat and nod.

There are two men in the beige guardhouse. One of them sticks his head out of the window and waves for us to pull up to the gate. Zian drives his car up slowly as he lowers his window.

"Hi there!" Zian says. "Boy, are we glad to see you!"

"What are you doing here?" the guard barks. "This is a restricted area."

"Oh, no. I'm sorry. We're lost," Zian says.

"Completely lost!" I chime in.

"We were visiting Gladstone Farms, and then must have driven the wrong direction." Zian adds.

The tall, muscular guard dressed in a black government uniform, steps out of the guardhouse and marches over to Zian's side of the vehicle. He leans his head into Zian's open window. His mustache twitches and he squints his eyes suspiciously as he asks, "Didn't you see the Restricted Area sign?"

"I'm so sorry. I must have missed it. We were talking and I wasn't paying attention," replies Zian, shrugging his shoulders and smiling apologetically. The guard doesn't look like he's buying it, so I chime in.

"I distracted him while he was driving, sir. It's my fault," I confess apologetically.

The guard glares at Zian, and then shifts his gaze to me. His stare sends chills up my spine. "What are your names?" he finally asks.

"My name is Zian Reddington. This is Ren."

"I need to scan your processors. Step out of the vehicle now," he commands.

We both open our doors, get out and stand in front of the car. The guard pulls out a handheld device and waves it over the back of Zian's neck. This appears in the screen of his scanner:

Name: *Zian Reddington*
Age: *18*
Address: *3015 NW Overlook Place, Capital City*
Order: *Intelligencia*
Occupation/Workplace/School: *Student, Pittock High School*
Current Location: *Mountain Region, Restricted Area*

Next, the guard holds his scanner over my neuroprocessor:

Name: *Ren Sterling*
Age: *17*
Address: *5535 NW Westbrook Lane, Capital City*
Order: *Intelligencia*
Occupation/Workplace/School: *Student, Pittock High School*
Current Location: *Mountain Region, Restricted Area*

The guard rubs his head and says, "Sterling. I know that name."

"Ren's father, Dr. Peter Sterling, was just killed in the bombing at Ash-Tech," explains Zian. "I was taking her out for a drive to help get her mind off everything when we got lost."

"Oh. I see," the guard replies, his tone of voice becoming

gentler. "Alright kids, I'm going to let you go with a warning, but next time you better watch where you're going. It can be dangerous near restricted areas. They're restricted for a reason. Now turn this vehicle around and go home!"

"Yes, sir," Zian nods.

I say, "Absolutely, sir."

The guard folds his arms across his chest, and nods gruffly. We quickly jump back in the car. Zian backs up, carefully turns around, and then heads back down the road under the watchful eye of the guard until we curve out of sight. Both of us exhale a huge sigh of relief at the same time, and then giggle.

"Good job playing along!" Zian says, giving my shoulder a playful push.

"I'm glad he let us go!" I laugh.

"Me too," Zian replies. He furrows his brow. "Not everyone is so lucky," he says.

Ugh. There's that weird feeling in my gut again. "I had no idea there are restricted areas around here, Zian."

Zian nods. "Most people don't. Only a few people outside of the government know what's really happening out here. But, there's more than one way to show you what they're hiding." Zian leans forward and peers through the windshield. "Here it is. Hold on tight!" he exclaims, as he abruptly turns the car onto a small, unmarked, dirt road. It appears as if we are on an old logging road, steep and narrow, with dense forest on both sides. We climb higher and higher, bouncing over deep ruts in the road as we go.

"You won't find this on any neuroprocessor map!" Zian says, raising his voice excitedly over the noise of the bumpy road. The forest is breathtakingly beautiful. How does Zian know about all this? After many twists and turns, we pull into a small clearing where the dirt road ends.

"We'll walk from here," Zian announces. He grabs a big, metal-framed backpack out of the trunk of his car, hoists it on his back, and then leads the way through the trees. We follow a stream as we hike even higher up into the forest. After walking for about two miles, Zian points to an unusual mark on a tree—one that I've never seen before.

"What's that?" I ask.

"It's a marker telling me we're heading in the right direction," Zian answers, and flashes me a warm smile. My heart flutters. "This will all make sense soon, Ren. I promise."

We leave the side of the stream, and then begin climbing up some large rocks before coming to a cliff with a view of the open expanse on the east side of the mountains. The sun is getting close to setting. It's a gorgeous view of farmlands with the fading autumn sunlight glowing across the landscape.

"It's beautiful," I say.

"Yes, it is. But we didn't come here for the scenery. Do you see those buildings in the distance, Ren?"

"Yes, barely."

"Look closely. Use the binocular function on your neuroprocessor."

I flip on my neuroprocessor and ignore the new messages. I immediately activate the binocular function and adjust the focus. A compound of buildings surrounded by a tall, barbed wire fence comes into view. There appears to be a large guard tower, buildings that look like barracks, and various types of farm equipment parked in one area. Men with government uniforms are stationed around the complex, as guards, I guess.

"What is this place..." I begin to ask, when one of the barrack's doors suddenly swings open. A boy—who appears to be about eleven or twelve years old, and is dressed in gray, ragged clothing—runs out the door. A guard sprints out after him and hits the boy across the back with a black baton, knocking him to the ground. Then, the guard kicks and stomps on the child.

I gasp, horrified. "Oh NO! What in The Order is this, Zian?!"

"I'm sorry you had to see that, Ren, but you have to know the truth. *This* is where our food really comes from. This is a typical Producer farm—it's what they're like." Zian shakes his head with disgust and adds, "Now, look over there." He points to the right, at something in the distance.

I magnify my binocular function again. Two huge, rectangular-shaped buildings with smoke billowing out of the chimneys and many smaller barracks come into focus. There's another guard tower. A high, barbed wire fence surrounds the buildings.

"What is that?" I ask.

"It's a factory complex. Like hundreds of other ones, it produces common household products, parts for our vehicles, and pretty much everything else we use in daily life. The government runs these farms and factories with slave labor, using low-class Producer families and subversives."

"This is crazy," I say, shaking my head in disbelief. "What are subversives?"

In a matter-of-fact way, Zian replies, "A subversive is anyone the government deems to be rebellious or disloyal to The Order."

A shiver runs down my spine. "That makes no sense, Zian. We've always been taught that Producers are proud of their contributions to The Order."

"Producers *are* essential to the survival of The Order," Zian asserts, "but they don't have the freedom to choose their path. There's no pride without freedom, Ren, only oppression."

My head pounds as I stare in disbelief. I feel crushed by guilt. "How could I not know about this?" I ask as Zian gently takes my hand. His big, warm hand cradles mine.

"As I said before, outside of certain government divisions, very few people know, Ren. Our government doesn't acknowledge the existence of these slave camps. It could threaten The Order."

"Oh. Of course," I mutter.

Zian squeezes my hand reassuringly. "There's a lot of things they don't teach us about in school. They don't want us to question the way things are. Such as, do you ever wonder why so few women are in positions of power in The Order?"

The question catches me off-guard. I stammer, "But what about the Central Advisor for Intelligencia?"

"Yes, but it took almost 70 years to have our first female Central Advisor. The Order is not exactly a beacon of equity and social progress," he retorts sarcastically. "And do you ever ask yourself why there are gates around your neighborhood, Ren? There's virtually no crime in The Order. Everyone stays in their assigned neighborhoods and does their assigned jobs. Why would you need a gate?"

I think about it for a moment but can't come up with any plausible reason. "I really don't know," I reply.

After a long pause Zian says, "The gates aren't there to keep people out. They're there to *keep you in?*"

All I can do in response is slowly shake my head, which is starting to throb. It's all too much to take in. My world feels like it's melting. Suddenly I'm questioning everything I thought I knew about my life. Even though I've always felt that there was much more happening in my world than meets the eye, the weight of all this new information is overwhelming... terrifying.

Zian and I hold hands, staring at the farm and factory for a long time. Eventually, Zian pulls a thick blanket out of his backpack and lays it out on the ground. We sit down together on the blanket. Zian wraps his arms around me as we watch the sunset, leaving streaks of orange across the sky and clouds.

"Don't worry about hiking back to the car in the dark, I have headlamps in my backpack," Zian says, and then gives my forehead a kiss. A shiver ripples through my body. I nestle my head into Zian's shoulder and neck, and he pulls me closer to him.

"Are you cold?" he asks.

I nod. "A little bit."

Zian reaches over into his big backpack and pulls out a cozy-looking sleeping bag. He unzips it, and then wraps it around us like a cocoon. We sit, gently rocking back and forth in each other's arms, watching the sky change colors. "I know I should go home," I whisper, "but I wish I could stay here with you forever."

The sun sets, and stars are beginning to pepper the sky. I snuggle even closer to Zian. He looks down at me, lovingly, with his beautiful blue eyes, leans in, and gently kisses me on the lips. As soon as Zian's lips touch mine, the whole world falls away—the guards, the gates, the factory complex, The Order, even my father's death. Everything just… disappears. I melt into Zian's full, soft lips. Eventually Zian pulls back but continues caressing my cheek.

"I should get you home," he whispers, "or your Mom will worry."

I nod. "Yes, but first, let's watch the stars just a little bit longer?"

"It's one of my favorite things to do, too," Zian says, smiling. We lie back on the blanket, cuddling under the unzipped sleeping bag, and staring up at the twinkling stars. We're quiet for a long time.

◆ ◆ ◆

The back of my neck begins to burn. I move my head a little, but the burning won't stop. Then a pressure in the center of my forehead starts, too. A strange sound enters my ears, like the wind whistling. It quickly shifts and sounds like many voices rising and falling, chanting, and singing. I close my eyes, burrow my head into Zian's arm and shoulder, and hope it will stop.

Suddenly, I'm a raven flying, circling overhead the Restricted Area guardhouse we saw earlier. I flap my black, shiny wings, and fly towards the Producer Farm compound. As I circle above, I begin to observe the same scene I saw unfold this afternoon. I can see the boy leaving the barrack, and then the guard chasing after and beating him. I flap my wings and cry out, but there's nothing I can do to stop it from happening. The guard stomps on the boy, and then steps away. I land by the boy's hands, cock my head and peer into his brown eyes. They're filled with tears.

I open my beak and cry out. The boy reaches his fingers toward me, opens his swollen, bloody lips, but no words come out.

My wings become arms and I'm no longer a raven. Guards surround me, and they lift me off the ground. I hit and kick at the guards, trying to fight against them, but they hold fast, and half drag, half carry me inside the barrack. I scream and cry for help, but they ignore me, and then slam me down into a metal chair. One guard pins me down while another straps my wrists and ankles to the chair. I can feel a needle puncturing the base of my skull. I try to fight it, but my whole body begins to go numb—they've injected something into me. As my body goes limp, suddenly Special Agent Rudy's sinister face looms in front of mine.

The barrack fades, and then disappears from my sight. I'm in darkness, but I can hear chanting, singing, and the wind whistling again. The burning feeling in the back of my neck returns, as does the pressure in the center of my forehead. I sit up, sweaty and breathing hard.

Zian is sound asleep on the blanket next to me. When did he fall asleep? I glance up at the sky. The stars have disappeared, and the sun has risen in the east. Oh no! What happened?! How did that much time pass without me knowing? I don't even remember falling asleep. Was I asleep? Was it a nightmare—or was it a daymare? Was kissing Zian last night a dream, too? I touch my face and lips with my cold fingers. My lips feel a smidge swollen, and I can feel where his stubble scratched my chin a little. I smile to myself. We kissed. I didn't dream that.

I flip on my neuroprocessor. It's 7:02 A.M. A reminder notice shoots before my eyes. **Pick up for meeting with Special Agent Rudy at 8:30 A.M.** Oh no! Mom's going to kill me.
"Zian, get up! We have to go!" I exclaim, shaking Zian awake.

CHAPTER NINE

Zian quickly slings the backpack over his shoulder, and we scramble down the large rocks we'd climbed up the afternoon before. We sprint the two miles through the forest back to the car. Fortunately, we're both good athletes. Once in the car, Zian drives as fast as he can over the ruts in the logging road. We bump around a lot, and skid a few times, but finally make it back to the main road.

Once we're on pavement, I summon the courage to tell Zian about my dream. Unlike when I've told others about my nightmares, he doesn't seem surprised or bothered. In fact, he seems weirdly happy about it. "Whoa, that's amazing!" Zian exclaims, as we speed past the apple orchards, fields, and Gladstone Farms. "You were a raven in your dream?"

"Yeah, but then the guards pinned me in a chair and injected something in me, and I saw that horrible Special Agent Rudy..." I shudder just thinking about it.

"What do you think it means?" Zian asks.

I shake my head. "I don't know. Honestly, all I can think about right now is how furious my mom is going to be with me. We have a meeting with Agent Rudy at the Central Government Building this morning."

"You *do*?" A look of fear crosses Zian's face.

"I tried to get out of it, and just have Mom go, but Agent Rudy insisted. He says I'm the one they really to need to speak with. I have no idea what he's talking about."

Zian is silent. I glance over at him, and his brow is furrowed. He bites his lip the way he does during particularly difficult tests in class.

Zian speeds up to the gated entrance of my neighborhood. The weekday guard waves when he sees me and opens the gate. Zian zips his little silver car into my driveway—right behind a black government vehicle. Oh no. I'm late. Mom is going to be so mad! My heart is pounding and my palms are sweating, fearful of facing her. At least all the media vans are gone. I guess the reporters have moved on to more exciting stories.

"Just tell the SED what you know," Zian blurts out. "They'll find out eventually."

"What do you mean? I don't know anything," I reply, undoing my seatbelt. "Thank you, Zian. Thank you for an amazing night," I say, turning to look at him. Zian leans across the front seat, kisses my cheek with his soft, full lips.

He whispers in my ear, "I don't know when I'll see you again. Stay strong, Ren."

I push him away a little so I can look up into his eyes. "What? What do you mean? Won't I see you in school later today?"

"I don't know," Zian says softly. He leans toward me again and kisses me tenderly on the lips. "You need to go. Everything will be okay," he says, as he caresses my cheek. I grasp his warm hand in mine and raise it to my lips. I gently kiss the back of his hand and gaze into his beautiful eyes. I don't want to leave him. For a moment, I consider not going inside, and running away with Zian instead, but then the responsible part of me quickly regains control.

I drag myself out of the passenger seat, and wave as Zian pulls his car out of the driveway. I run to the front door and open it. Aunt Bliss and Mom are sitting on the couch in the living room, looking like they haven't slept all night. Uh oh. I'm going to be grounded for a year. Two government agents wearing SED uniforms are sitting on the chairs we rented for Dad's memorial.

As soon as she sees me, Mom jumps up, yelling. "Where have you been, young lady? You had me worried sick. You just disappear in the middle of your father's service? And then you don't come home all night or respond to any of my messages?

What were you thinking?! I was scared you were dead!" Mom's fury gives way to tears. I wish the floor could open up and swallow me whole. Suddenly, I feel so selfish.

"I'm so, so sorry, Mom. I wasn't thinking. It's a really long story," I sputter.

"Well, you better start talking!" Mom yells, her eyes bulging with more anger.

Aunt Bliss stands up and calmly touches Mom's arm, and then gently places her hands on my shoulders. She looks directly into my eyes and asks, "Are you okay, Ren?"

I nod my head.

"That's all that matters right now. We can find out what happened later. Now run upstairs and change into some clean clothes." I nod, and race through the house, tearing up the stairs. Piper yips happily when I enter my room. I quickly strip down out of my boots, tights, and sweater dress. I debate about leaving the shell necklace on, and then decide to take it off. I slip it into my jewelry box for safekeeping. I shimmy into a pair of jeans, toss on a long sleeve shirt, and grab a sweater. I slide on clean socks, zip up my boots, and sprint back downstairs again.

When they see me, the agents stand impatiently.

"Let me get you something to eat, Ren," Aunt Bliss says.

"There isn't time for food," one of the SED agents asserts. "We need to leave now."

"Yes, there is!" protests Aunt Bliss as she runs to the kitchen. I can hear the refrigerator door open and close. Aunt Bliss returns with a mozzarella sandwich in a small bag and tosses it to me. "Here, leftovers." She winks at me. I gratefully catch the sandwich. It's been three days since I've eaten, and I'm literally starving.

Tia storms into the living room, dressed in heels, and wearing a ton of make-up, as if she's going to a party. "Great job, Ren. Now you've made us late." Clearly, Tia can't leave the house without looking fashionable, even under these circumstances. Mom, Tia, and I are escorted out of the house and into the back of the government vehicle, which roars to life. I wolf down the sandwich while we speed away, racing through the streets until we arrive at a large, ominous looking, gray government building in the heart of downtown Capitol City.

As we pull up to the front of the building, Mom says nervously to Tia and me, "Just tell them everything you know, so we can be done with this as quickly as possible." Mom touches my arm as I start to exit the vehicle. "Ren, you don't know anything about this, do you?"

I wonder silently, *do I*? Certainly, I learned some very disturbing things about The Order yesterday. Could anything I saw with Zian be related to the investigation of Dad's death? All I can do is slowly shake my head.

◆ ◆ ◆

The Central Government Building has our national flag and the Emblem of The Order over its large, wood, main doors. Our flag is black, with Cascasdia written across the top in green and the Emblem of The Order in gold in the middle of it. The Emblem represents the four segments, or pillars, of The Order. The word ORDER appears across the top in a semi-circle. Just under it, on the left, is a picture of the Federal bank, which represents financial stability offered by the Financiers. To the right of the bank is an open book, which represents knowledge offered by the Intelligencia. Under the bank is a muscular arm, which represents pride in service offered by the Providers. Under the book is a field of crops, which represents sustenance offered by the Producers. Like most people, I've always felt a lot of pride at the sight of our national flag and the Emblem. Every citizen knows the stability that The Order brings to our world. After what I saw yesterday, though, I'm not sure what I believe.

The agents escort us into the building and down a wide, gray corridor. Tia's heels click loudly on the polished cement floor. The Emblem of The Order is above every door along both sides of the hallway. We're taken into the office at the end of the hall, which is enormous, and contains about twenty desks and chairs. Men and women in black uniforms are working at their desks, while others are busily walking around the office.

Special Agent Rudy struts in from another room. It's hard for me to even look at him—I find him so distasteful. "Thank you for coming in this morning," he begins, in a somber tone. "This is what is going to happen today. We'll be asking each of you a few questions separately, which shouldn't take very long. Then, you can get back to your day."

This seems like a lot of fuss for just a few questions. Why couldn't they just ask us at home? Mom, Tia, and I exchange nervous glances. We're each escorted by two agents into different rooms. Agent Rudy leads the two agents escorting me. Once in the smaller room, Agent Rudy directs me to have a seat in a metal chair. He sits at a desk, across from me.

"How are you holding up, Ren?" he asks in a neutral voice.

Ha! As if he cares. The room smells like stale coffee, and the walls are blank and gray, except for a big monitor. The metal seat is cold and hard beneath me. Clearly, they're not really into comfort here at the SED. "It's been tough," I reply as I settle into my chair.

"I can only imagine," Agent Rudy says robotically. "Now, let's get started. I have a few questions I need to ask you. First, tell me about your nightmares. How long have you been having them?"

"A couple of months," I reply without thinking. An uneasy feeling begins in the pit of my stomach. "How did *you* know I've been having nightmares?"

Agent Rudy's lips curl into a slight smile, which quickly disappears. He ignores my question. "I hear that your neuroprocessor has been giving you some trouble, Ren. Is this true?"

"I don't understand. What do my dreams and my processor have to do with anything? I thought we were here to talk about what happened to my father," I reply, furrowing my brow.

A look of frustration crosses Agent Rudy's face. "We're here to investigate crimes against The Order. You may have important information you don't even know you have. So, please just answer my questions," he barks. Agent Rudy takes a deep breath, and then calmly asks, "What about the note in your locker? Tell me about that."

I dutifully respond, "Right after I arrived at school on Friday, I stopped at my locker on the way to Tech Lab..." I pause, remembering that I told Mr. Johns, my Tech Lab teacher, about my nightmares and my neuroprocessor flickering. Mr. Johns must be the one that told Agent Rudy! I wonder if Agent Rudy was the person he was communicating with as Noelle and I were leaving his classroom. That jerk! He totally betrayed me. My stomach begins to hurt.

"Go on," Agent Rudy commands.

"When I opened my locker, there was a piece of paper with the word, Conation, written on it, and a symbol of an open eye. That's it. Like I already told you, I didn't see who put it in there. I don't know anything about it or what it means. That's all I know," I state as calmly as I can.

"Yes, so you've said. There must be some details that you're not remembering."

"I don't think so. I told you precisely what happened."

"Do you still have the piece of paper?" asks Agent Rudy, frustrated.

"No," I reply, wishing I hadn't thrown it away.

"Of course you don't," Agent Rudy sneers as he stands. "Okay, Ren. I need to scan your neuroprocessor to see how it's working."

"Do I have a choice?" I ask timidly.

A sinister smile comes across Agent Rudy's face as he leans toward me and says, "Choice. Ah... that's an interesting concept." Without answering my question, he stands up, and removes a handheld scanner from a locked, black, metal cabinet along the wall of his office. The scanner looks different from other ones I've seen. It's slightly larger and has two antennae coming out the top. Agent Rudy walks behind me and waves the scanner over the back of my neck.

73

"Well, your neuroprocessor seems to be working correctly," he says, after a minute. "I'm going to deep scan your processor now. Neuroimaging, we also call it. It's painless. It produces a mild sensation that some people find relaxing." He taps the scanner, which turns on the large monitor mounted on the wall on my left. "Just relax and let's see if we can find some details that might help identify your father's killers."

My stomach feels like it's twisting in a knot. "I don't understand. What's a deep scan?" I ask.

"Just relax," Agent Rudy repeats as he types something into the scanner.

Suddenly, I have the weirdest sensation, as if my brain and spinal cord are being gently tickled from the inside. I shiver. The monitor on the wall illuminates with images that move quickly across the screen, as if someone is using a fast-forward function. The pictures are of my school. It appears as if someone with a camera is walking through Pittock High's hallways. The camera pans down, and on the screen pops a picture my favorite boots. The images must be coming through *my eyes*! There's Noelle and she's talking… Agent Rudy types something into the scanner. The footage of Noelle reverses and then plays forward slowly, with sound.

"**What's up, girl?**"

"**Not much. I'm just pumped about our soccer game tonight. Rawr!**"

"**Rock solid! Yeah, me too. I'm pretty tired, though. I had another nightmare, then my processor flickered again this morning. It's so annoying. I want to stop by Tech Lab during study period to get it checked.**"

"**Sorry about the nightmare, Ren. I slept so well. It's weird that your processor keeps flickering… want me to come with you to Tech Lab? I've finished my homework. No need for Study Hall.**"

"**Yes, please. I just need to stop by my locker first.**"

"**Me too.**"

The camera shifts to my locker. I'm opening the locker,

and now there is the piece of paper attached to the top shelf. I watch myself pick it up. On the paper is the word, Conation, and the symbol of a wide-open eye.

"WAIT! STOP!" I yell, as I push away from the desk and spring out of the metal chair. "This is wrong—it's an invasion of my privacy. I don't want to do this anymore."

"Please sit down, Ms. Sterling," Agent Rudy requests calmly. "I know it can feel odd the first time you have a deep scan."

I cross my arms in front of my chest. "Yes, it feels really bizarre. I don't want you to deep scan me anymore! You don't have the right to look at my personal life. It's private."

"Oh really?" Agent Rudy rocks back on his heels, with a smirk on his face. "In fact, I do, Ms. Sterling. The government has practically given me free reign to investigate crimes against The Order."

"But I haven't committed any crimes!" I exclaim, raising my arms in frustration. "I've already told you everything I know!"

"Ms. Sterling, we can either do this with your cooperation or without it," Agent Rudy gives me a smug smile. Frantic, I spin around to see if I can get out of the room. The two other agents are now standing in front of the door, blocking any attempt I might make to get away. I turn back to Agent Rudy.

"I want to see my mom!" I exclaim. Mom will put a stop to all of this.

"When we get the information we need, you'll be free to go. Now sit back down," Agent Rudy growls.

No. No way. I cross my arms in front of my chest, and defiantly state, "I'M NOT SITTING DOWN UNTIL YOU LET ME TALK TO MY MOM!"

Agent Rudy angrily gestures to the other agents. They grab my arms and force me to sit, and then strap my ankles and wrists to the metal chair as I buck and writhe, trying to escape. Agent Rudy lifts a black leather bag out of the metal cabinet behind the desk, and then sets it down in the middle of the table.

He pulls a syringe and vial out of the bag. The vial is full of an amber colored liquid. Agent Rudy plunges the syringe into the vial, withdraws the liquid, and then sets the vial down. He strides toward me, holding the syringe high in the air.

"What are you doing?!" I ask, panic welling up inside me.

"I'm going to give you a sedative," Agent Rudy replies calmly. "It will help you relax. It'll also speed the downloading process. Once we download your memories from your neuroprocessor, you'll be able to leave. Then we can analyze the file and look for details that might help the investigation. Hold as still as possible—it will hurt less if you hold still."

Agent Rudy motions for the agents to hold my head while he injects the serum into both sides of my neck just below my skull. I feel a burning sensation as the needle punctures my skin. Intense pain lasts for a few seconds during each injection, and then a dull, burning sensation remains.

"Remember, Ren, we're doing this to catch your father's killers and to protect The Order from terrorists," he says. I try to hold as still as possible. The agents' fingers dig into my scalp as they squeeze my head from both sides. Tears run down my face as I let out a muffled scream.

"No! Stop it!" I cry, terrified. This is exactly what happened in my nightmare last night. How could I possibly know this would happen today?!

"The serum will enable us to get better images and sounds. It'll make the whole process proceed much more smoothly. Relax, and let the medicine do its work," Agent Rudy says, sounding as if he's actually expecting me to enjoy this.

Finally, the agents let go of my head. The burning sensation in my neck is slowly replaced with a warm, fuzzy feeling, which begins in my head, and then travels down my spine, until my whole body is relaxed and calm. My body feels paralyzed, but I don't really care. I have no energy or motivation to move at all—I'm in a state of relaxed numbness.

Agent Rudy picks up his scanner and begins anew. The images and sounds of my day at school on Friday are displayed again through the monitor. Then, the pictures accelerate at an amazingly fast speed, causing them to blend together. Uncomfortable tingling rushes through my head and spine. Agent Rudy chuckles condescendingly, "Don't worry. I'm only recording your memories from the last week up until you came here this morning. So, I hope you haven't done anything *too* embarrassing."

Oh no! He'll see my adventure with Zian yesterday! He'll see everything—the Restricted Area, the Producer Farm, the factory compound… I will myself to move, to stop it, but I can't. I'm trapped. My sense of being comfortably numb is now replaced with feelings of utter violation, helplessness, and fear.

CHAPTER TEN

Agent Rudy continues to use the scanner to replay the events of my life from the past few days. It feels as if it takes hours, but I'm not sure. I can't check my neuroprocessor, and there's no clock on the wall. I'm paralyzed—I can't move a muscle, or say a thing while Agent Rudy speeds up through some of my memories and reduces others into slow motion. I've never hated anyone so much as I loathe this smug, spiteful man in front of me right now.

Agent Rudy studies my conversation with Mr. Johns, repeatedly replaying the moment where I spoke about my nightmares. He watches my school lunch conversation with Zian and Noelle several times in slow motion, and then he speeds up through the next few days. Once Agent Rudy reaches my conversation with Uncle Patterson at my father's memorial service, he slows down the footage once again. He freezes it when he reaches the image of Uncle Patterson's ring. Panic rises inside me, but I can't move.

"Well, well, what do we have here?!" Agent Rudy practically squeals with excitement. "It appears as though your Uncle has been associating with terrorists." He peers over at me, as if expecting some reaction. I can't react. I can't even blink. Agent Rudy paces back and forth in front of me with his fists clenched. "Perhaps your Uncle *is* a terrorist. The SED will have to pay him a visit and have a little 'conversation' about this," Rudy says, menacingly. If I could shudder, I would. Poor Uncle Patterson. I hope they don't do *this* to him.

"Let's see what else we can find!" Agent Rudy says, almost gleefully, as he picks up the scanner and continues fast forwarding through the footage to my adventure with Zian. Once he sees the Restricted Area, though, he slows it down. He shakes his head, frowning, when he sees the Producer farm and then Zian pointing out the factories to me. Agent Rudy freezes the picture, and then enlarges the image of Zian's excited face. Oh no, oh no!

"LOOK AT THIS!" Agent Rudy shouts. The other two guards step in for a closer look. "Can you believe this punk?!" Agent Rudy asks, shaking his bald head angrily as he stares at the image of Zian's face on the screen.

One of the guards nods his head. "I recognize him, sir," he says. "His name is Zian Reddington. He's a student at Pittock High School. His father was William Reddington."

Agent Rudy's eyes widen. "Well, well," he says, nodding slowly. "It all makes sense now. Find this subversive and bring him to me!" he commands.

Hot tears flood my eyes and roll down my cheeks. *Subversive?* Zian said subversives are forced to work as prisoners at Producer Farms. Does that mean he's going to imprison Zian?! As the two guards rush to the door, I open my mouth to scream 'NO!' and with all my might I arch my back to try to stand. Only a whisper leaves my lips though, and Agent Rudy easily shoves me back down in the metal chair again. He jams another needle into the skin at the base of my skull. My body goes limp and I lose consciousness.

◆ ◆ ◆

My eyes open and I'm staring at my bedroom ceiling. I blink. I don't remember getting here. I try to move, but I feel like I've been hit by a truck. Why does everything hurt? Even the base of my skull stings. I touch it, and then immediately remember exactly what happened. I feel adrenaline, and then rage surge through me.

I struggle to sit up. My body feels like a limp noodle. How dare Agent Rudy do that to me! Now, Uncle Patterson and Zian are in danger... my lungs suddenly feel crushed by guilt, and it's hard for me to catch my breath. Will Agent Rudy arrest them? What will happen to them if they're arrested? Will the SED come after me again? What about Tia and Mom—are they Okay?

Piper gazes up at me, lovingly, from the foot of my bed and wags his tail—thump, thump thumping it on my white down comforter. I try to stretch my hand out to pet him. It feels like it takes me forever to reach him. Ugh, I hate feeling this way. I despise Agent Rudy for doing this to me!

It's dark outside, and I can hear the pitter-patter of rain falling softly on the roof.

I flip on my neuroprocessor. It flickers, dims, and then brightens. **6:17 A.M.**, and **53 unread messages**. Whoa. I try to move my head side-to-side, to clear the fuzziness from my brain. I wish all of this was just a stupid nightmare, every bit of it—and that any moment now, when I wake up, everyone I love will be safe and my dad will still be alive.

I drag my body out of bed, and begin a slow, dizzy, shuffle to the bathroom. I hold onto the sink and wall in the bathroom for balance. When I finish, I shuffle back through my bedroom, clinging to the wall for support. I open my bedroom door and reach for the railing at the top of the stairs. I cling to it as I struggle to lower one leg at a time down each wood stair. It seems like it takes forever for me to reach the bottom of the stairs, but when I finally do, I peek around the corner.

Everything seems normal. Aunt Bliss is in her PJ's, with an apron tied around her waist, humming, while making omelets at the stove. Coffee is brewing. Mom enters the kitchen, carrying an arrangement of flowers. "I'm going to take these down to my studio, Bliss." Mom looks up and sees me. "Ren! Good morning. How are you feeling?" Mom asks, sounding almost... chipper.

I have no idea what to say. Doesn't she know what Agent Rudy and his goons did to me? "How did I..." my voice sounds weirdly far away and frog-like, "how did I get home?" I ask, tentatively.

Aunt Bliss and Mom exchange a quick glance. "SED agents drove us home, sweetie. We were at the government building for an hour or so," Mom replies.

An HOUR?! No. That's impossible. It felt like Agent Rudy scanned me all day long. I shake my head. "No. No, I was there much longer. Are you and Tia Okay? Did they deep scan your neuroprocessor too? Did you get injections?" I ask, my voice still shaky. I release the stair railing and try to walk into the kitchen. I wobble as I reach the kitchen table, and almost fall when I try to pull out a chair. Aunt Bliss catches me. Mom and Aunt Bliss exchange a second glance, this time, more worried.

"What are you talking about, Ren?" Mom asks, furrowing her brow.

I slowly lower myself into the chair and then stare up at Mom and Aunt Bliss, bewildered. Don't they know? "They strapped me to a chair, gave me an injection, and then Agent Rudy used some scanner thing to download my memories from my neuroprocessor. Didn't they do that to you?" I ask.

Mom slowly shakes her head, confused. Then, her face brightens. "OH! I know what's going on here!" she exclaims. "Agent Rudy said they gave you a mild sedative because you were so upset about your father. He mentioned you might have some slight memory loss or dreams because of the medication. You were *very* out of it when they brought you out of his office. The agents had to practically carry you to the car! You must have had one of your nightmares last night while under the influence of the sedative," Mom replies, shrugging her shoulders.

I flush with fury. "*Mild* sedative?! He injected me multiple times until I blacked out, Mom! Look at me. I can hardly stand. I didn't dream any of this! Agent Rudy used some sort of scanner to watch my memories, and now Zian and Uncle Patterson are in danger. Agent Rudy is going to go after them!" I shout, slamming my hand on the kitchen table for emphasis.

Mom crosses her arms in front of her chest and shakes her head. "Ren Sterling, calm down. No one is in danger. No one scanned your memories—there's no such technology! Agent

Rudy reported that you're having trouble discerning reality from fiction. He said we may have to take you to the doctor because you might be having a nervous breakdown. He hoped the sedative would help you, but now I can see that it hasn't..."

"Are you trying to say I'm crazy, Mom?!" I pull myself up and stand, clinging to the kitchen table. "I'M NOT MAKING THIS UP!" I scream.

Mom's face flushes with anger. "Well, either it's your nightmares acting up again, or you need psychiatric help, Ren!" she snaps.

"Hold on, hold on," Aunt Bliss says calmly as she steps between Mom and me. "No one is saying you're crazy, Ren! You and your father were very close. Grief and stress can do strange things to people. Also, sedatives *can* make your memory fuzzy. I can assure you that you were home and in bed by 11 A.M. yesterday. You slept for almost 20 hours straight."

My jaw drops as I stare at Aunt Bliss in utter confusion. "Now, I need to go home and help Charlene get off to school," Aunt Bliss continues. "I think your cousin wants her mom back—she's getting tired of her dad's cooking!" she says, chuckling. She places one hand on my shoulder, and another on Mom's. "Now, you two stay calm and be kind to one another. Everything will be Okay." Aunt Bliss lets go of Mom's shoulder and takes both my hands reassuringly in hers, saying, "I think it's best if you go back to school today, Ren. Get back into a routine. It should help you feel more stable, and it'll be good for you to see your friends."

"Maybe you're right, Aunt Bliss," I reply, hopefully.

"I usually am!" she exclaims, laughing. "Now, sit down and eat some breakfast. It's Aunt Bliss's special eggs. I'll check in on you later. I've gotta go!" Aunt Bliss unties the apron from around her waist, slips on her coat, picks up her purse, and scoots out of the kitchen. Tia strolls in, already dressed for school in a tight skirt and a sparkly shirt.

"Yum! Bacon omelets! Thanks Aunt Bliss!" Tia calls out. Mom hands each of us a plate. My stomach growls. I haven't eaten since yesterday morning. I sit and devour a huge amount of food. Boy, I do love Aunt Bliss's cooking! I begin to feel more relaxed and clear-headed. My body starts feeling a little bit stronger and more normal.

◆ ◆ ◆

After breakfast, I haul myself upstairs to get dressed for school. I head for my jewelry box first. I want to wear the shell necklace Dad gave me—it makes me feel close to him. Once I'm dressed, I begin responding to my unread communications, most of which are condolences and best wishes from friends. There are so many to wade through! I take a break and send Noelle a message.

"Hey you. Are you coming to school today?"

"From Noelle: "Of course. Are you feeling well enough to come?"

"I think so. It'll be good for me to get back into a routine."

"From Noelle: Great! I can't wait to hear what happened between you and Zian. I want details!"

My stomach flip-flops when I see his name in print. I don't know if Agent Rudy really saw my memories or not, but oh, please let Zian be Okay. I'll never forgive myself if I get Zian in trouble, although I can't help but wonder how he knew about the Producer farm and factory in the first place. Unless... did I dream about that too? Impulsively, I send Zian a message. **"Will you be at school today? I need to talk to you."** There's no response, which isn't unusual for Zian, since he rarely uses his neuroprocessor—but it sends a jolt of worry through me.

"Let's go, Ren!" Tia calls from downstairs. "Don't make us late again!"

"Seriously? I was late *once*. You're late *every day*, Tia!" I shout as I grab my backpack, and rush downstairs as quickly as my noodle-like body allows.

CHAPTER ELEVEN

As Mom drives us through our neighborhood, all the pretty houses and perfect, manicured lawns appear oddly artificial. I wonder why Mom and Tia don't see it. We pull up to the gate, and Mom announces, "I'm taking the girls to school." The guard nods and opens the gate.

"Have a great day!" he replies, waving. Mom waves back. I can't believe I never realized how weird it is that we are supposed to tell the guards where we're going every time we leave the neighborhood. Why should the guards care, unless their job is to be watching us? Is it possible that we live in a very pretty *prison*?

When Mom pulls up to the drop off zone at Pittock High, Tia jumps out and quickly disappears into the throng of students. I gather up my backpack and slowly open the car door—my body is still wobbly. Mom gazes over at me and her eyes well up with tears. "Just do your best today, honey. We're all dealing with so much… I love you, Ren," she says, reaching out and rubbing me gently on the back.

I nod. "I love you too, Mom." I struggle to give her a smile. I know she's doing her best, but I miss Dad so much, sometimes it hurts to breathe. I drag myself out of the car and close the door. As Mom pulls away from the curb, I feel very alone. I wonder if I'll have the energy to make it through the whole school day. Maybe I should have just stayed home today.

I trudge up the stone stairs through the bustling crowd of students. Suddenly, in the corner of my eye, I can see several men dressed in black uniforms watching me. What the…? I turn my head to look at them, but they've vanished. I take a deep breath and try to calm down. I'm probably just being paranoid. Why would SED agents be watching me at school? I'm not that important. Get it together, Sterling. I shake my head and walk through the open doors to the school.

Just inside, Noelle—dressed in jeans and a flannel—rushes up to me. She must have been waiting. "Hey you!" she exclaims. Noelle gives me the once over, observing my shaky state. "Are you *sure* you're ready to be back here?" she asks, concerned. Noelle's kindness makes me tear up. I shake my head.

"I'm not sure, but I just want life to be normal again," I reply. There's so much I wish I could tell Noelle, but I don't want to overwhelm her with my drama or get her in trouble with the SED, so I keep my mouth shut. Noelle wraps her arms around me and gives me a big hug.

"Don't worry, we'll get through the day together," Noelle comforts me as she links her arm in mine to hold me steady as we walk down the hall. I'm so grateful. What would I do without her?

I clear my throat nervously. "Have you... seen Zian today?"

Noelle shakes her head. "We don't usually see him until lunch, remember?"

Right. Maybe I dreamt the whole thing with Zian. Maybe I dreamt the whole thing with Agent Rudy calling Zian a subversive. Maybe I'm crazy and everybody else is fine. I clear my throat again. "May I... ask you a silly question, Noelle?"

Noelle grins. "Sure, what?"

"Did I leave my house with Zian during my dad's memorial service?"

Noelle furrows her brow in bewilderment. "What? Of course you did, silly! Why would you ask that?"

I shake my head and gaze down at my boots. "Umm... I've just been under so much stress... my dad, the nightmares... I've been having trouble keeping everything clear in my mind," I mumble.

"Well, your time with Zian must not have been too memorable, then!" Noelle tosses her head back and laughs.

Nothing could be further from the truth, but I give Noelle a small smile anyway. I'm not sure what to say. Even though I want to tell her everything, I don't want to put her in any danger.

"Well, when you're ready to talk, I want to hear all about your time with Zian. I'm dying to know what happened!" Noelle giggles as she wraps her arm around my shoulders.

I change the subject. "I need to stop at my locker before first period."

"Of course," Noelle replies.

As we approach my locker, I feel an odd sense of dread. What if there's another note? Honestly, a small part of me hopes there is another note and an even bigger part of me hopes there's not. I hold my breath as I enter the code with my processor. My locker door pops open and I peek inside. I can see my advanced chemistry and math books, but no notes—nothing unusual. I exhale slowly. Well, good. Maybe life will become normal again.

◆ ◆ ◆

Tuesday is a B day, which means my first period is an elective. I'm taking Introduction to Psychology this year with Ms. McNally. It's the only course she teaches at Pittock, because she also teaches at Capitol University—where Uncle Patterson works. I always look forward to this class. Ms. McNally is one of my favorite teachers, and I love the subject. Psychology is so fascinating.

So far this term, we've been focusing on social psychology. We've read studies on obedience, where the researchers urged participants to enslave or hurt other research participants. And the participants did it—they engaged in behavior that was brutal and horrific. How anyone could be induced to hurt someone as part of a study is beyond me, but it happened, and the studies have been replicated.

Ms. McNally clears her slender throat and straightens her brown corduroy jacket. "Okay. Let's get started with today's lecture, open your books--" Suddenly, she's interrupted by a neuroprocessor message from Principal Chapman.

"From PHS Principal: There will be a change in the schedule today to accommodate a special event planned for this afternoon. Right after fourth period lunch, there will be a campus-wide assembly in the main auditorium. The President of The Order will be giving a speech that will be shown on the large screen in the auditorium. Because of the importance of the information that President Coldstone will be conveying, this is a mandatory assembly for all Pittock students, teachers, and staff. I look forward to seeing you all at the assembly. Thank you and have a great rest of your morning."

Our classroom is suddenly abuzz with speculation. It's typical for President Coldstone to give State of The Order speeches periodically, and the speeches are always available through our neuroprocessors. What's odd this time is that he's giving the speech during the school day, rather than in the evening, and that it's mandatory viewing. Everyone in class is wondering what's so important about President Coldstone's speech today, including me.

◆ ◆ ◆

The rest of the morning feels like it drags on forever. I can't wait to see Zian at lunch—he's all I can think about. I have so many questions about what we saw together, and I'm dying to tell him what happened with that horrible Agent Rudy. IF... what happened with Agent Rudy really happened... I don't know. Mom has me doubting myself.

At lunch, Noelle and I take our usual seats at one of the senior Intelligencia tables. I scan the lunchroom looking for Zian, but he's nowhere to be seen. I ask around, but none of the other students at the table have seen him, either. The lunch period passes by with the usual topics of conversation—soccer, Foundation Team, tests, homework, music, and the upcoming homecoming dance. It's hard for me to talk. I feel more and more anxious as each minute passes and Zian is nowhere to be found.

When the next period bell rings we all rise to go to the assembly. *Where is Zian?* I hope he's safe. One of the last things he said to me was he didn't know when we would see each other again. Did he know the SED agents would find out that he showed me the Producer farms and factories? If so, how did he know? I fidget with the gold shell necklace Dad gave me as Noelle and I walk to the auditorium, trying to talk myself out of my fears. Maybe this whole mess is just in my head, and Zian will walk up to me any minute.

◆ ◆ ◆

Our school's enormous, elegant, state-of-the art auditorium is filled to capacity with all of Pittock's students and staff. The maroon colored seats are cushy and even rock back and forth slightly. The national flag and the Pittock school flag are mounted on each side of the black, glistening stage. Mr. Chapman, our tall, stately, greying Principal—wearing a navy suit and a maroon ascot—glides onto the stage, followed by short, portly Vice-Principal Davis and my bow-tied Tech Lab teacher, Mr. Johns. I can't help but have a bad taste in my mouth when I see Mr. Johns. I'll never trust him again.

Principal Chapman steps up to the podium, which is adorned with the Emblem of The Order. Mr. Davis and Mr. Johns position themselves on each side of Principal Chapman as he welcomes the assembly. As Principal Chapman begins to speak, I scan the seats of the auditorium, looking for Zian.

"Welcome Pittock High School student body and staff. It's so nice to see the entire Pittock community here for such an important event!" There's a round of applause, and then

Principal Chapman continues. "In just a few moments, President Coldstone will be addressing our nation with news of vital importance. Like all good citizens of The Order, we do our part to make our society work effectively, and our President's words will surely give us inspiration to continue our focus on our collective mission and values." More applause. I've spied Tia's long, blonde hair and sparkly shirt in the crowd, but I can't find Zian anywhere. I feel desperate to see him. What if he's in trouble because of me?

The large screen behind Principal Chapman illuminates with the Emblem of The Order. The Emblem is then quickly replaced by an image of President Coldstone sitting at his presidential desk. He's dressed in a crisp, grey suit and is wearing a light blue tie which matches his eyes. His silver hair is perfectly coiffed. Chapman, Davis, and Mr. Johns scurry off the stage as soon as President Coldstone leans forward and begins to speak.

"Citizens of The Order, it is with a sad heart and a steady resolve that I, President Xavier Coldstone, speak to you today. As you already know, last week we experienced an act of terrorism—the likes of which has not been seen since The Order was formed seventy years ago. One of our lead scientists at the Ash-Tech Corporation was brutally assassinated. This is a monumental loss for not only Ash-Tech, but for our great nation. Dr. Peter Sterling was overseeing some of the most advanced and rigorous research focused on the continued improvement of our neuroprocessor technology. Today, we honor Dr. Sterling for his outstanding and innovative research. He gave his life for the betterment of The Order. We grieve for, and along with, his family, friends, and colleagues. He leaves behind a wife and two daughters, as well as a legacy of exceptional contributions to The Order."

A lump forms in the back of my throat. I feel like I'm going to burst into tears. I reach up and gently hold the shell pendant against the hollow of my throat. President Coldstone leans back slightly in his chair. "We believe that the high quality of Dr. Sterling's research is precisely why he was targeted by the terrorist organization, known as Conation. From what we can gather, their sole purpose is to disrupt the technological advances of The Order, for reasons that are not rational or understandable. These criminals erroneously seem to believe that the technological advances that have brought us so many wonderful medical, educational, and social improvements need to be eliminated. I simply cannot fathom it. They are motivated by an ideology of madness."

There are anxious murmurs across the auditorium. Principal Chapman raises his long, slender hand, and the quiet resumes. President Coldstone leans forward and continues. "My intention is not to alarm you by sharing this information. My only goal is to strengthen your resolve to help us locate and destroy these terrorists. If we work together, we will protect the cherished values of The Order. I don't need to remind you of how The Order saved our nation. Due to the wisdom of the Founding Fathers of The Order, everyone in our society has a clear purpose, which supports the well-being of all. Do we wish to return to a time when chaos, crime, and inefficient financial and social structures dominated our crumbling nation? Like you, I'm certain the answer is no."

There are more murmurs—this time, of agreement. "Thankfully, the terrorists are only a small group of *individuals*. We *will* prevail in eradicating this scourge from our nation. We will stamp them out, like the many diseases that have been crushed by our medical and technological advances. Together, we will protect The Order and all that it provides for us. *Together, we will prevail.* Long Live Cascadia. Long live The Order."

President Coldstone's image disappears from the giant screen, and cheers erupt throughout the auditorium as feelings of civic pride sweep through the crowd. We have a collective mission and purpose: The Order must be maintained.

Principal Chapman steps forward as he addresses the auditorium again. "Well, that was truly inspirational!" he exclaims. "We've just been informed that the President's speech is available to watch again on your neuroprocessors. I know that all of us wish to help in any way that we possibly can. If anyone has, or receives information, that can assist with identifying these terrorists, please contact me directly, Mr. Davis, or any of your teachers. Thank you. We'll now be moving to sixth period class. Enjoy the rest of your day."

As the auditorium slowly empties, students and teachers walk up to me, shake my hand, pat me on the shoulder, and even hug me—offering support for me and my family. Across the auditorium I see Tia is also surrounded by supportive friends and teachers. While it feels good to receive support and encouragement, it's very confusing. If Dad died for the good of The Order, as President Coldstone said, then he may have died for a nation that is good for the well-being of some but not for all. What if our prosperity is built on the backs of those who are enslaved? I don't have any answers, and I don't dare express my thoughts to anyone—not even Noelle.

◆ ◆ ◆

When the school day ends, Noelle and I grab our usual pre-soccer meal of a veggie burrito and chicken bowl. I'm hoping the food will give me the strength I'll need to practice today. I'm still not quite myself, but it'll feel good to be out on the soccer field again, as long as I can keep up. Noelle and I sprint up the steps to Pittock, hurry through the hallways, and then head downstairs to the locker room, which is noisy with the usual end-of-day chatter. As soon as I enter, though, the room becomes silent. My teammates line up to give me hugs and words of encouragement. Even Donna Royce, the Financier, flashes me a supportive look.

"Sterling," Coach Cari bellows as she strides into the locker room. She's chewing gum, as usual. "I'd like to speak with you in my office."

Noelle gives me an inquisitive look. I shrug my shoulders. I quickly follow Coach Cari down the hall. Once in her office, she closes the door behind us, and directs me to have a seat. She sits down behind her large metal desk and runs her fingers through her dirty blonde hair.

"Ren, I can only imagine how difficult things have been for you lately," Coach begins. "I'm so sorry for your loss. I'm not sure that soccer is the best thing for you right now, however. I've asked your mother to pick you up. I'd like you to take the rest of the week off so you can come back strong next week."

I can't believe what I'm hearing—Coach Cari has always told us that sports are the best thing for kids, especially if we're dealing with stressful life events. 'Sports help cultivate focus and purpose,' she's said many times. I stare at Coach Cari with a stunned look on my face, and then finally blurt out, "But I'm okay, Coach. I'd really like to go to practice today!"

Coach shakes her head. "Nope. I've discussed this with the assistant coaches. We all agree it's best for you to take some time off. Just come back strong next week, kiddo."

I nod. "Okay." I guess I don't have a choice. It's probably for the best. I'm still feeling a little weak and tired—my burrito hasn't exactly given me superpowers yet. Coach Cari stands and gestures for me to join her at the back door of her office. I grab my backpack and follow. She pushes the door open, and then escorts me into the parking area behind the gym.

Mom's car is nowhere to be seen, but a large, black van pulls up in front of us. Two people dressed in all black and full-face masks jump out and lunge at me. What the...?! I scream and start to recoil, but Coach Cari clamps a hand over my mouth and holds me still. "Shhh..." she hushes me. "Everything will be okay, Ren."

The masked individuals pick me up and carry me to the van. Panicked, I crane my neck to look back at Coach Cari just before being placed into the back of the van. She mouths the words again, "Everything will be okay," and her face is the last thing I see before a black hood is forced over my head.

CHAPTER TWELVE

"This will go more smoothly if you stop fighting us, Ren!" A woman's voice shouts from the front seat as the van roars out of the parking lot. "Now stay down!"

I don't know how I could possibly get up. I'm face down in the back of the van with a knee pressed firmly against my back and a hood over my head. My arms are wrenched behind my back and my wrists have been bound together with some sort of zip tie. The air is being squeezed out of my lungs by the knee. If this is one of my horrible nightmares, I sure hope I wake up soon.

"Who are you? Why are you doing this to me?" I ask, gasping for air. The hood is suffocating.

"Be quiet. Answers will come. I promise," the woman in the front of the van replies.

Something cold touches the back of my neck. After about 30 seconds, a man says, "Okay. Her locator function has been disabled, and her neuroprocessor interrupted. It's now 4:07 P.M. Set the timers on your processors. We have exactly ninety minutes."

I don't think these people are SED agents. I don't know what's happening to me, but I get the feeling I should just follow their instructions, at least for now. I stop struggling and try to slow down my breathing. What choice do I have, anyway? Once I stop struggling, my kidnappers loosen their grip on me and eventually the knee is removed from my back. I start to catch my breath, even with the hot, black hood still on my head.

No one speaks again while the van is moving. At one point, I try turning on my side to get a little more comfortable, but then I'm told to stay down. We seem to be leaving downtown Capitol City, but I'm not sure. I can see only slivers of light coming around the base of my neck where the hood ends. I try to activate my processor, but it won't turn on. Finally, the van stops. The back of the van is opened, and I'm lifted out. My kidnappers stand me upright on my unsteady legs. Two people hold my arms and lead me into some sort of building. I hear the door close loudly behind us as I am guided forward. We walk through what must be a hallway, and then enter a room, where they sit me down on a low stool that must have wheels, because I slide a little when they let me go.

The hood is removed, and I can finally breathe! One of the masked men cuts the zip tie, freeing my wrists. It takes a few moments for my eyes to adjust to the bright light in the room, and then I peer all around me, still blinking, trying to get a sense of where I am. There are two men in black wearing masks guarding the door. The room looks like a lab, with various machines, monitors, work desks, and equipment. The floor is cement, the walls are green tile, and the room smells… sterile.

I sit quietly until a woman dressed in all black, wearing a dark green, full-face mask enters the lab. She rolls another low stool up in front of me and sits down. She's tall—six feet or more—and quite thin. "Hello, Ren," she says. Her voice is gravelly. "I'm sorry we have to go to such extreme measures to meet with you, but we must take the necessary precautions to protect you and us."

"How do you know my name? Where am I? Who are you? What do you want with me?" I ask, rapid fire. I'm so relieved someone is finally going to tell me what is going on.

"Slow down. One question at a time," the woman in the green mask replies. "First, I can't tell you right now how we know you, or where you are, that would be too dangerous. And I can't tell you who I am either—also too dangerous. As for why we need to meet with you, I need to find out what you know, and what has happened to you over the last few days. There's something you're going to help us accomplish."

Well, she didn't answer *anything*. Frustrated, I exclaim, "Accomplish? I don't understand what you're talking about!"

"Okay, Ren. Let me try to explain it to you," the woman calmly replies. "First, I'm going to ask you a few questions to see what you know. Please, just relax--"

Seriously?! "I'm getting really tired of people doing things to me that are in no way relaxing—like kidnapping, and then telling me to relax!" I snap.

The woman's voice becomes even gentler. "Focus, Ren. Tell me about your interview with the SED. What did you tell them?"

I take a deep breath and exhale slowly. "I'm not even sure any of this happened, because my mom says it isn't possible, that I must have been dreaming, but... they stuck needles in my neck, sedated me, and then used some kind of device to deep scan my neuroprocessor. Agent Rudy downloaded my personal memories, and then watched them. It was horrible," I reply. Then, I shake my head, confused. "I told my mom, but she didn't believe me."

The woman shoots a glance at the men guarding the door, and nods her head, as if I've said something of great significance. She leans forward, resting her elbows on her thighs. "So, it's true," she replies in her gravelly voice, tapping her fingertips together. "We had heard that the government recently developed this type of technology—deep scanning, they call it. We suspected that had happened to you, which is why we have to take such extraordinary precautions with you today."

I didn't dream it? It happened. "What do you mean? Why are you taking these 'precautions'?" I ask.

"If they scanned your memories once, they'll likely do it again, which could put us all in danger," the woman replies. She sits up straight and gazes directly into my eyes. Her brown eyes are surprisingly kind. "Do you know what they saw, Ren?"

"They saw everything," I say softly, and then helplessly shrug my shoulders.

She nods slowly, as if she understands exactly what I

mean. "That's what we were afraid of. We're going to do a painless procedure on your neuroprocessor. It won't take very long--"

"Oh NO!" I protest, rolling my stool backwards. "I'm not letting anyone else touch me until you answer my questions."

The woman smiles, which looks kind of funny because of the mask. "Wonderful. You're making progress, Ren."

I squint my eyes suspiciously, and stare into hers. They appear sincere. "What do you mean, *progress*?" I ask.

"You've always been very intelligent and exceptionally intuitive, from what I understand. Now, however, your courage, strength, and sense of free will are emerging. I'd heard it was so, but it's good to see first-hand." There's that funny smile again.

I begin to smile back, but then realize what she's just implied. Goosebumps rise on my arms. "What do you mean, *my free will is emerging*? Suddenly, we're interrupted by loud voices and a commotion coming from outside the door of the lab.

"Excuse me." The woman ignores my question, stands, and quickly exits the room.

"Let me see her, please! I need to see her!" I hear someone shout in the hallway. I know that voice... It's Zian! I start to stand too, but the two guards step forward threateningly.

"Sit," the bigger guard commands. So, I sit and listen. Fortunately, there's a gap between the bottom of the lab door and the floor.

"No," I can hear the woman who just left the lab say. "It's too dangerous."

"She has a right to know what's happening to her," insists Zian.

"Stop. Think rationally about this. If the procedure doesn't work, it could expose you and all the others working for the cause," the woman argues back. "There are a *lot* of people who could be endangered. Besides, Ren isn't ready to know the truth yet. She's making progress, but she isn't ready."

"No, *you* stop and think. If the government has already deep scanned her processor, then they already know about me.

CONATION

There's no harm in letting me speak with Ren about what's happening, even if the procedure fails. I won't mention any names or expose anything that could put our people at risk... I promise. Trust me. Please," Zian pleads.

"No, Zian, and that's final! Ren's not ready. The timing has to be right or it could backfire on us. When it *is* the right time, you'll be with her again. Our time today is very short. We need to do the procedure and then immerse her back into her life as soon as possible."

With that, the lab door opens, and the masked woman returns. She sits down in front of me again.

"Please, I want to see Zian!" I exclaim.

The woman shakes her head, sighing. "It's unfortunate you heard that, Ren. I sure hope this procedure works. Okay, listen. I have some answers for you, but I don't have time to explain anything further, Okay?"

"Okay..." I nod my head slowly.

"It was rumored—and now it seems it's true—that the government has developed the technology to be able to deep scan neuroprocessors in order to reveal what a person has experienced, even when their processor is turned off. They can download and store anyone's memories. They can find details that your conscious brain doesn't even remember. They can probably even download your dreams."

"Whoa. Even my *dreams*...?"

The woman in the mask nods. "Most likely. It's very frightening, and it's a complete violation of privacy. To combat this intrusion and protect our people, we've been developing a procedure which will replace select memories with the ones we've designed. That way, even if you *are* deep scanned, the government is prevented from seeing memories we don't want them to see. Or, at least, that's how it's supposed to work. You'll be the first person to try the procedure under real life conditions, not just in a lab."

"Oh great," I say, sighing. "So now I'm *your* guinea pig, too?"

"In some ways, yes," the woman concedes, shrugging.

"I don't understand—why are you so afraid of the government? Aren't they here to help us?" I ask.

Her eyes stare into mine again. "What do *you* think, Ren? Did the SED help you when they stole your personal and private experiences?"

Okay, she has a point there. "One more question. What's the name of your organization?" I ask. The woman reaches under her mask, rubs her chin, and shakes her head.

"I don't have time to go into this right now, Ren. Your locator function will become enabled again very soon. We need to replace the memories of your time with us and get you back in your life before the SED realizes you're missing. Please, I need for you to lay down on this table--" she says, pointing to a medical table near the lab equipment.

I recoil. "Let me get this straight. You want to play around with my neuroprocessor, distort my brain, and then replace my memories? No, no way! I don't want anybody else messing with my head. I've been toyed with enough. I feel like I've been going crazy lately."

"I love your feistiness and sense of freedom, Ren. Again, it shows real progress. But right now, *I just need you to trust me*," the masked woman replies.

"Trust you?! I don't even *know* you!" I exclaim. The masked woman stands, and the two guards move closer. "Zian!" I cry, "Zian, help me!" The three of them surround me. "Get away from me!" I shout. They step even closer, and I raise my arms, getting ready to strike out if needed.

"Ren, listen to me!" the woman shouts. "We don't have time for this! If you want to protect yourself and your loved ones, then you have to let me do this. *Please*."

I stare into her eyes, and suddenly, I know, without a doubt, that she's telling me the truth. I don't know how I know, but I know. I lower my arms. "Okay." I walk to the medical table, and then climb on top. The woman takes out a set of medical equipment, fills a syringe with clear liquid, and then wipes the side of my neck with cotton. She lifts my necklace gently with her calloused hand.

"Did your father give this to you?"

I'm astonished. "Yes, how did you know?"

She ignores my question and injects the syringe into my neck. "This is a sedative to help you relax, Ren. It'll help the procedure go faster."

"But I don't want any more sedatives--" I begin to reply, and then suddenly feel warm and relaxed all over.

"Okay Ren, you'll feel tickling in your brain and spine during the procedure. That's normal."

Normal... what about this whole thing is normal? I'm supposed to be at soccer practice with a dad that's alive, instead of being a guinea pig for mysterious people in masks. One of the guards wheels over a small desk with a machine and a monitor on top. The machine has thick wires that are attached to a small paddle, with a two-inch elastic band hanging from it. The woman lifts my head up off the table, and the paddle is placed on the back of my neck. The paddle is held firmly in place by the elastic band, which is wrapped around my head. Once secured, my head is lowered back down on the table.

"Very good. Now, we're going to replace all your memories from the school locker room until now. If the SED deep scans you again, they shouldn't find any evidence of your time with us. You won't have any memory of this, either."

"What do you mean, no memory?" I try to ask, but I think I end up babbling some nonsense instead. The sedative has taken full effect.

The woman begins typing on a keyboard. I feel a tickling sensation inside my head and along my spine. Images of the locker room and Coach Cari flash before my eyes, and I see Aunt Bliss' smiling face. Then, I feel the woman unfasten my necklace. She slips it off my neck. Stop, that's mine, I want to say, but my lips won't move. Instead, I hear the woman say, "The memory replacement seems to be working. Fingers crossed that it holds up. Now, let's get her out of here."

CHAPTER THIRTEEN

I wake up groggy. My sheets and pillow feel softer than usual. When did I get flannel sheets? I reach for Piper, but I don't feel him on the foot of my bed. I sit up and look, but I don't see him either. Why is my comforter yellow? Where am I? My mind is blank and my heart starts to pound as I frantically look around the strange room.

Suddenly, I remember—I slept at Aunt Bliss and Uncle Ray's house last night! The butter yellow guest room has Aunt Bliss's beautiful, framed photography of flowers on the walls. Whew. I take a deep breath and exhale. I lie back down and stretch my toes—rubbing them against the fuzzy, warm sheets. So cozy. I need to get some of these for my bed at home. I didn't even have any nightmares last night!

I can hear the faint hum of voices and clanking of dishes. Eventually, I climb out of bed and head downstairs, stopping at the small bathroom across the hall on my way. In the kitchen, Aunt Bliss is baking cinnamon rolls and frying bacon, while Uncle Ray empties the dishwasher. Aunt Bliss's cooking smells so delicious I'm practically drooling.

"Hey there, sleepy head," Uncle Ray calls out playfully, as I enter the bright white and yellow kitchen. Aunt Bliss adores yellow.

"Hi, Uncle Ray. Hi, Aunt Bliss."

"How'd you sleep, Ren?" asks Aunt Bliss, with a cheerful smile.

"Amazing! I always sleep well here."

"I'm so glad, sweetie." She gives me a hug and a kiss on my head. She smells like cinnamon and sugar. "You were completely exhausted yesterday. I was worried you were coming down with something. So, you're feeling better?"

"Yes. I think I just needed a good night's sleep," I reply. "Thank you so much for picking me up at school yesterday, Aunt Bliss. Coach Cari was probably annoyed that I had to leave soccer practice, but it was the best decision. Obviously, I needed the rest."

"Of course! You're so welcome. I'm glad it worked out that I could come and get you in-between hair appointments. Don't worry, I'm sure Coach Cari will get over it." Aunt Bliss kisses me on the head again and rests her cheek on my forehead. "Well, you don't have a temperature. Do you think you're up for going to school today?" she asks.

"I think so," I reply.

Just then, my tall, honey hair-colored cousin Charlene comes bounding into the kitchen. "Cinnamon rolls, yum! Ren! You're awake!" Charlene exclaims, and gives me an enthusiastic bear hug.

I laugh. "Hi Cuz!" I say.

Charlene is fifteen. She's the youngest of the three Bixby kids, and is a freshman at one of the large Provider high schools. Her older siblings, Josh and Whitney, are at trade schools. Josh is training to be an electrician, while Whitney is becoming a hair stylist, like her mom. Mom told me that it was a big surprise when Aunt Bliss got pregnant with Charlene because Aunt Bliss thought she was too old to have another child. Aunt Bliss always says how lucky they are that Charlene came to them. She calls Charlene her 'Gift' because of the joy she's brought into their lives.

"Okay you two. It's time to sit down for some breakfast," Aunt Bliss announces, pointing to the delicious spread on the kitchen table.

"YUM!" Charlene and I exclaim in unison. What a breakfast—hot, crispy bacon, and warm, doughy, sweet cinnamon rolls! Uncle Ray, Aunt Bliss, Charlene and I eat until our bellies are stuffed. We keep our conversation light—chatting about friends, soccer, and school. Charlene is one of the best players on her freshmen soccer team. She may even be named to the all-star team in the Provider division. We laugh a lot. I'm actually starting to feel normal again, like my old self.

"Charlene, dear, will you let Ren borrow an outfit?" Aunt Bliss asks, as we help clean up after breakfast. "She came here straight from school yesterday. We didn't have time to stop at her house to pick up a change of clothes."

"Of course! Let's go to my bedroom, Ren. Race ya!" Charlene exclaims. We run upstairs, giggling. I love Charlene's sense of humor. She's so much fun, and so easy to get along with—compared to Tia. Charlene's a genuinely sweet girl with a positive attitude about life. She's a lot like her mom.

Once in her room, Charlene gives me multiple outfits to try on, and we end up laughing hysterically while I model her clothes. Although I'm almost three years older than Charlene, she's as tall as I am, so her clothes fit me well. Eventually, a group communication flashes to me and Charlene, interrupting our fun.

"From Aunt Bliss: I'm going to name you two, the giggle girls. Maybe GG, for short. It's time to go to school, GG."

"Coming!" we both respond. We bound playfully back down the stairs and out the front door. Aunt Bliss is already in the car waiting for us. As we hop into the back seat, I smile to myself. I've had so much fun this morning with Charlene and Aunt Bliss! I haven't felt this happy since before Dad died.

◆ ◆ ◆

Unfortunately, my happiness is short-lived. As we pull out of the driveway, I observe a black government vehicle with tinted windows parked across the street. Just as we pass it, the car pulls out from the curb, and then follows close behind us as we drive through the neighborhood—riding our bumper. "What the heck!?" Aunt Bliss exclaims, annoyed. Suddenly the black car races past us, and then abruptly pulls in front of Aunt Bliss' car, blocking her way. She slams on her brakes to avoid hitting it. "Are you kidding me?!" yells Aunt Bliss. "What's *wrong* with them?"

Two men wearing black SED uniforms step out and walk over to our car—one on each side. Aunt Bliss cautiously lowers her window. "What's this about?" she asks, barely controlling her frustration. "You almost killed us."

"I need to scan your processor, ma'am," an agent sternly replies.

Aunt Bliss retorts, "Why? I didn't do anything wrong."

The agent doesn't answer. He simply waves a handheld device near the back of Aunt Bliss's neck for a few seconds. He glances at the device and then says, "Mrs. Bixby, we need to speak with Ms. Sterling. She needs to come with us." As he talks, the other agent opens the rear door of Aunt Bliss' car, gesturing for me to step out.

No, please, I don't want to go with them. My heart starts to race, and all the calm and happy feelings drain from my body. I don't move a muscle.

"Please come with us, Ms. Sterling. Now!" the agent commands.

My pleading eyes meet Aunt Bliss's. Please do something, anything to protect me, I beg her, silently. Compassion and then anger appear on her face. Aunt Bliss barks with authority, "Listen! Ren needs to go to school. What is *wrong* with you people? She was just there a day or so ago. She told you all she knows."

The agent nearest Aunt Bliss leans his face into her open window, and replies calmly, "We'll take her to school once we speak with her at the Central Government Building." Then he peers into the back seat at me and commands, "Ms. Sterling, you will exit the vehicle and come with us now, or we will remove you forcibly."

I still don't move a muscle. My heart pounds even faster. I wish I could just run away. Aunt Bliss flashes me a worried look, and then says with false bravado, "Go ahead, Ren. It'll be fine, sweetie. I'll come find you downtown after I drop Charlene off at school. Don't worry. We'll get you back to school as soon as possible."

Charlene looks shocked. Tears well up in her eyes. I do my best to appear brave, even though I'm trembling on the inside. I reach over, and gently squeeze Charlene's arm goodbye.

As I step out of Aunt Bliss's car, my legs are shaking from the nervous energy coursing through my body. I can't believe this is happening again. Why won't they just leave me alone? Once I'm in the back of the government vehicle, I turn around to gaze out the back window at Aunt Bliss and Charlene. I wonder when I'll see them again.

◆ ◆ ◆

We drive downtown in silence until we come to a stop in front of the imposing Central Government Building. Just seeing the building makes me want to cry. I don't want to be here. My heart is still racing, and I'm shaking with fear as they escort me into the building. They lead me down the hall to the same large office I was in a few days ago.

When we enter, all the agents cease what they're doing, and turn to stare at me. One of the agents points for me to sit in a chair along the wall. I quickly send a communication to Mom. **"SED agents took me to the Central Government Building. Why won't they leave me alone?"**

She responds instantly. **"From Mom: Yes, I just heard from Aunt Bliss. I'm sorry, honey. Just answer their questions and then Aunt Bliss will take you to school."**

Mom's probably working in her studio. She doesn't seem concerned at all—maybe I have nothing to worry about either…? My body keeps telling me differently, though. I can't get my hands to stop shaking. I wish I could run out of here and never look back. After fifteen long minutes, one of the agents directs me to rise and follow him. Once we enter Agent Rudy's office, the door is abruptly slammed behind us.

Agent Rudy is seated at his desk with his back to me. The SED agent shoves me by the shoulders into the metal chair on the other side of the desk. When Agent Rudy finally turns to face me, he just stares without acknowledging me. His facial expression is so ice cold and steely, I look away.

As we sit in awkward silence, questions speed through my mind. What does he want this time? Will he do another deep scan? Will he give me more injections? Have they arrested Zian? Nervous energy courses through my body as I painfully wait.

CHAPTER FOURTEEN

After a few long, intimidating minutes of complete silence, SED Director Rudy finally speaks. "Okay, Ren. This is what's going to happen. You're going to tell me everything I want to know and cooperate with me fully, or we'll just have a repeat of our last visit. We can do this the easy way or the hard way. *Do you understand?*" He leans forward and puts his elbows on the desk, angrily. Ugh. I can smell his stinky breath from here.

I nod my head. "Of course, sir! But I don't know anything. Nothing has happened since the last time I saw you," I respectfully reply.

Agent Rudy slams his hand down on his desk. "DON'T LIE TO ME!" he shouts.

I startle from the violent sudden movement. I try to think as quickly as I can, but I still can't remember anything that's happened. I'm pretty sure I haven't done anything wrong. I don't remember doing anything wrong, anyway. Tears suddenly sting my eyes. "I truly don't know what you're asking of me, Agent Rudy," I say, my voice trembling. "I can't think of anything that has occurred that would be important to you. I don't know what you want to know."

"I want the complete truth!" Agent Rudy exclaims as he stands and begins pacing. "I'm going to give you one chance to tell me the truth before I deep scan your processor. What did you do after school yesterday?"

To appease him, I speak as quickly as I can. "Noelle and I went for some food before soccer practice, like we always do. Then we went to the locker room, and…" I pause. I can't… I don't… for some reason I can't remember what happened next.

My mind is totally blank.

"Go on," Agent Rudy urges, leaning down at me.

I close my eyes, shake my head, and try to recall any memories. Sweat is beginning to bead on my forehead. Suddenly, in a flash, I remember. "Oh right! I was feeling sick, so I went into Coach Cari's office. She couldn't get a hold of my mom, so she contacted my aunt instead. Aunt Bliss came and picked me up. I went straight to bed when I reached Aunt Bliss's house and slept until this morning. That's it." I say, exhaling—deeply relieved I finally remember what happened.

"*Wrong!*" Agent Rudy angrily replies. "The locator function on your neuroprocessor was disabled for ninety minutes shortly after you entered the locker room yesterday. My agents were unable to locate you when you did not emerge for soccer practice. How and why was your locator function disabled? *AND DON'T LIE TO ME.*" Agent Rudy commands, pointing his thick finger in my face.

What is he saying?! "I have no idea what you're talking about, sir. I didn't *do* anything. Please believe me," I plead. My stomach is in knots, and my palms are sweating.

"I want to believe you, Ms. Sterling, but tracking functions on neuroprocessors don't just stop working on their own."

"Tracking functions?! The SED tracks people through their neuroprocessors? Isn't that an invasion of privacy?!" I ask, dismayed.

Without answering my questions, Agent Rudy plops back down at his desk, folds his arms across his chest and then asks, "Have you seen Zian Reddington? His locator function has also been disabled."

My mouth drops open and I shake my head with genuine bewilderment. "No. Zian wasn't at school yesterday."

Agent Rudy studies me for a moment, and then says matter-of-factly, "I'm going to scan and download your memories now, Ms. Sterling. I'm going to see every detail of your life since the moment you were last in this office. You better be telling me the truth." Agent Rudy removes the strange looking scanner out of the cabinet. "Will you cooperate, or do I need to give you an injection again?" he asks, threateningly.

"I've told you the truth. Nothing has happened. Please don't give me another injection... please. I'll cooperate."

Agent Rudy stands up, marches behind me, and then places the scanner on the back of my neck. He taps the device. The large monitor mounted on the wall illuminates, revealing the Emblem of The Order. My brain and spinal cord begin to feel gently tickled. It's an unpleasant, but not necessarily painful sensation. The Emblem on the monitor shifts into images from my life. Agent Rudy uses the fast-forward function, and then slows down to reveal images of Mom and Aunt Bliss in the kitchen of my house. He turns up the volume.

"Ren! Good morning. How are you feeling?"

"How did I... how did I get home?"

"SED agents drove us home, sweetie. We were at the government building for an hour or so."

"No. No, I was there much longer. Are you and Tia okay? Did they deep scan your neuroprocessor too? Did you get injections?"

"What are you talking about, Ren?"

"They strapped me to a chair, gave me an injection, and then Agent Rudy used some scanner thing to download my memories from my neuroprocessor. Didn't they do that to you?"

"OH! I know what's going on here! Agent Rudy said that they gave you a mild sedative because you were so upset about your Dad. He mentioned you might have some slight memory loss or dreams because of the medication. You were very out of it when they brought you out of his office. The agents had to practically carry you to the car. You must have had one of your nightmares last night while under the influence of the sedative."

"*Mild* sedative?! He injected me multiple times until I blacked out, Mom! Look at me, I can hardly stand now. I didn't dream any of this! Agent Rudy used some sort of scanner to watch my memories, and now Zian and Uncle Patterson are in danger. Agent Rudy is going to go after them!"

"Ren Sterling, calm down. No one is in danger, no one scanned your memories—there's no such thing! Agent Rudy told me you're having trouble discerning reality from fiction. He said we may have to take you to the doctor because you might be having a nervous breakdown. He hoped the sedative would help you, but now I can see that it hasn't…"

"Are you trying to say I'm crazy, Mom?! I'M NOT MAKING THIS UP!"

"Well either it's your nightmares acting up again, or you need psychiatric help!"

"Hold on, hold on. No one is saying you're crazy, Ren! You and your father were very close. Grief and stress can do strange things to people. Also, sedatives *can* make your memory fuzzy. I can assure you; you were home and in bed by 11 A.M. yesterday. You slept for almost 20 hours straight."

"Well—unlike you—your mom and aunt are behaving like good citizens of The Order," Agent Rudy says, scathingly. Then he fast-forwards through my day, including President Coldstone's speech. He slows down when I enter the locker room. There are images of my teammates giving me hugs and encouragement, and then… there is a millisecond blip in the images. It's barely noticeable, but Agent Rudy rewinds and replays the blip in slow motion.

"Just what in The Order is that?" he asks, incredulously.

"I have no idea, sir." I respectfully reply.

"That distortion shouldn't be there," Agent Rudy grunts, furrowing his brow. "The scanner indicates your processor is working fine, but that blip is very strange. It must have occurred when your locator function became disabled. Your neuroprocessor seems to have malfunctioned." Mystified, he shakes his head, and then continues playing images. The monitor on the wall reveals that I'm walking down the hall to Coach Cari's office. I knock on the door.

"Come in."

"Hi Coach, I'm sorry to bother you, but I don't know if I can practice today. I'm not feeling well."

"Ren, you've been through so much, but I think athletics are the best thing to get your mind off your troubles. My advice would be for you to come to practice and be with your teammates."

"I know, and I don't want to disappoint you, Coach. But I'm feeling really light-headed and dizzy. I think I might be getting sick."

"Okay. I'll call your mom to come get you... Well, she's not answering her processor. It looks like your aunt is next on your emergency call list. Hi Bliss. This is Cari Werth at Pittock High School. I'm here with Ren. She's not feeling well. Would it possible for you to come pick her up?"

Agent Rudy speeds up the images, which show Coach Cari escorting me out the back of her office and walking me to Aunt Bliss's car. Then I ride to Aunt Bliss's house. Once inside, I climb the stairs and go straight to bed in the guest room.

A frown forms on Agent Rudy's lips. "Well, I will have your memories analyzed, but it appears you're telling the truth," he says, sounding disappointed. "One of the agents will take you to school now. He motions for the other agent in the room to escort me out.

As I rise to leave, Agent Rudy leans back in his seat with a little smirk on his face. "For your own good, Ren, don't tell anyone about our little conversations and the memory scanning. No one will believe you anyway, and it could get you put away in a special treatment facility, if you know what I mean. It might also lead to some people that you care about getting hurt," he says, ominously.

I don't reply. I just stare Agent Rudy directly in his cold, gray eyes, and then walk past his desk toward the door. As I do, Agent Rudy reaches out and touches me on the arm. I shirk from his touch. "One more thing, Ms. Sterling. If you see or hear from Zian Reddington, you are required to get in touch with me right away. Not telling me about any contact you have with him will be viewed as a subversive act against The Order. Do you understand?" Agent Rudy stands. I say nothing. "*Am I making myself perfectly clear?*" he asks, leaning into my face.

I try to keep my facial expression neutral. I don't want to give Agent Rudy the satisfaction of seeing the fear inside me. Instead, I slowly nod my head, and then exit the office. That man really needs to brush his teeth.

CHAPTER FIFTEEN

Relief courses through me as soon as I exit Agent Rudy's office. I can't wait to get out of this horrible place. When I walk into the open area—filled with all the agents at their desks—I can see Aunt Bliss seated against the wall, waiting for me. She jumps up and practically sprints over to me. "Are you okay, Ren?"

No. Not even close. I'm pretty sure I'm scarred for life, actually. Instead, I reply, "Yes, let's get out of here."

"Okay, boys. I'll take it from here," Aunt Bliss says as she gives the agents a dismissive wave of her hand. She drapes one arm around my shoulder, and I lean into her as she guides me down the hall and out of the building to her car. "What kind of things did they ask you?" she asks curiously, as we climb into her car.

I wish I could tell Aunt Bliss about the interrogation and memory scanning, but I'm afraid of what Agent Rudy might do. I hesitate, because I don't know what to say. Finally, I answer, "They just asked the same old questions about what happened to my dad. It was no big deal." I keep my gaze straight ahead. If I look Aunt Bliss in the eyes, she'll know I'm lying.

Aunt Bliss gives me a sideways glance. Obviously, she knows I'm not telling the whole truth, but she lets it go, saying. "Alright, sweetie. Just know that you can talk to me about anything."

I nod my head. I appreciate Aunt Bliss's reassurance, but I know I can't tell her about this. Clearly, Agent Rudy will stop at nothing to get the information he wants, no matter how many people he hurts—and I couldn't bear it if Aunt Bliss were to get in trouble because of me.

♦ ♦ ♦

When we drive up to the front of Pittock High School, I notice that a black government vehicle has also pulled into the side parking lot. They must have been following us the whole way here! Ugh. Why won't they just leave me alone? Then it dawns on me: They expect me to bring them to Zian. Suddenly, I feel sick with dread that I might unintentionally lead them to him.

"Okay, sweetie. We're here. I'll let your mom know that you arrived at school safely," Aunt Bliss chirps cheerfully.

"Thanks, Aunt Bliss, but I'm not entirely sure Mom will even notice. She's always in her studio, even more than usual. She can't handle things since Dad died. She just wants everything to go back to normal—not that I can blame her, I do too." I'm a little taken aback by my directness and honesty. Maybe I'm making up for the fact that I can't talk about Agent Rudy.

"Of course your mom notices, Ren! She just gets overwhelmed at times, and her artwork helps her calm down. It always has. Everyone deals with grief and tragedy differently," Aunt Bliss says compassionately.

I know Aunt Bliss understands my feelings, but I also realize she's hesitant to say anything critical of Mom. "Yeah, I know. Thanks for always being there for me, Aunt Bliss." I lean over and give her a hug.

"Of course, sweetie. Have a good day. Slow and steady today, okay? I love you."

"I love you too!" I shout, as I jump out of her car. I know I'm being watched, so I scurry up the stone stairs and through the large, wooden, entry doors. The halls are empty because classes have already started. It seems like it's been a long time since I was last at school. It feels different being here. *I* feel different.

When I walk into the main office to check-in, the office staff looks at me strangely, and then exchange knowing, worried glances with each other. At least, I think they do. I don't know. Maybe I'm just being paranoid. Ms. Norella, one of the office Providers, stands up and picks up a handheld scanner from behind her desk. She waves it near the back of my neck saying, "Okay Ms. Student Body President, you're checked-in. I love this new neuroprocessor attendance function. It's so simple. Don't you think?" she asks, a little nervously. I wonder why she's being so awkward.

I nod my head silently. I have no energy for small talk. I leave the office and trudge down the hall. I really don't want to be here. Everything I once took for granted seems unsettled and uncertain now—my family, my friends, the Foundation Team, being in student government, and even soccer. A wave of sadness and exhaustion crashes over me as I think about the death of my dad. I feel so alone. At this moment, nothing seems to matter to me anymore. Nothing seems real. It all feels so pointless and overwhelming.

I sit down on the floor and lean against the wall outside my third period class. I wish it would stay this quiet forever, but in a few minutes the halls will be filled with noisy students rushing to fourth period classes.

Suddenly, the bell rings and all the classroom doors swing open. As students stream into the hall, I stand up on my tippy toes so I can catch a glimpse of Noelle as she exits class. When I finally see her, I reach forward and tap her on the shoulder.

Noelle spins toward me. "Ren! How are you?!" she exclaims, over the noise, as she gives me a big hug. "You've been crying!" Noelle says as she steps back and looks at my face. Have I? I didn't even notice. Noelle grabs my hand and pulls me into a nook in the hallway to avoid the mass of students. "Are you sure you're ready to be back at school, Ren?" she asks.

"I don't know if I'm ready to be anywhere," I reply pitifully.

"I'm so sorry," Noelle murmurs, as she gives me another hug. "Maybe you should go home?"

"No. I'm so far behind in my classes. I have to be here."

Practical as usual, Noelle says, "Well, let's get to fourth period, then. We can catch up when we have more time during lunch."

◆ ◆ ◆

My mind wanders in my seemingly endless math class. I'm not paying attention to anything my teacher is saying. I even manage to ignore the lecture slides that flash in my eyes, courtesy of the most recent, academic neuroprocessor application. Instead, my mind replays all the events that have happened to me over the past few weeks—the frightening nightmares, my dad's tragic death, his service, my brief encounter with Uncle Patterson, my wonderful and disturbing adventure with Zian, my argument with Mom, and two *very unpleasant* trips to the Central Government Building. If I never go to that horrid place again, it'll be too soon.

I think about tall, smart, handsome Zian. I miss him so much and wonder if I'll see him at lunch today. If so, SED agents are probably watching, and might arrest him. I feel panicky just thinking about it. I wish I could warn Zian or get a message to him. I'm so scared for him, and for myself. I know I'll never tell Agent Rudy if I see Zian, but he'll find out if he deep scans my processor again. My stomach twists and hurts.

The bell ending fourth period rings, jarring me back to reality. Noelle and I stroll to our lockers before heading to the lunchroom. My heart begins racing in anticipation when we enter the cafeteria, and I scan all the tables looking for Zian, but he's nowhere to be found. I wonder if the SED agents have already caught him. They could be interrogating him right now…

"So, how are you Ren, really?" Noelle asks, as we sit down at the far end of our usual Intelligencia table. "Tell me."

I stare at Noelle silently for a few moments, unsure of what to say. "I don't want to drag you into my mess, Noelle," I finally reply.

Noelle rolls her eyes. "What are you talking about, Ren? We're always here for each other. There isn't anything you can't tell me." She reaches across the table and gently squeezes my arm.

I keep staring down at the table. "I know, Noelle, but there are some things happening that I can't talk about..." Realizing this will only make Noelle *more* curious, I begin to speak about some of the things on my mind, without giving any details about the SED agents or Zian. I gaze into Noelle's curious, concerned, brown eyes. "Do you ever feel as if there's more to life than school, soccer, going to the mall, and all the stuff we usually do?" I ask.

Noelle laughs and nods. "Yeah. Sometimes I think about that, but then I remind myself that we're seniors. Everything will change very soon when we go to college. We'll have brand new experiences."

"But even college seems too safe," I reply, shaking my head. "It seems sort of fake, as if it's been laid out for us. I feel like there must be something more. I think there *is* something more, but I can't figure it out because we're so busy following the rules and the path which has already been set for us as Intelligencia.

Noelle stares back at me, in shock. She furrows her brow, clearly worried. "I don't know what you're talking about, Ren. This must be about your father... which I can totally understand. I mean... we have a good life, we're at a great school, we have great friends. We're on one of the best soccer teams in Capitol City... We're Intelligencia, so we'll attend good colleges and study whatever we want. We're set."

A sense of injustice stirs inside me. I know I sound frustrated, but I can't help it. "Right. *We're set.* What about the other segments of The Order, though? Have you ever asked yourself why Producers don't get to go to college? Why are only certain levels of Providers allowed to go? In reality, are any of us *truly free to do what we want, Noelle*?" I ask. Noelle recoils. "Maybe it's just my dad's death, but this is the stuff I've been thinking about." I say, trying to soften the impact a little.

"Sheesh, Ren. You've always been a deep thinker—much deeper than me, but you're kind of starting to scare me," Noelle replies, and then looks down at her lunch.

I sigh. "Me too, Noelle. I've been scaring myself. But why should I be afraid of these thoughts? Why are we so afraid to ask questions about The Order?"

Noelle stares at me in silence, before finally stammering, "I... I can honestly say that I don't think about things like this. I believe it's better to enjoy what we have, rather than focus on why things are the way they are. We have The Order for many reasons—which you know more about than any of our friends because you're on Foundation Team. The Order gives us all clear purpose," Noelle says, robotically repeating what we've been taught.

"At least that's what we've been *taught* our whole lives," I counter. "But what if it's not *true*? I've seen things, Noelle. Things I can't tell you about."

"What are you talking about, Ren?" Confusion and fear flood her face, and suddenly, I realize I shouldn't be saying any of this to Noelle. It's not fair to shatter her world the way mine has been shattered. It may not even be safe for her to hear what I could tell her. I don't want the SED to start following Noelle around or interrogating her. I love Noelle, and I don't want her in danger!

I shake my head and try to think of a way I can quickly change the topic. I force a smile. "I don't know what I'm saying. I'm just all messed up about my dad," I say. "You're right, Noelle, we should just focus on what's good in our lives. Grief does weird things to people. I'll get back to my old self—just be patient with me."

Noelle sighs with relief. "Thank goodness! I thought you were really losing it for a second. Everything will be okay, Ren, you'll see," she reassures me, with a warm smile. I smile back. Our conversation is abruptly interrupted when Vice-Principal Davis taps me on my shoulder.

"Ren, Principal Chapman needs to speak with you," he

says, wrinkling his sweaty brow.

"Oh! Right now?" I ask, a little confused. I wonder if he wants to talk to me about the SED. Or Zian.

"Yes. Right now. It's urgent," Vice-Principal Davis says. Noelle and I exchange a worried glance.

"May I come with her?" asks Noelle as she starts to rise from the table.

"No," Vice-Principal Davis says, shaking his head. "Principal Chapman needs to see Ren alone." Noelle sinks back down and mouths, "Sorry!"

I nod my head. "Thanks for trying!" I say, giving Noelle another small smile before following the waddling Mr. Davis out of the lunchroom. We walk briskly down the hall into the main office, and past the twittering office staff. They fall silent as soon as they see me. Vice-Principal Davis directs me to enter the Principal's office. The door is open, so I walk right in. Mr. Davis quickly shuts the door behind me. Principal Chapman is seated behind his desk, looking tall and elegant, yet uncomfortable. He nervously smooths his greying hair.

"Uh, have a seat, Ren," Principal Chapman directs me. I sit on the edge of the chair, anxious. "You have been through so much recently, Ren, but unfortunately... I have some more bad news to share with you." Principal Chapman clears his throat, hesitating.

Oh no, is it Zian? Was Zian arrested?

"Ren, your Uncle, Patterson Sterling, was found dead in his university office today. Apparently, he had a heart attack last night and was found by the cleaning crew early this morning. I'm so sorry."

I stare at Principal Chapman, trying to register what he just said, and then shake my head. *Uncle Patterson?* "No." I say. "That's impossible. I just saw him a few days ago at my dad's service. He was fine. He was healthy."

"I'm very sorry, Ren." Principal Chapman furrows his brow, and looks down at his long, tapered fingers.

"This can't be happening. I don't understand--" I begin

saying, then suddenly I remember that Agent Rudy saw Uncle Patterson's ring when he was downloading my memories, and then made threatening comments about Uncle Patterson. Fear, anger, and guilt wash over me. I can hardly breathe. Uncle Patterson is dead... because of me. I drop my head in my hands.

"It's my fault," I moan.

Startled, Principal Chapman leans back in his chair. "What are you talking about, Ren? How could a heart attack possibly be your fault? Sometimes things just happen. Even with all of our advanced medical technology—we're still mortal."

As pain rips through my heart, I shake my head. Tears fill my eyes and drip down my cheeks. Principal Chapman sits silently for a moment, and then leans forward compassionately. "I think you should go home and be with your family, Ren. Perhaps you should take a few weeks off from school to process all of this. I'll have each of your teachers send you the classwork and homework through your neuroprocessor, so you can keep up with your studies. Take a break from Student Government, from Foundation Team, and from soccer. I want you to be able to graduate with your class, Ren, but you need to take some time off. You've been through so much..."

I've stopped listening. Uncle Patterson is dead and it's all my fault. I feel nauseous as Principal Chapman guides me out of his office and down the hall.

CHAPTER SIXTEEN

"Your mother and sister are waiting for you in front of the school," Principal Chapman says, as he escorts me out the front of the building. I don't reply because I'm still nauseous. I'm afraid if I open my mouth, I'll throw up all over the Principal's expensive shoes. We walk down the front stairs of Pittock High to Mom's parked car. Principal Chapman opens the back door, and I climb in the seat next to Tia, who looks unusually pale, and is wringing her hands. Mom looks like she's been crying.

"Did you hear about Uncle Patterson?" Tia asks, dramatically, in a half-whisper, as I slide in next to her. "I can't believe it. What's happening to our family?"

I shake my head in disbelief and shock—I can't think of anything to say.

"Thank you so much, Mr. Chapman," Mom says. "I appreciate your thoughtfulness during such a hard time for our family." She holds out her hand and Mr. Chapman shakes it.

"Of course, Mrs. Sterling. It's the least I can do," he replies kindly. "All of Ren and Tia's coursework will be forwarded to their neuroprocessors. We'll help you get through this. Please let me know if there's anything I can do to assist your family further."

Mom and I close our car doors. Principal Chapman gives a gentle tap on the top of the car, and then waves goodbye as we drive away.

◆ ◆ ◆

We drive home in silence, until I eventually blurt out, "Mom, I *told you* Uncle Patterson was in danger." Mom doesn't react. Tia glances over at me with a look of horror on her face. Mom's lack of response frustrates me further, so I raise my voice. "Why didn't you listen to me when I told you he was in danger? Please, you can't just ignore this, Mom," I plead. Mom's cheeks and neck flush a deep red.

"I can't believe you would bring up your conspiracy theories again and blame *me*, Ren! I don't want to hear any more of your delusions. Uncle Paterson died of a heart attack. That's it. It's a tragedy, nothing more!" Mom replies angrily.

"And you believe that?" I ask, my voice rising to match my growing fury.

"What's gotten into you, Ren Sterling?!" Mom snaps back at me. "I know your father's death has been hard on you—it's been hard on all of us—but you've got to get a grip on yourself and stop with these wild fantasies. JUST STOP IT!" she shouts.

I sit back in my seat, stunned. I'm not used to Mom yelling at me. I take a deep breath and decide to try again—to calmly explain what's happened. Maybe she'll listen this time and see what's right in front of her eyes. "Mom, I've seen things —things I can't tell you about. But what I *can* say is that the government is not as nice as you think they are. The SED does horrible things. They have devices that can scan and download our private memories against our will and they've done it to me twice," I explain, keeping my voice steady and soft.

Frustrated, Mom shakes her head. "We've been through this already, Ren! You're confusing dreams with reality. Just because you say something more than once doesn't make it true."

Stung, my calm devolves into rage. "You're in complete denial, Mom!" I snap. "When unpleasant things happen, you either get overwhelmed or do what you're doing right now: You ignore what's happening around you. Either way, you never open your eyes and see what's actually happening!"

"Ren Sterling, I will ground you for a month if you don't

stop talking to me like this," Mom growls furiously. "You're not the only one who misses your father. This is hard on all of us!" Her voice breaks and tears begin to roll down her cheeks. "You're usually not this cruel, Ren. What's wrong with you? I used to be able to count on you when I was having a hard time."

Typically, I feel guilty when I say what I really think to Mom and end up apologizing. Right now, though, my anger is stronger than my guilt and watching Mom cry doesn't make me feel sorry for her—it makes me furious. "I guess I'm just tired of taking care of you," I reply bitterly. "There are really unpleasant things in the world, and you have to face them, Mom. They're happening all around us. They've happened to Dad, to Uncle Patterson, and they've even happened to me. *Why won't you believe me?*" I ask, anguished.

Tia jumps in, "Ren! Stop it. Just stop it. Please. Please stop talking like this," she pleads, half-whining, half-screaming.

"All I'm saying is..." I begin to defend myself, but then stop speaking mid-sentence. Sitting in frustrated silence for a few moments, I eventually conclude that there's nothing I can say—Tia and Mom won't hear me, can't hear me. Quietly, I continue, "...forget it, it's not worth trying to explain it to either of you." Hugging my arms to my twisting stomach and staring out the window, I don't know whether to feel sorry for Mom and Tia or to loathe them for their denial. I know they haven't seen what I've seen, but it really sucks they don't believe me. I feel so alone.

◆ ◆ ◆

As soon as Mom parks the car, I jump out and sprint into the house. Piper yips when he hears the front door open and follows me as I race up the stairs into my bedroom. I slam the door closed behind me. Suddenly, my twisting stomach takes charge. I barely make it to my bathroom in time before my lunch comes up and I cling to my toilet, shaking and sweating.

When my body is finally finished purging, I wash my face at the sink and brush my teeth. Then, the tears come. Sobbing, I make my way back across my bedroom, flop on my bed, and nuzzle up to Piper. I can't shake the thought that I'm somehow at fault for Uncle Patterson's death. It loops through my brain over and over again and hurts every time I think it. I've never felt so scared, guilty, angry, and alone all at once in my life.

I hold Piper's warm furry body and bury my face in my fluffy comforter and cry. Whatever dam existed inside of me containing all my grief and anger has been shattered. I cry for Uncle Patterson, for Dad, and for my frustration with Mom and Tia. I cry out my rage at Agent Rudy, and the powerlessness I feel over how he's treated me. I cry over my loss of Noelle, because normally when I feel sad, she's the one who comforts me. Now, not only does Noelle have no idea of what I'm experiencing, if I share my feelings with her, I could be putting her in danger. My ribcage feels like it's splitting in two. I've lost everything and everyone who is important to me. More and more feelings pour out of me until there is nothing left.

Zian pops into my mind and my heart leaps. I know *he* would understand how I'm feeling. He knows what it's like to lose a father. He's also the one who showed me the slave farms and factories; he's the only person who understands my fears and confusion. I couldn't fully recognize and voice my own feelings until he helped me. If I could just connect with him, I wouldn't feel so alone. I wonder what would happen if I tried to contact his neuroprocessor...?

I begin to send Zian a message, and then stop myself when I have a terrifying thought: What if the SED are monitoring my neuroprocessor communications remotely? I wouldn't put it past them. The risk is too great, so I don't reach out. It then dawns on me that I might have lost Zian forever, and the tears come pouring out again.

My mind drifts to Uncle Patterson. The last time I saw him was at the service for Dad, and he was wearing a ring with the symbol of Conation. Agent Rudy and President Coldstone both said that Conation is the terrorist organization that murdered my dad. Agent Rudy told me Uncle Patterson was associating with terrorists, but I know Uncle Patterson would *never* be part of a terrorist group. He certainly wouldn't kill his own brother—he loved Dad! So, what's really going on?

My brain hurts as I struggle to put the pieces together. Was Uncle Patterson's death truly caused by a heart attack? I seriously doubt it. I bet the SED killed him and made it look like a heart attack. Agent Rudy certainly seemed angry enough to have Uncle Patterson assassinated. I wonder if they deep scanned Uncle Patterson's memories before they murdered him. *If* they murdered him… is it possible Uncle Patterson just died of a heart attack?

I'm so confused. I can't make sense of any of it. I shake my head, focus on taking deep breaths, and try to slow my thoughts. Eventually, I close my eyes, bury my head under my pillow, and drift off to sleep.

CHAPTER SEVENTEEN

Over the next few days, I continue to feel utterly alone. Mom retreats to her art studio every chance she gets. Tia won't speak to me and stomps around the house, alternating between tears and anger. Thankfully, Aunt Bliss pops in and out of the house, and keeps us all fed—but I don't dare tell her what's really going on with me. If the SED harmed her in any way, I couldn't bear it.

◆ ◆ ◆

The day of Uncle Patterson's memorial service arrives, and I feel a strange sense of déjà vu while getting dressed. I'm wearing the same navy dress I wore to Dad's service, and my favorite brown boots. Brushing my long hair in front of my dresser, I catch my eyes in the mirror. I look tired, sad, and... older. Setting my brush down, I open my jewelry box so I can wear the shell necklace Dad gave me, but when I look inside, it's empty.

Immediately, my hand flies to my neck, but the necklace isn't there either. Panicked, I search the top of my dresser, my floor, my bed, my backpack, and my closet, but I can't find it anywhere. I frantically toss things left and right, trying to find it. Did I lose it? How? When? Crumpling to the floor, I can't hold back tears. On top of everything else I've lost, now this. How could I be so careless?

"Ren! We're waiting for you!" Aunt Bliss calls from downstairs. Sighing, I stand up, wipe my eyes, and trudge downstairs with an aching heart.

◆ ◆ ◆

Besides making us meals, dependable, heroic Aunt Bliss helped organize Uncle Patterson's funeral service with his grieving wife, Aunt Vanessa, who is also a professor at Capital University. Because Uncle Patterson was such a beloved professor, many students and colleagues wish to give their testimonies about his contribution to The Order, in addition to family and friends —so the memorial will be much longer and bigger in size than Dad's service. Aunt Bliss and Aunt Vanessa decided that the main ballroom of the Community Center was the perfect fit as it's large enough accommodate all the people who wish to attend.

The Community Center is located on the edge of the Capital University campus in a historic brick building. The parking lot is already almost full when we arrive. White flower arrangements decorate both sides of the massive, carved wooden doors as we enter. An informational message, which automatically activates when anyone steps into the main foyer, flashes across my neuroprocessor: **"A Celebration of the Life and Contributions of Professor Patterson Sterling. 1-4 P.M. Digital recordings of the service and presentations will be available for download."**

Mom, Tia, Aunt Bliss and I are escorted to our reserved seats at the front of the ballroom, along with the other relatives in attendance. Almost all the other seats in the room have been filled. I wonder if Zian's here. I'm dying to find out more of what he knows—and honestly, to feel his strong body holding me again. I could really use a hug. Glancing around, I don't see him anywhere. Part of me is sad while another part is relieved. Surely the SED will be here watching, and as much as I'm desperate to see Zian, I don't want him in danger.

I spy Noelle, though. She's sitting toward the back with her family and some of our soccer friends. I'm glad she's here. I can't get up to talk to her because the service is about to start, so I send her a quick neuroprocessor message: **"Thanks for coming. I really appreciate it."**

"From Noelle: Of course! I love you!" flashes back.

The service begins with the singing of the Anthem of The Order. Once the song ends, our neuroprocessors illuminate with pictures documenting Uncle Patterson's life set to instrumental music piping through the ballroom. Many of the pictures include my father, who was just a few years older. My heart feels like it's being slowly crushed in my chest. Soft sounds of weeping echo through the room.

Then, Uncle Patterson's best friend and fellow professor Bob Robin stands to give his testimony. Bob, and then many others, speak of Uncle Patterson's intelligence, strong work ethic, caring spirit, inspirational teaching style, and all the other ways he contributed to the lives of so many in the university, the community, and The Order. I listen closely to every speaker, hoping to glean some clues about what has happened to my family. How can one family lose two members in such a short amount of time? I wonder if anyone will allude, even subtly, to Conation—but no one does.

The last scheduled speaker is Aunt Vanessa, who is dressed in a flowing black dress covered by a black cardigan sweater. The crowd is silent as Aunt Vanessa takes the podium. She seems remarkably composed as she begins. "Dr. Patterson Sterling was an amazing husband, father, son, brother, friend, professor, community member, and human being. He gave of himself tirelessly. He was my best friend for over fifteen years, and my loving husband for twelve of those years. He was completely engaged as a father, devoting himself to our intelligent and thoughtful daughter, Chloe. I truly could not have asked for a better life-partner, and Chloe could not have asked for a better father." Aunt Vanessa's voice breaks. She tucks a stray silver curl behind her ear, and takes a deep breath to compose herself again, before continuing.

"Patterson was also a deep thinker and a gifted teacher, a true Intelligencia. He believed that we could all learn to listen to our inner-wisdom, intuition, impulses, and desires, and to express them with intentional striving and action. Rather than retreat into defensive beliefs, stereotypical principles, and slogans, Patterson encouraged others to stay open and present with the experience of living while using the discernment of inner-generated wisdom and convictions. He believed and taught that each of us is responsible, first and foremost, to our own personally-defined values." Aunt Vanessa pauses to let that last sentence land for a moment, looking out at the audience. She clears her throat, and then continues.

"Patterson had a beautiful way of questioning students and others about their ideas. His goal was to create just the right level of challenge. His intent was to encourage free-thinking and volition, without overwhelming anyone's sense of safety—although some ultimately became threatened by his contributions. His death did not have to occur if not for fear—fear that is propagated by ignorance, complacency, and blind obedience."

Anger flashes across Aunt Vanessa's regal face. She takes a deep breath and steadies herself. "May you rest in peace, my beloved, Patterson. You will be missed. I assure you that your ideas and intentions will not cease with your passing. We will carry on... with *eyes wide open*."

Aunt Vanessa exits the podium and sits next to my younger cousin Chloe, whose eyes are red from weeping. The crowd is silent. I don't think anybody knows how to react. It's rare for anyone to speak so openly about individual values and choice as compared to the needs of the collective, of The Order. Some of what Aunt Vanessa said was a not so veiled criticism of The Order, especially her accusation that Uncle Patterson's ideas were threatening to others. What did Aunt Vanessa mean when she said that his death was avoidable "if not for fear that is propagated by ignorance, complacency, and blind obedience"?

Scattered clapping quickly follows the stunned silence. Clearly, there's a small group of individuals that understand and support Aunt Vanessa's words. A thought suddenly occurs to me: What if Aunt Vanessa is expressing the ideas of Conation? I do a quick neuroprocessor search for the definition, and again find: **"Conation: an inclination or impulse to act purposefully and intentionally; volition. Pronounced: kō-nā-shən."** Wait a minute. *Were* Uncle Patterson and Aunt Vanessa part of Conation? How could they possibly be part of the terrorist organization that killed my dad? Neither of them would ever want to hurt Dad. What am I not understanding about all of this?

As we stand to exit the room and enter the reception hall, I turn and quietly ask Mom, "What did you think about Aunt Vanessa's testimony?"

"She loved Uncle Patterson so much," Mom tearfully replies. "They were so deeply connected."

"Really?! That's all you heard?" I ask, accusingly.

"What? I think what Aunt Vanessa said was beautiful," Mom replies, bewildered.

Losing patience, I retort, "You've got to be kidding me—there was so much more to what she said--"

Tia interrupts me. "Stop it! Leave Mom alone. I thought it was a beautiful service too."

Frustrated, I shake my head as we're escorted out of the ballroom and into the main reception hall where food and beverages are set up for the guests. I need to get away from Mom and Tia. Their inability to perceive what's really happening is both astonishing and appalling. I excuse myself and find a chair at an empty table in the far back part of the reception area, away from everyone. I plunk my elbow on the table and rest my chin in my hand. I need to make sense of what's happening to me.

While deep in thought, I don't notice the smartly dressed, familiar-looking woman in a black pantsuit who has approached my table. I glance up and startle to see her standing over me, looking down at me with kind, compassionate eyes. "I'm so sorry for your losses, Ren," she says, as she reaches out and shakes my hand. "Hi. My name is Abigail Zimmer. I'm the Director of Presidential Communications and Personal Assistant to President Coldstone. The President was unable to attend due to previous obligations but instructed me to come on his behalf and to express his deepest condolences to you and your family," she says, warmly.

In shock, I nod my head. "Thank you," I manage to answer. I've seen Ms. Zimmer many times on my neuroprocessor, providing news briefings and informational messages from the government. She's even more beautiful in person—tall and slender with jet-black hair, extremely fair skin, and strikingly beautiful, blue-green eyes. In contrast to her pale skin and dark hair, Ms. Zimmer's eyes shimmer and sparkle. Her long, black hair is pulled back from her face, and held in place with a small, blue-green bow at the back of her head.

"May I have a seat?" she asks, pointing to the chair next to me.

"Yes, of course, Ms. Zimmer," I reply politely, still in shock that Abigail Zimmer is speaking with me.

She sits in the chair and turns to face me directly. "On behalf of the President, we're deeply sorry for all that has happened to you and your family, Ren. Your father and uncle were wonderful men. Both were such valuable contributors to The Order."

"Thank you... thank you, Ms. Zimmer," I stammer.

"Please call me Abi."

"Okay. Thank you, Abi. Thanks for attending my uncle's service."

"You're welcome. President Coldstone has been deeply affected by these recent tragedies, especially your father's assassination." I nod my head, but don't speak. Suddenly I feel nervous. I wonder if she'll start grilling me about what I know about Dad's death. I look away so I can't make eye-contact. After an awkward pause, Abi asks, "Ren, what do you know about the upcoming platinum celebration?"

Her question surprises me. "Um...well... It's the 70th anniversary of the founding of The Order. There will be extra events and festivities on Order Day this year," I answer.

"Yes. Right. This year there will be a four-day long series of events marking the anniversary, rather than just a national holiday and the usual Order Day Parade.

"Oh, I didn't realize it was a four-day long celebration."

"Well, you've been a little preoccupied." Abi smiles compassionately. Her kindness makes me weepy. I nod, trying to hold back tears. "In fact, in addition to sending his condolences, President Coldstone sent me here to meet you—specifically to see if you'd be interested in being part of the celebration." Abi raises her eyebrows with a hopeful look.

"What? Why... why would the President want me to be part of the celebration?" I ask, confused.

Abi's eyes light up, and her voice is impassioned as she speaks. "President Coldstone believes you can be the face and voice of the young people in The Order—a role model. Because of your father's and uncle's deaths, you and your story are of great interest to many people. You're a figure of resilience and patriotism—providing messages of strength and hope—which perfectly represent the core values of the founding of The Order. And being Pittock High School's Student Body President and Captain of the Foundation Team makes you the ideal spokesperson!"

Not knowing how to respond, I sit in stunned silence. After a long pause, Abi leans over and asks softly, "What do you think about what I'm saying, Ren?"

I'm shocked and overwhelmed. I don't know what to say. Finally, I manage, "I'm flattered, but I don't know if I'm the right person for this. I've been so confused and upset about all that has happened. My dad's death has been so overwhelming. And now Uncle Patterson..." I trail off as my eyes fill with tears. Abi gently places her hand on my arm.

"I can only imagine how hard it's been on you, Ren," she says sincerely. "You don't have to decide right at this moment. Would you be willing to meet with President Coldstone to talk about this special opportunity to serve The Order?"

I can't help it. My mouth drops open in shock. "Meet with... *President Coldstone*?"

"Yes. He wants you to meet with him at the Presidential Compound. I've been directed by the President to escort you there this evening after the service ends. In fact, the President would like you to spend a few days at the Compound. He's taken a special interest in you."

Fear sends an icy chill through me, and I tense up—which Abi immediately senses. Smiling, she gently squeezes my arm. "Don't worry, Ren! Everything will be fine. The President just wants to support you through this difficult time and to assess your interest in being part of the celebration. No pressure. On the way to the Compound we can stop by your house to pick up some clothes and personal items. We'll make sure you're well cared for. All of your needs will be met, I promise."

Boy, I don't know. After all that's happened, I'm not sure if I can handle more stress. What does President Coldstone *really* want? "Uh... I need to ask my Mom. I'm not sure--" I begin to reply.

Abi releases my arm and holds up her hand. "Hold on, Ren," she says, as she receives a message through her neuroprocessor. Then she looks me in the eyes and smiles happily. "Great! Your mother has given her permission for you to come to the Compound. She just sent you a message. Check your processor."

With a quick blink, a message flashes in front of my eyes. **"From Mom: What an amazing opportunity, Ren. It could help you through this difficult time. Go and enjoy the Presidential Compound! I can't wait to hear what it's like. Love you."**

My stomach twists and my heart skips a beat. What if this is a ploy to take me back to Agent Rudy, or worse? Now that Mom's given her blessing, I have no excuse to get out of the invitation. Or is it a demand, rather than an invitation? Do I even have a choice?

Abi smiles again and gently nudges my shoulder with her hand. "Come on, Ren, it'll be fun! Most people would practically kill to meet the President and to visit the Presidential Compound!"

I peer into Abi's eyes, and I see she believes what she's saying. She means me no harm. I think... I think I can trust her. Besides, if Agent Rudy really wants to interrogate me again, there's no where I can hide to escape him, anyway.

I take a deep breath, and then slowly exhale. "Okay," I say, nodding my head. "Let's go."

Abi grins. "Wonderful!" She wraps a slender arm around me and ushers me out a back door of the Community Center and into the back of an idling government vehicle. I can't help but feel anxious as the car roars to life and carries us across downtown. What have I gotten myself into now?

CHAPTER EIGHTEEN

Anxious and excited, I peer through the tinted car window as we pull up to a white guardhouse and a tall, black, wrought iron gate. On top of the gate is the Emblem of The Order, and underneath the emblem is the Presidential Seal. This is it—the Presidential Compound! The driver of our car lowers his window and a guard marches over to wave a scanner by the driver's neuroprocessor. Nodding approval, the guard signals our driver to proceed forward. The gate slowly begins to open, and my heartbeat speeds up.

    Ever since I was a little girl, I've always wanted to visit the Compound. I've dreamt of working here someday as Central Advisor for the Intelligencia, or maybe even as The Order's first female President. As we travel slowly along a cobblestone road through acres of perfectly landscaped, lush gardens, bright afternoon sunlight illuminates the gorgeous reds and golds of the autumn foliage. There's a large pond with a charming, arched-shaped bridge stretching across the width of it.

    I make a mental note to myself to walk across the bridge if I'm permitted to—if I'm not too busy being locked up and interrogated. Catching myself thinking fearfully, I try to snap myself out of it. "Just be polite and don't show your fear, Ren," I tell myself. "Then, maybe they won't give you a reason to feel afraid."

    Abigail's voice interrupts my thoughts. "The Presidential Compound is situated on 300 acres and consists of a series of buildings—the first being constructed just as The Order was instituted 70 years ago. As you know, The Order was founded in 2047 after years of war and terrorism had ravaged the former United States.

"The Modern Dark Age," I add.

Abi nods. "Precisely. With much of what used to be the country unlivable due to nuclear fallout, the Founders of the Order placed the seat of government at this location, outside of what was Portland, Oregon—now Capitol City. This move was not only logistically necessary due to the contamination and destruction of the former Washington, DC, it also signified a break from the inefficient, ideologically-confused laws and processes that contributed to the lack of purpose and clarity of our previous nation."

"Yes. Very cool!" I exclaim. Hearing Abi speak is like being in a Foundation Team class with Ms. Eyke, only better.

Abi grins in reaction to my excitement, and then continues. "Well, along with developing the philosophical and practical dimensions of The Order, the Founders formed a nimble, responsive, and decisive system of government by consolidating the decision-making power to a President and four Central Advisors, one from each segment of The Order. There's a statue in front of four of the buildings in the Compound, and each statue represents one of the segments."

Abi hesitates and smiles. "Of course, you already know this from Foundation Team, correct?"

"Oh, yes, but it's much more fascinating to hear about the history when I'm here in-person," I reply.

The car rolls to a stop as the road curves in front of a large, box-shaped, three-story red brick building. In front of the building, there's a statue of a Producer holding a hoe, and two stone stairways leading up on each side of the statue to the building's entrance on the second floor. The front of the building has open-air porches on the second and third levels, which are framed by white columns that rise across all three levels. White dormers decorate the roof and chimneys on each side of the building.

"Here we are!" Abi says, as she opens her door. Stepping out of the car, Abi continues proudly, "This is Reception Hall, which serves as the receiving area for guests as well as a ballroom for events. As you can see, there's a statue of a Producer in front. This is significant because the Founders recognized that Producers are the backbone of the entire Order. Thus, it's fitting that a Producer adorns the first building in the Compound."

At this, I feel a twang of guilt and suspicion. Yes, Producers are the backbone, but are they *free*? I follow Abi as we step up one set of stairs to the porch on the second floor, and then through the entrance doors into a foyer area. My neuroprocessor activates automatically and the following message appears before my eyes: **"Welcome to Reception Hall, Ms. Sterling. We hope you enjoy your stay at the Presidential Compound."**

"How'd they know I was coming?!" I ask, sheepishly. Abi just grins. I don't know whether to be creeped out or impressed.

Thick, golden-brown wooden beams stretch across the crisp, white ceiling, and frame the sleek reception desk on our right. A woman behind the desk immediately stands and smiles graciously. "Good afternoon Ms. Zimmer. Hello, Ms. Sterling. Welcome to the Presidential Compound. The President and Mrs. Coldstone are very much looking forward to meeting you." I smile back politely and then blush, suddenly feeling awkward at being the center of attention.

"Good afternoon, Ms. Jorgenson," Abi replies with a smile and nod, as she leads me forward to a shiny wood door at the back of the foyer. The door opens to an exceptionally large room, with a very high ceiling covered in murals and wood floors so glossy I can see my reflection in them. "As you can see, Ren, this is the Event Ballroom. The ceiling has hand-painted murals that depict the founding of The Order. Each segment is represented through traditional folk art and illustrates the segment's unique contributions," Abi explains with pride. "The walls of the Ballroom are also adorned with paintings, which express the essence and contributions of each segment." She places her hand over her heart and sighs. "I just love the history of this building. Think about all the events which have occurred in here over the last 70 years!"

I stroll around the center of the ballroom, taking in the

beauty and majesty of the expansive room, and the artwork. Even with all my doubts about The Order, I can't help but feel a sense of awe and civic pride. I can't believe I'm seeing first-hand the building I've read about so many times in school.

"Are you ready to see more of the Compound?" Abi asks.

"Sure" I say, even though I'm not quite ready to leave Reception Hall. I could stay here for hours. "I love this room. It's so light, airy, and peaceful. May I come back in here before I have to leave the Compound?"

"Of course," Abi answers with a smile. "As we discussed earlier, you'll be our pampered guest for the next few days. You'll have plenty of opportunities to return to this building and enjoy all the grounds. Follow me, Ren."

Abi escorts me down a marble hallway and out a back door of Reception Hall. We enter a large courtyard, which has a reflecting pool in the center and manicured grounds around. There are paved paths weaving though the grounds, which lead to four buildings. Abi points across the reflecting pool. "As I'm sure you already know from seeing pictures of the Compound, the building directly facing us across the reflecting pool is the Presidential Residence. President Coldstone lives there with his wife, Dolores. The Presidential Residence, or PR as we call it, has additional security and privacy. President Coldstone refuses to conduct official business at the Residence. He sees it as his private family sanctuary."

I'm feeling star-struck as Abi points to her left and continues, "Instead, all official business occurs at the building on our immediate left, Commitment Hall. There's a statue of an Intelligencia reading a book in front of the building, signifying our never-ending commitment to research, technological advances, and respectful academic debate and discussion. This is where the President gives his State of the Order addresses to the public. It's also where he meets with the Central Advisors, along with the many other constituents that visit the Compound."

"Wow! It's as if my history classes and Foundation Team are coming alive before my eyes!" I exclaim. I can't help myself.

Abi grins and points at a large, three-story, U-shaped building behind and just to the left of the Presidential Residence. "That's the Provider Dorm. As you'd expect, there's a statue of a Provider in front. Almost all the highly valued Providers who serve the many, varied needs of the Compound live in that building. The dorm also has rooms for any guests that spend the night at the Compound, in what we call the guest quarters."

Curious, I ask, "Do you live in the Provider Dorm, Ms. Zimmer?"

"It's Abi, Ren." she gently reminds me. "Yes. I live in the dorm. I've lived there for the past seven years. When a person is chosen to serve The Order by serving the Compound, it's a complete life commitment."

"Do you like living there? Is it weird to live where you work? How often do you see President Coldstone?" I ask, rapid fire. I can't help it. I'm so fascinated.

Abi smiles and replies sincerely, "It's great. It's such an honor. There's no higher calling than serving The Order. I get to work with the President every day and am so grateful to have the opportunity. And, it's not really a dorm, although that's what we call it. It contains many lovely and spacious one-bedroom apartments."

"Do married couples live there too? Are you married?" I ask, before realizing I'm being too nosey. I shake my head. "I'm sorry, that was a personal question."

Abi laughs. "It's okay. I usually tell people that I'm married to my calling, which is working for the President and The Order, although my mother wants me to actually *get* married!" she replies with another laugh. "Sometimes the Providers who work at the Compound do get married, but most people are married to their jobs, like me. Married couples can live here, but children are not permitted. If a couple conceives a child while working here, they either leave their positions or the child is raised by family members outside the Compound."

"Oh," I reply, shocked. Even though kids are not allowed

to live here, I could still imagine myself working at the Presidential Compound like I have dreamt about for many years.

Abi cheerfully continues. "Okay, back to our tour! The last major building, which is to the right of the Presidential Residence, has the offices of the four Central Advisors, and is called Foundation Hall. The statue in front is of a Financier, signifying the importance of the strong financial institutions that provide capital to The Order. In addition to their offices and the offices of their staffers, each Central Advisor also has an apartment in Foundation Hall, in case they choose to spend the night at the Compound. I hope you'll have the chance to meet a few of the Advisors over the next few days."

"Really?!" I ask, amazed. Interrogation and torture are sounding less and less likely—maybe they really are going to treat me like a special guest.

"I hope so. But for now, I'd like to show you where you'll be staying. We need to get you settled before dinner. Okay?" Abi asks. I nod as she leads me down one of the trails around the reflecting pool. When we encounter a fork in the trail, I begin down the path toward the Provider Dorm, but Abi gently touches my arm and says, "Oh, you aren't staying in the typical guest quarters."

A confused look crosses my face. "What? Why not?"

"The President and Mrs. Coldstone are offering you the rare privilege of staying at the Presidential Residence. The President wants to spend some extended time with you. He has some important topics he'd like to discuss with you, and Mrs. Coldstone is quite interested in getting to know you too."

"*Really?!* I... I don't know what to say." I reply, shocked.

"Just say 'thank you' when you meet the President and Mrs. Coldstone. It's quite an honor! In the seven years that I've lived here, only a handful of people have been invited to stay in the Presidential Residence—you're a lucky duck!" Abi adds, with a wink.

CHAPTER NINETEEN

I'm going to be staying at the Presidential Residence! My mind begins racing. What do I say? How do I act? *Why* does President Coldstone want to spend time with me? I can't shake the fear that I'm going to be interrogated again. Abi senses my discomfort and gently touches my shoulder reassuringly, saying, "Everything will be fine, Ren. Don't worry. I'll be with you much of the time. The President is a wonderful man. He's very kind and warm, much like a caring grandfather. He'll make you feel safe and welcome. Don't worry," she repeats, as she gently wraps her arm around my shoulder and guides me down the paved trail leading to the Presidential Residence. "And Mrs. Coldstone is one of the most genuine, caring people I've ever met. You'll see."

If I knew Abi better, I'd ask her to pinch me, so I'd know for certain I'm awake. Today has already been so surreal that I can't help but wonder if I'm dreaming as we approach the Presidential Residence. There are two guards in front, one on each side at the bottom of the large staircase leading up to the Residence.

Built in the same style as Reception Hall, the Presidential Residence is a box-shaped building with four levels and impressive white columns that frame the stairs. Unlike Reception Hall, the bricks are white rather than red. The window frames are cement, with ornate designs around the edges. White brick chimneys adorn the length of the building on both sides. In the center, on the Residence wall, is a large Emblem of The Order, which stands out against the white bricks.

As we approach, the guards smile. One of them steps forward, saying, "Good afternoon, Ms. Zimmer. Hello, Ms. Sterling. Welcome to the Presidential Residence."

"Hello, Mr. Jacobs. Mr. Andrews," Abi replies, nodding politely to both guards. "As you know, Ren will be staying with us for a few days. Please allow her the freedom to access and exit the Residence as she chooses during her stay here. She is our trusted and honored guest." Both Mr. Jacobs and Mr. Andrews nod.

As Abi and I begin walking up the stairs, Mr. Jacobs calls after us, "Please let us know if there is anything we can do to assist you during your stay, Ms. Sterling. We're here to serve."

"Thank you," I mumble in reply, still in shock. I can't believe this is happening. It's hard not to feel special. I'm about to enter the most private and revered building of all! I've heard about the Presidential Compound and the Presidential Residence my entire life, and now I'm here! Everyone has been kind so far... maybe I can relax and just enjoy what's happening. After what I experienced in Agent Rudy's office, though, it's difficult for me to let down my guard.

The wooden door to the Residence is painted black and has a large brass handle. Abi opens it to reveal a grand foyer. The first thing I notice is the shiny marble floor. It's gorgeous. A reception desk sits in the middle of the back end of the foyer, with marble staircases rising up and around either side.

"Hello Ms. Zimmer," a voice rings out from behind the desk. A woman with striking silver-gray hair stands up and reaches out her hand to me. "And welcome, Ms. Sterling," she says, greeting me with a warm smile. "My name is Ms. Parsons. I'm the Receptionist and Concierge for the Presidential Residence. I can set up any activity you would like during your stay here. Please don't hesitate to call upon me for anything."

I blush and nod, saying, "Thank you so much, Ms. Parsons." I feel like I should curtsy or something.

"Ms. Parsons has been here for over forty years. Longer than anyone else, I think," Abi explains, smiling. "She knows everything about the Compound."

"Several of the gardeners and one of the dinner staff have been here just a little bit longer," Ms. Parsons corrects. "But yes, I've been here a long time, forty-seven years to be exact. There's no other place I'd rather be."

"Forty-seven years!" I exclaim. "You've practically been here since the founding of The Order!"

"Just twenty-three years shy," laughs Ms. Parsons. "You're going to have a wonderful time staying here, Ms. Sterling. Your suite is ready. Your first appointment is already up there waiting for you."

"My first appointment...?" I ask, nervously. I hope it's not some SED agent—worse, Special Agent Rudy.

Ms. Parsons smiles. "Yes. Mrs. Coldstone's personal seamstress is waiting to take your measurements. You will be receiving a new, custom-made dress with matching shoes and a matching handbag. The President and Mrs. Coldstone have decided that your first dinner here will be a formal one. They usually prefer their meals to be quite casual, but tonight they want to treat you to a special dinner in the private, formal dining room. It's an experience that's reserved for our most important guests. It should be quite memorable."

Personal seamstress?! Agent Rudy drugs and interrogates me, but the Coldstones want to *dress me and feed me*? What a bizarre twist! Absolutely floored, I stammer, "Okay. Um, thank you, Ms. Parsons!" as Abi leads me toward the staircase on the right.

She points to an office door near the foot of the stairs and says, "That's my office. I'll show it to you later. We need to get you up to the smart suite for your fitting."

"Smart suite?"

Abi grins. "It's amazing. You'll see."

We hurry up two flights of stairs to the fourth floor. There's a small marble foyer, and a hallway leading down the center of the building. We glide down the hallway, past several doors on each side, until we reach a door at the back of the building. A small wooden placard over the door reads, "Suite A."

This must be the smart suite. I can't lie, I'm excited. I've heard of this kind of tech, but very little of it is available to the public yet.

"There are five suites on the fourth floor of this building. Two on each side, and one at the back. Suite A is the most luxurious. You're going to love it!" Abi exclaims with a wink.

My jaw drops open as we enter the suite. It's gorgeous! It's an open floor design connecting the sleek, modern kitchen to the large living and dining areas, and is decorated with elegant, yet cozy-looking furniture. The colors are neutral beige and cream, with cheery accents from red throw pillows and deep orange candles.

My neuroprocessor activates automatically, synching with the technology of the suite. A menu pops up before my eyes, revealing choices related to interfacing with the many features in the apartment, such as the entertainment center, lights, doors and windows, fans, temperature controls, and the kitchen, bath, and laundry appliances. "Wow, wow, wow" I repeat.

Abi giggles. "Amazing, huh, Ren? You can monitor and adjust almost everything in the suite with your processor. You'll get used to it quickly. Suite A is intuitive and will interact with your preferences and thoughts. All the latest and greatest tech has been integrated into this apartment!"

I nod my head, astonished. "You're right. It *is* amazing!" A slender, silver-haired woman who looks like she's in her sixties enters from one of the rooms at the back of the suite. She's carrying a black dress over one of her arms. "Hello, Ms. Zimmer. Nice to meet you, Ms. Sterling. My name is Ms. Elderberry. I'm the clothing designer and seamstress in the Residence. I've been instructed to take your measurements so that I might complete a new dress for you for a formal dinner tonight. We only have about an hour before you need to be dressed, so I had the dress and shoes made based on what I know about your size, but I would like to double-check so we can make sure everything fits perfectly. Are you ready for me to measure you? It should only take a moment or two."

I nod in agreement and stand in stunned silence as Ms. Elderberry takes the necessary measurements. I wonder how she knows my dress and foot sizes? After a few moments, she says, "Okay. Great. The shoes fit perfectly, and the dress will need only minor alterations. It should take me less than 30 minutes to complete. I'll be back soon. Go ahead and start getting ready for dinner. Ms. Torres will be here in a few minutes to assist you with your hair and makeup," she says, smiling as she rushes out the front door of the suite.

"Thank you, Ms. Elderberry," Abi calls after her. "Okay, Ren. Let's get you in the shower. Choose the bathroom option from the menu in the lower left-hand corner of your left eye, and then start the shower with your processor. In the future, Suite A will remember your preferred temperature and water pressure for your shower." Abi leads me down a plush, carpeted hall to the master bedroom, which has a king-sized bed brimming with big, soft pillows. There are two reclining chairs, a massive walk-in closet—which already contains the clothes I brought from home—and an entertainment center that automatically turns on when we enter the room. Music from one of my favorite bands starts to play through the speakers in the ceiling. Abi explains, "The entertainment system has already synched with your neuroprocessor, so it will play songs from your most recent playlist. Of course, you can always make any changes to the songs and artists that you want, and the system will adapt to your interests. Just use the entertainment option in the menu. Okay, time to shower. You don't want to be late for dinner!"

I nod and thank Abby as I enter the bathroom. Again, my jaw drops open with astonishment. "OH MY... WOW!" I exclaim. The entire master bathroom is tiled in beautiful marble and quartz. There are gold-plated accents along the walls with gold-plated fixtures in the sinks and bathtub.

Chuckling, Abi pokes her head in the bathroom. "I know. I told you, amazing, right? You can gawk later. Now get cleaned up!" Laughing, Abi closes the bathroom door behind her with a click.

Once I set the water temperature and pressure for the shower, I strip off my navy dress and brown boots and climb inside. There's a marble bench built into the wall, and the water is streaming in on every side of me. I sit, grateful for a moment alone with my thoughts, though I know I'm supposed to hurry. Was I really at Uncle Patterson's memorial just a few hours ago? It seems like years. What an odd day. My childhood dream of living at the Presidential Compound… in the Presidential Residence—okay, not as President, *yet*,—has come true. I don't know if I can trust any of it, though. None of this erases Agent Rudy's treatment of me, or what Zian showed me.

◆ ◆ ◆

After my shower, I enter the bedroom wrapped in luxuriously thick and fluffy towels to discover Ms. Torres waiting to do my hair and make-up. She's petite, curvy, and looks like she's in her early twenties. I like her immediately. We chat comfortably as she brushes, blow dries, and styles my hair and then begins on my makeup.

"I understand you typically use very little make-up, Ren. You can get away with it—you have radiant skin and high cheekbones. However, I'd like to apply just a hint of this lightly-toned bronzing make-up to give you a little color, paired with this bright peach lipstick. I think the color of the lipstick will compliment your skin beautifully and contrast perfectly with your black dress. May I?"

She asks so politely, how can I refuse? "Sure. Thank you," I reply.

While Ms. Torres is finishing my makeup, Ms. Elderberry returns to the suite and places the newly completed dress in the closet. "Thank you, Ms. Elderberry," I say, as she whisks out of the room again. After helping me into the dress, Ms. Torres fastens some sparkling jewelry around my neck, and then hands me a matching handbag. We walk to the front of the suite where Abi is waiting for us.

"Right on time. You look beautiful, Ren. Just stunning!" she exclaims. Ms. Torres coos in agreement. Abi's also wearing a formal dress. The black velvet compliments her alabaster skin perfectly.

"Thank you. You look stunning too, Abi! I'm so glad you'll be with me for dinner."

"We're both knockouts," Abi replies, linking her arm through mine.

I'm not used to wearing heels, so we descend the marble staircase slowly and carefully to the third floor, and then enter the formal dining room where the white-haired President and Mrs. Coldstone are already seated. There's a photographer dressed in a black suit and tie standing in the corner of the dining room. He begins snapping pictures as soon as Abi and I enter. I give Abi an inquisitive look—she didn't say anything about photographs—but she just smiles reassuringly at me as the President and Mrs. Coldstone stand to greet us.

Mrs. Coldstone immediately walks over and gives me a big, comforting hug. Then, she gently cups my face in her hands and gazes at me with her dark-brown eyes. Snap, snap—the photographer captures the moment. "Ren, we couldn't be happier that you are able to join us for dinner! Welcome to our home," she says, her voice ringing with sincerity.

"I'm honored to be here. Thank you," I politely reply. I keep feeling like I should curtsy or bow, but I don't want to look absurd. President Coldstone steps forward.

"It is *our* honor, Ren," replies President Coldstone as he shakes my hand with both of his. "With all you've been through, we're the ones that should be thanking you for your sacrifice to The Order. I'm so sorry for your losses." Snap, snap, snap, goes the camera. I'm distracted by the noise, but then the President's pale blue eyes peer deeply into mine and penetrate my heart with his warmth and kindness. I immediately feel comfortable, safe, and relaxed in his presence. Mrs. Coldstone continues smiling at me while patting my arm gently. I don't know what's happening exactly, but at this moment, I feel as if I would do anything for the Coldstones.

Snap, snap, the photographer steps in closer, and the lovely spell is broken. Irritated, I spin around to look at him. President Coldstone waves his hand. "That's enough George, thank you." George bows his head slightly and exits the dining room.

We sit at the table, which is covered with a white linen tablecloth and formal dinnerware. Several of the dinner staff quietly appear, carrying drinks and appetizers. "We don't usually eat this much," Mrs. Coldstone, laughs apologetically. "At our age, we need to watch our weight. But it is so nice to splurge with such a lovely and important young lady!"

I feel like I've entered the loveliest dream I've ever had, but I'm still confused as to why I'm here. "Mr. President," I finally manage to say, "I'm so grateful for the invitation to stay, but I don't understand how I'm worthy of such an honor." President Coldstone looks a bit uncomfortable with my question.

Abi reaches across the table and gently touches my arm. "Ren, remember, President Coldstone doesn't discuss business in his personal residence."

"Oh, right! I'm so sorry," I apologize, blushing with embarrassment.

"Please don't worry, Ren," the President reassures me, giving a slight wave of his hand. "Everything will be explained and discussed in time. You and I will be having some serious talks tomorrow. This dinner is about fun and relaxation, however. We just want to get to know you and for you to get to know us. Is that okay?"

"Yes, of course, Mr. President," I reply, blushing even more.

"Excellent," he replies, with a sincere smile. I have the sense that President Coldstone truly means what he's saying. Usually when I become embarrassed, the feeling lingers for a long time. Surprisingly, though, I feel comfortable again almost immediately, and my comfort continues to grow throughout the evening as we chat about Pittock High, soccer, and the history of the Presidential Compound. I'm so engrossed in the relaxed conversation and delicious food that I forget my nervousness entirely.

CHAPTER TWENTY

I awake slowly, feeling as if I am floating. Every bit of my body is relaxed and supported—oh it's dreamy! I just had the best night's sleep of my life. At least, I can't remember having a better sleep in a long, long time. I didn't have any nightmares, or daymares, for that matter. Nothing traumatizing occurred—just a long, deep, relaxing sleep. I lounge in bed for a while, enjoying the blissful comfort of what I'm now convinced is the most perfect bed in the world. I don't want this peaceful feeling to end. As my brain begins to wake up, I start feeling excited about the possibilities for the day. Finally, I hop out of bed. My neuroprocessor automatically springs to life and seems to be working perfectly—no flickering.

"**From Suite A: Good morning, Ms. Sterling. How can I serve you? Please choose among the options that you see. Coffee?**" flashes before my eyes.

NO WAY! Suite A is talking to me. With a few quick eye movements, I choose a shower and a vanilla latte with extra milk. Another message suddenly appears before my eyes.

"**From Ms. Parsons: Good morning, Ren. Suite A notified me that you are awake. How did you sleep?**"

I respond: "**I just had the best sleep of my life!**"

"**From Ms. Parsons: I'm not surprised. Your bed synchs with your processor. It adjusts to your weight and changing positions throughout the night, optimizing sleep. You have an appointment with President Coldstone in 50 minutes in front of the Presidential Residence. I'm sending some breakfast to your suite, now. Do you need any assistance with the suite controls?**"

I shake my head in amazement and reply: **"I'm figuring it out pretty well. Thanks for everything, Ms. Parsons."**

"From Ms. Parsons: "You're welcome, Ms. Sterling. Enjoy your time with the President."

◆ ◆ ◆

After another perfect shower, as well as a delicious pancake breakfast, I bound down the marble stairs and through the main foyer—cheerfully waving goodbye to Ms. Parsons as I exit the foyer and sprint downstairs to the front of the building. Incredible what a good night's sleep can do! I feel so energetic and refreshed. In front of me, the reflecting pool and surrounding dew-covered grounds glimmer in the bright, October morning sun. I take in the scene—I still can't believe I'm here.

"Good Morning, Ms. Sterling," Mr. Jacobs calls cheerfully from his post at the bottom corner of the stairs. "The President will be here shortly."

"Thank you, Mr. Jacobs!" I say as I turn back to face him. Just then, Mr. Jacobs and the other guard snap to attention and salute. I spin around to see President Coldstone standing directly behind me, wearing a cardigan sweater.

"Good morning, Ren! I hear from Ms. Parson that you slept well. That's wonderful. The technology in the beds and suites boggles the mind, doesn't it?"

"Honestly, I'm in awe, Mr. President. I just had the best sleep of my life!" I exclaim. President Coldstone chuckles and gives me a warm smile.

"Ren, I was hoping we could take a walk around the grounds and discuss why I invited you here," he begins quietly, as he ushers me toward the reflecting pool. "I understand Abigail has already initiated the conversation with you, but it's vital that we discuss this personally."

"Yes sir," I reply, mirroring his tone and matching his lengthy stride. When we reach the reflecting pool, President

Coldstone stops walking and gazes at me with compassion and warmth.

"I believe many citizens of The Order have strong feelings about you due to the circumstances of your father's death. I, too, have been deeply moved by your loss. If you can find the inner strength and resolve to contribute to The Order by being part of the platinum celebration, you would lift the spirits of so many. You would show that we will *not* be beaten by cowardly acts of terrorism. Our way of life and our core values will not be undermined by a few misguided individuals! Am I making sense, Ren?"

"Yes. I think so," I nod. Sunlight dances on the water's surface and reflects on President Coldstone's face as bright golden ripples and waves.

"I believe our citizens will rally around The Order to combat this scourge—and you will be a source of inspiration for many—especially the young people. You are the face and voice that resonate with your generation. Becoming Pittock High's Student Body President and the Captain of your Foundation Team indicate you're already a leader with a thoughtful understanding of The Order. Therefore, Ren, I'd like you to play an important role in the upcoming celebration. The festivities begin in just a few weeks."

He pauses for a moment before continuing to escort me on the path alongside the shimmering pool. "Now, I also understand that you have some questions, based on some things you saw with a young man named, Zian Reddington. Please ask me any questions you may have. I have nothing to hide from you, Ren."

The mention of Zian sends an initial wave of panic through me, but my nervousness quickly subsides, and a feeling of trust immediately replaces it. "Well, Mr. President, I do have a few questions..." I trail off, unsure if I want to explain what I've seen and experienced.

"It's okay, Ren. Please ask away. Nothing is off limits. If you're going to be part of the celebration and represent The

Order, you need to be completely sure and comfortable. Please. Tell me your concerns."

I'm silent for a moment. I want to choose my words well. "I... saw some very disturbing things out in the countryside, Mr. President. There were slave farms and factories, and a young boy was beaten by a guard."

The President shakes his head in disbelief. "I really can't believe they're saying that our farms and factories have slaves? That is completely preposterous!"

My voice rises as I quickly respond, "With all due respect, Mr. President, I saw it with my own eyes! Maybe you don't know what's happening out there?"

President Coldstone regains his composure and smiles. "Let's go into Commitment Hall, Ren. I would like to show you something."

◆ ◆ ◆

As we enter Commitment Hall, President Coldstone warmly addresses each staff person we encounter. Previously on our walk, the President messaged Abigail to meet us in the main conference room, so that she would be in the room when we arrive. The conference room is vast, and the glossy, oval-shaped maple table in the center of the room is enormous. Abigail is stunning in a cherry red business suit. She smiles and stands as we enter. My boots sink into the plush navy carpet as we approach the table.

The President smiles courteously. "Good morning, Abigail!"

Abi nods her head graciously. "Good morning, Mr. President!"

All three of us sit in the plush leather rolling chairs pulled out from the table. "Abigail, please display Ren's neuroprocessor file—the segment on the farms and factories." The file the SED downloaded from my processor pops up on a large screen on the wall in front of us, and the footage begins. I can't help but recoil. It's shockingly painful to see Zian and my personal memories on display.

The President notices my discomfort and furrows his brow. "I'm sorry, Ren. This must be quite intrusive. But there's no other way to show you the truth."

Abi nods in agreement. "Yes, unfortunately, Ren, but there are only two possibilities. Either Mr. Reddington was misguided and confused by terrorist propaganda, and thus unintentionally gave you incorrect information, or he was intentionally giving you false information—in which case he was intentionally manipulating you. Either way, I'm so sorry to have to inform you that Zian Reddington is a member of the terrorist organization called Conation."

My heart pounds and stomach twists, hearing Zian is connected to Conation. I seriously doubt Zian would ever give me false information, however.

Abi continues, "The proud Producers who work in these farms and factories are not slaves, Ren, far from it. They're honored members of The Order. Yes, they work hard, especially during harvest seasons, but they take great pride in their contributions and know that they're deeply valued by the other segments." Abi peers directly into my eyes and asks, "Did you know that they enjoy a fabulous, rotating vacation schedule? There are trips to various retreat centers that are set up exclusively for their renewal throughout the year. I bet Mr. Reddington didn't tell you about that."

Images of Producer children and families enjoying various activities amidst mountain cabins and lakes fill the large screen. "No, Zian didn't tell me about that," I reply, quietly.

President Coldstone chuckles, "Well, to be fair, we don't publicize that perk, do we Abi? We don't want the other segments of The Order to also start demanding trips to resorts." Abi laughs as well.

"If they're free, why are there barbed wire fences?" I ask, pressing the issue. I don't quite believe what they're telling me.

Something isn't right. Once again, the screen displays my neuroprocessor images.

"There *are* high fences around the living quarters, but they're not there to keep people in. They're there to keep wild animals out," Abi explains. "The crops are stored onsite, before being transported throughout Cascadia. Our environmental and wild animal protection policies have been extremely effective—perhaps too effective, because the animal population in the countryside has exploded. Even the most endangered species have made remarkable recoveries over the past few decades. One of the most popular vacation options for Producers, in fact, is hunting—which is necessary to curb the animal numbers to minimize their starvation."

We're veering off topic. "Okay. That sounds plausible," I interject, "but I saw a guard attack a young boy."

"You're correct, Ren, you did." Abi replies. "That was a very unfortunate incident—one which we take *very* seriously. The man that struck the boy was not a guard, however. There are no guards at the farms and factories, only safety monitors."

My face flushes angrily. "Well, it's horrific that a safety monitor beat that boy!" I exclaim.

"I agree with you, Ren," Abi calmly replies, nodding her head. "While the man who beat the boy was indeed a safety monitor, it's more complicated than that. He wasn't acting in an official capacity. The man is the boy's father." I feel like cold water has been suddenly dumped all over my fury.

President Coldstone adds, "For all our strides in promoting strong family health through education and support programs, we have yet to stamp out domestic violence entirely. It's a tragic, but not completely uncommon problem across all segments of The Order. I'm pleased to say that we've intervened effectively in this case. The father has been removed from the home and the entire family has begun to receive state-of-the-art treatment. While there is always the possibility of a relapse, the expert mental health Providers have informed me that the prognosis is excellent." The President locks his eyes onto mine with the sincerest look I've ever seen. A sense of trust and warmth well-up in me. However, through the haze of warm feelings, a painful thought occurs to me.

I ask, hesitantly, "If Zian is part of the terrorist organization, did he... did he have anything to do with my dad's death?"

President Coldstone and Abi exchange sorrowful glances, and the President reaches over to gently squeeze my shoulder.

"No!" I gasp.

Abi nods her head slowly. "Ren, I'm sorry to tell you this, but yes, it seems that Zian was part of your father's assassination. Our intel indicates he was involved, or at the very least he knew what was about to happen."

Hot tears flood my eyes. I feel as if my world is collapsing in on itself. It can't be true! How could Zian have played a role in my dad's death, and then spent the night kissing and holding me? Waves of nausea course through me.

"Are you *sure*?" I plead, desperately fighting the urge to throw up on the floor.

Abi nods. "We're not one hundred percent certain he was part of the planning or execution of the act, but he definitely knew it was happening. The SED has intercepted neuroprocessor transmissions which are quite conclusive." Abi adds gently, "I'm so sorry, Ren."

I'm blinded by more tears. My heart feels like it's been blown up by a grenade. "I can't believe I trusted him. I'm such a fool. I have no one left now," I sob.

Abi wraps her arms around me, holding me while I cry, and President Coldstone gently rubs my back. When I finally catch my breath, I lift my head again and ask, "Tell me... was my Uncle Patterson involved with Conation and the planning of my dad's death?"

President Coldstone pats my back and answers softly, "It appears he was a terrorist sympathizer, but he was not involved in your father's death in any way. For some reason, he was interested in their ideology, but there's no evidence he was formally part of the group. And to be perfectly clear, the SED had no part in your Uncle's death. He died of natural causes. I've been assured of this by the Director of the SED and have been shown your Uncle's medical documentation as well as the hospital report."

"Okay," I reply, dropping my head into my hands. At least Uncle Patterson didn't harm Dad.

Eventually, I lift my head and mutter, "I think I need to be by myself for a little while."

Abi and President Coldstone rise from their seats and escort me outside Commitment Hall, where I sit down on a bench facing the reflecting pool. "Again, I'm so sorry, Ren," the President says soothingly, as he gently squeezes my shoulder one more time. "Please contact Abi or Ms. Parsons if you need anything. We'll speak again tomorrow, if you're able. Take all the time you need."

After President Coldstone and Abi leave, waves of loss rock through me. How could Zian do this to me? Suddenly, I hear a voice behind me.

"May I sit down with you, Ren?" I look up to see the kind face of Mrs. Coldstone.

"Yes, of course, Mrs. Coldstone," I reply, trying to regain my composure.

She holds out a plate of chocolate chip cookies as she sits down next to me. "Please have some. Sometimes a girl needs chocolate when dealing with grief and matters of the heart."

Although food is the last thing on my mind, Mrs. Coldstone's comment strikes me as funny. I laugh, tearfully, and then pick up a particularly decadent-looking cookie. I close my eyes and savor the sweet, gooey goodness that fills my mouth, and eat the entire cookie.

"Wow! Thank you. That was delicious," I declare as I lick the chocolate from my lips.

"Have another. Sometimes we just need to eat our feelings," Mrs. Coldstone shrugs and giggles.

I nod tearfully and help myself to another cookie. "It's so good!" I coo, through a full mouth.

Mrs. Coldstone pats my hand and gives me a wink. "Now that you have your blood sugar up a bit, Ren, we can talk. I'm so, so sorry, my dear. I can only imagine how sad you must be about your father's passing, and how betrayed you must feel by that young man's actions."

I swallow and nod, blinking back more tears. Mrs. Coldstone continues, "Now, I'm not making any excuses for your friend, but I do think the loss of his father must have left him vulnerable to unscrupulous influences. This can happen when a young person doesn't have enough parental guidance. Everyone needs guidance to develop a strong moral compass, Ren, and I'm afraid the void that was created in the wake of his father's death seems to have been filled with radical, violent ideology."

As I contemplate this, I find myself agreeing. I know how much Zian's father's death hurt him and left a hole in his life. I certainly can empathize. Mrs. Coldstone pats my hand again. "One reason my husband and I want you to stay here is to support you through this difficult time—to provide you with meaningful, moral guidance. You're not alone, Ren. We're here for you."

I don't know if it's the chocolate or Mrs. Coldstone's words, but I'm starting to feel a bit better. "You're a strong, bright young woman," she continues. "You have the potential to be a leader in the best sense of the Intelligencia tradition! Stay the course. Stay on the path. Don't entertain any provocative or rebellious ideology. Stay with the flock and the people that love you. Am I making sense, Ren?"

"Yes, I think so," I reply.

Mrs. Coldstone smiles. "Good. You're a thoughtful, intelligent, amazing young woman. You have so much to offer The Order! I hope you'll find the strength to help us with the platinum celebration... but I get ahead of myself. You take all the time you need. I'll be keeping you in my heart." She pats me gently on the back and leaves the plate of cookies next to me on the bench as she walks back toward the Presidential Residence.

CHAPTER TWENTY-ONE

I feel like I'm floating. Slowly, I open my sleepy eyes to see that I'm in Suite A, lying on what truly must be the most comfortable bed in the world. I had no nightmares again last night, and no 'daymares' either. Suddenly, I remember Zian's betrayal and sit up, feeling like I've been shot through the gut with a cannon ball. Instead of crying, though, I feel like yelling or hitting something.

Overnight, my sadness has turned into outrage. How dare Zian pretend to care about me while knowing that my dad was going to be murdered, and then console me after Dad's death? How could he be so horrifically deceitful and manipulative?! I can't believe I was falling in love with him. The first thing I'll do if I see him again is turn him straight over to the SED.

"From Suite A: Good morning, Ms. Sterling," flashes before my eyes and startles me out of my contemplative fury. **"Should I start your vanilla latte? Are you ready for your shower?"**

Despite my seething anger, I smile. I could get used to this luxury. **"Yes please to both,"** I reply. Suite A must have notified Ms. Parsons that I'm awake, because she chimes in: **"Good morning Ms. Sterling! How did you sleep? Are you feeling well enough to meet with President Coldstone this morning?"**

"I had another perfect sleep," I reply. "Yes. I'm ready to meet with the President."

"From Ms. Parsons: Wonderful. The President and Abi

are bringing a special guest—the Central Advisor of the Intelligencia, Dr. Bagai. Please be at Commitment Hall by 9:00 am. Breakfast will be delivered to your suite shortly."

"Okay, thank you!"

Dr. Bagai is the first woman to be appointed as a Central Advisor. In Foundation Team, we learned she has a doctorate in Utilitarian philosophy, which is based on the idea that actions are right if they benefit the majority. She's an outspoken supporter of the President. I'm so excited to meet her!

Once I'm showered, dressed, and fed, I bound down the stairs and through the foyer, waving at Ms. Parsons as I sprint out into the light, misty rain. "Good morning, Mr. Jacobs and Mr. Andrews," I say as I trot past the guards and down the trail to Commitment Hall.

My neuroprocessor automatically activates as I enter the building. **"The President will meet you in Boardroom 127."** As I enter the boardroom—a smaller, more intimate room than the conference room I was in the day before—I see that President Coldstone, Abi, and Central Advisor Bagai are already seated at the rectangular mahogany table, waiting for me. They stand to greet me.

"Good morning, Ren," the President begins, "I'd like to introduce you to Central Advisor Dr. Das Bagai." Dr. Bagai is a strikingly beautiful woman in her 60s, with perfectly styled shoulder-length silver hair. She is wearing a deep purple pantsuit that accentuates the radiance of her smooth olive skin, with barely any lines. She smiles warmly at me, flashing straight white teeth. She holds out her hand and I shake it firmly. I hope my hand isn't sweaty.

The President continues. "As you know, Ren, Dr. Bagai is the Advisor representing the Intelligencia. I consider Das to be one of my closest, most trusted friends and colleagues. Her philosophical ideas are a strong part of the guiding principles of The Order."

I smile timidly, suddenly unsure of what to say. I'm in awe at meeting such a famous figure in The Order.

Dr. Bagai nods and replies, "Thank you, Mr. President. I'm honored by your introduction. Ren, I've heard so much about you, I just had to meet you in person. President Coldstone invited me to attend this meeting in hopes that I might assist in addressing some questions or concerns you may have about The Order."

The President motions for us to sit. "Ren, ask away. We have plenty of time."

Flustered, I reply, "Well, I'm not sure where to begin... yesterday... yesterday was very emotional for me. I'm so angry and embarrassed that I trusted Zian."

Dr. Bagai nods sympathetically. "Terrorists are very manipulative, Ren, and sometimes Intelligencia can be the most susceptible because we tend to be the most interested in and open to innovative ideas. It's part of our make-up. It's our greatest strength, but also our greatest vulnerability. Don't beat yourself up—Mr. Reddington was also manipulated. The terrorists played on his vulnerabilities as well." The President and Abi nod in agreement.

Blinking back tears, I reply, "I'm sure you're right—it just hurts." I take a deep breath and will the tears to stop. I don't want to break down crying again.

After a moment of collecting myself, I muster the courage to ask about the SED. "I do have a question. Twice, SED agents scanned my memories from my neuroprocessor without my permission. It was an invasion of my privacy. Why are they permitted to do this?"

President Coldstone gestures to Abi, prompting her to respond. Abi nods. "Ren, it's unfortunate you had to go through that. However, at the time of your interviews, the SED didn't know if you were involved with Conation in some way, or what you knew about Mr. Reddington. To deal with threats as serious as Conation we must take certain actions to gather intelligence. The SED needed to be sure you didn't have some information which could assist the investigation, including information that you didn't remember or realize might be of significance."

Nodding thoughtfully, I reply, "I guess I see your point, but doesn't trampling on individual freedoms and privacy undermine the trust of the citizens, therefore ultimately weakening the integrity of The Order? It just doesn't seem right to me."

Central Advisor Bagai smiles broadly as she brings her palms together. "Spoken like the true Intelligencia that you are, Ren! Please let me respond to this Abi—I do love a good debate! While I agree with you in principle, Ren, the SED serves a vital purpose to protect the *majority* by sometimes encroaching on the rights of a select *few*. This is one way that we ensure the maintenance of The Order. Our strength comes from working as a team for the betterment of the whole."

Forcefully, I reply, "That encroachment comes with a big cost to those select few. It was really violating."

Dr. Bagai nods sympathetically. "I'm very sorry to hear that. However, while individual rights matter, they must be weighed against the need to maintain the system that works for everyone," she counters. "As you learned in Foundation Team, excessive focus on individual rights was a big part of the problem that led to the chaos and societal breakdown before The Order was formed! Too much focus on the individual destroyed the harmony of the whole. Individual rights became confused with personal entitlement, and the value in sacrificing for the larger whole was lost."

I nod. "Yes, you make sense, Dr. Bagai, but the SED goes too far."

"Well... sometimes their methods bump right up against the rules, but very rarely do they cross the line," Dr. Bagai replies, shrugging. "The SED has strict procedures that must be followed. One of the tasks of the four Central Advisors, in fact, is oversight of the SED. We have a committee, chaired by the Central Advisor of the Financiers, Mr. Wallace, which works very closely with the SED Director to monitor policies and training. The committee helped write the ethics codes for the SED. We also investigate any suspected violations and then report back to the President. I can assure you that a priority for President Coldstone and the Central Advisors is finding the proper balance between individual rights and what most benefits the majority of the citizens of The Order."

President Coldstone chimes in. "That's correct, Das," he confirms, nodding his head. "It *is* a priority. But it's important to realize that our highly efficient systems of financial and social processes require necessary maintenance and sacrifices. The Order is the glue that keeps it all together. The Order is what creates and supports our prosperity. Without it, selfishness, chaos, and fear will surely return. Does this make sense, Ren?"

He exudes such genuineness and sincerity; I can't stop the feelings of trust and safety which well-up in me—despite my misgivings. "Yes, of course, Mr. President. I'm so grateful for all you do for The Order, and for the leadership of the Central Advisors."

"Do you have any other concerns or questions, Ren? We want you to be completely comfortable," President Coldstone says, reassuringly.

I can't think of anything. My mind is a blank. "I don't think so Mr. President. Thank you so much. It's a privilege to be able to talk about this issue with all of you—especially here at the Presidential Compound. Dr. Bagai, it's been a pleasure to meet you. I hope someday to follow in your footsteps. It's always been my dream to represent the Intelligencia as a Central Advisor or perhaps even the first female President of The Order someday."

"You are a bright and thoughtful young woman, Ren! You are well on your way." Dr. Bagai responds with a smile.

"Duly noted!" The President chuckles. "I think you would make an excellent Central Advisor or President someday, Ren. Now, I have a question for you: Would you like to be part of our platinum celebration?" he asks, with a charming smile.

Sure. Why not? "Yes, Mr. President." I reply. "I'd be honored. What do you need me to do?"

"Wonderful! Welcome aboard!" the President exclaims,

as he stands and gives me a grandfatherly hug.

Dr. Bagai claps her hands and exclaims, "Oh, it will be fun to have another Intelligencia join the planning!"

"I'm picturing that you will play an important role in the opening ceremony as well as the closing parade," President Coldstone continues. "Perhaps we can also have you do some neuroprocessor promotional spots, but I'll leave the details to you and Abi. I trust you two can come up with some creative ideas about how to highlight your participation. Thank you, Ren. You are going to be an inspiration to many people, especially the youth, who will look up to you as a role model." He gives me another one of his warm, sincere smiles. "Oh, and one more thing, to most efficiently support your work on this, I'd like you to continue to stay at the Presidential Residence until the celebration is completed. Abi has already received permission from your mother. We'll have more of your clothes and personal items brought here, and a tutor will be coming to the Compound for a few hours each day so you can keep up with your schoolwork. Sound good?"

Although I'm not exactly sure what I just agreed to, I nod. If Abi's helping me, and I'm allowed to continue to stay in Suite A, I'm probably going to have a blast. After a round of handshakes and celebratory smiles, President Coldstone and Dr. Bagai excuse themselves and exit the room.

I look over at Abi and she grins, showing her dimples. "Well, are you ready to begin, Ren? We might as well get busy brainstorming about the possibilities."

"Sure—but where do we start?" I ask, becoming both excited and a little bit nervous.

"I suggest that the first thing we do is film several thirty-second, promotional clips for the celebration, which will be aired on all neuroprocessors via government informational alerts. The promotions will highlight how individual sacrifice for the betterment of the majority is the best way to embrace a clear purpose in life and overcome hardships. A production crew has been standing by just in case you agreed to be part of this. I'd like to film the promotional clips today. Are you up for it?" Abi asks. "This will be so much fun."

Today? Now I'm really nervous. "Um... Okay, I guess."

"Great!" Abi exclaims, standing up. "Let's go meet the crew."

Abi and I walk to another area in Commitment Hall where she introduces me to the director and members of the film crew who have been waiting. At first, I'm a little annoyed by the President and Abi's presumption that I'd say yes, but the crew is so kind, funny, and supportive, I forget to stay angry. They make me feel relaxed about being in front of the camera, too. In just under five hours, we complete three promotional clips for the platinum celebration.

◆ ◆ ◆

As soon as the first promotion is aired the next day through the Presidential Neuroprocessor Communications Division, or PNCD, positive feedback begins to pour in. Then, the other two promotions air, and the response is almost overwhelming. All three are a hit. They strike emotional chords and stir-up strong feelings of patriotism for The Order.

President Coldstone and Dr. Bagai are delighted by the response. Abby is thrilled and likes to tease me that I'm becoming a celebrity, because the promotions I'm in have received the highest number of neuroprocessor views and ratings ever recorded. I keep reminding her that she's the one who wrote them. A special neuroprocessor account is set-up to handle all the fan communications that continue to flow in for me. I read and respond to as many as I can, but am grateful for the PNCD, who manage most of the communications.

◆ ◆ ◆

The two weeks leading up to the platinum celebration

seem to fly by. The Presidential Compound is abuzz with excitement. I'm busy, have a deep sense of purpose, and every night continue to get the best sleep I've ever had, without nightmares. On top of tutoring and planning for the celebration, I manage to attend a few charity events with Mrs. Coldstone, who deeply inspires me by being a genuinely caring person to everyone she meets. She preaches that love is part of our clear purpose. She says, "Love your job and you will love yourself and be loving to everyone around you."

I connect with my mom daily through my neuroprocessor. She and Tia are struggling emotionally but are slowly recovering from all that has happened. I miss Dad every day and still get furious when I think about Zian. Despite this, and my nervousness about not messing up my role in the celebration, I can't think of a time in my life when I was happier than right now. I'm respected and feel as if I have an important role in The Order. A part of me wishes I won't ever have to return to my normal life.

CHAPTER TWENTY-TWO

Today's the day! I'm so excited—and anxious—that I can't lounge on Suite A's dreamy mattress for long. I spring out of bed and a moment later a communication from Ms. Parsons pops up on my processor: **"Good morning, Ren. The big day has arrived. After tutoring this morning, you'll have a meeting with President Coldstone and Ms. Zimmer. Your breakfast will be delivered to your suite momentarily. Have a great time today, and good luck!"**

I reply: **"Thanks! I'm nervous, I need all the luck I can get!"**

"From Ms. Parsons: We believe in you, Ren. You'll do just fine."

When I meet with Abi and the President, we review the events of the celebration—which officially begins this evening with an opening ceremony and ends Sunday evening with a big parade. Over the next four days, the city will be alive with a variety of sports, arts, and cultural activities. There will also be many exhibits highlighting all the technological advances of the past 70 years. I can't wait! I want to attend everything I possibly can.

After tutoring and the briefing with President Coldstone, Abi and I travel in one of the heavily guarded government vehicles as a part of the Presidential motorcade. We arrive at the City Stadium, the site of the opening ceremony, several hours before the crowd arrives. Abi, the President, Mrs. Coldstone, and

I are served a light, catered meal in the Presidential Box, but I can hardly eat. My whole body feels like it's trembling—I'm so nervous. We are then escorted to our assigned spots under the stadium, where we watch live-stream feeds on our neuroprocessors showing the activity above us. The noise from the crowd increases by the minute. Eventually, the giant outdoor stadium—which is often used for sporting events and concerts—is filled to capacity, and boy is it loud! Over 100,000 people are singing, dancing, and making as much noise as possible with small musical instruments.

The crowd is divided roughly into quarters—one for each segment of The Order. All the segments are distinguishable by their colors, logos, hand-held signs, chants, and songs. The Financiers are dressed in gold and silver colors, representing the currency of precious metals. They carry signs that have pictures of the federal bank, which is the symbol of their segment.
The Intelligencia are wearing blue and orange—the colors of the sky and sun—representing creative and visionary ideas. Their signs have the symbol of an open book, highlighting the knowledge they contribute to The Order. To show solidarity with my segment, I'm dressed in a beautifully tailored sky-blue pantsuit and a salmon-orange blouse, made for me by the fabulous Ms. Elderberry.

The Providers are wearing red and pink colors, demonstrating that they're the heart of The Order. Their symbol is of a muscular arm, boasting strength and pride in the services they contribute. The Producers are dressed in chocolate brown and bright greens, representing fertile soil and plants. Their symbol is a field of crops, highlighting the essential sustenance they contribute to The Order. Our national flag, with the Emblem of The Order on a black background, is posted everywhere. The atmosphere is like a giant party—the stadium is literally rocking with energy and excitement.

Suddenly, we receive a message on our neuroprocessors that the ceremony is about to begin. I give Abi's hand a quick squeeze as she enters the elevator that will take her up to the wings of the main stage. "Good luck, Abi!" I whisper.

Abi smiles and whispers back, "You too, Ren!"

Just as the sun is setting, the bright stadium lights are turned down low, and a loud roar of expectation erupts from the crowd. "Ladies and gentlemen, welcome to the platinum celebration!" the announcer's voice cuts through the din. "Please raise your voices to greet your hostess for the evening—Ms. Abigail Zimmer!" Abi enters the stage to deafening applause. Her pale skin glows alabaster in the stadium lights against Ms. Elderberry's creation of a scarlet dress with pink trim and matching pink bow in her hair.

"Welcome, one and all!" Abi exclaims as she waves to the crowd. Her amplified voice rings through the stadium and her face is displayed—on not only the massive screen above the stage—but on every neuroprocessor, television screen, and computer monitor in the country. "Thank you! Thank you!" She smiles and waves, and then clasps her hands in front of her—waiting patiently as the audience begins to quiet down. "Citizens, we have so much to be thankful for, and so much to be proud of!" Abi gestures sweepingly to the national flag directly behind her. Cheers and whistles erupt, and then eventually die down again.

Abi continues, "Our nation provides order and clear purpose for all. Everyone is useful and valued. The Order embraces technology, champions education, and supports advances in science and medicine—leading to the highest quality of life and longest life-expectancy ever recorded. Due to The Order, we have virtually no crime and all the citizens of Cascadia have financial prosperity, which has never occurred before in the history of civilization! We live in a society where individual rights are in balance with the needs of the majority. We are truly blessed to be living in such a golden age, one which has lasted for 70 years!"

She pauses to allow the crowd to shout its approval, and then continues. "With your contributions, our golden age will continue for many, many years to come. The citizens of The

Order forge our nation's health and prosperity. We *choose* to live by, and for The Order—each doing our part to contribute to the system that works so well for so many. Join me in thanking the President and Mrs. Coldstone, the four Central Advisors, and every citizen that does their part to contribute to the continued prosperity of The Order!"

As the crowd goes wild, fireworks erupt high above us. After a few moments, the stadium falls completely dark. Then, eerie, dark red lights illuminate a thick bank of theatrical smoke, which fills the stadium and intermingles with the smoke from the fireworks. Images are projected high above the stage, onto the smoke. The pictures are from almost 100 years ago, of urban police officers fighting with large crowds of demonstrators and rioters in the former United States.

Suddenly, hundreds of live reenactors dressed as police and protestors rush the center of the stadium floor and mimic the images of the riots still illuminated in the smoke above their heads. It's a wild, disturbing scene. Reenactors partially shrouded by blood-red smoke, battle each other while images of chaos rage above. While theatrical acts of violence continue, the images in the smoke shift in rapid succession—a homeless person sleeping under a bridge; hungry children begging for food; trash-lined streets; abandoned buildings; addicts using drugs; graffiti; broken down cars; long lines at food markets and various government buildings; closed banks; sick patients in drab-looking hospitals; crumbling roads and bridges; drinking and gambling; dilapidated schools; fields of unattended, dying crops; pollution in streams and lakes; armed robbery and various other acts of violent crime; overcrowded prisons; and finally a woman's face revealing a pained, vacant stare. She hovers in the smoke for what seems like a very long time.

While the actors on the field continue to battle and riot, projected words appear—one after the other—just below the woman's chin. Each word is visible for a few seconds before a new word or phrase takes its place:

self-centered

self-absorbed
individual
entitled
my needs
me
mine
uncooperative
unsupportive
uncaring
rebellious
vindictive
nihilistic
leading to ...
depression
alienation
loneliness
disconnection
violence
fear
addictions
crime
scarcity
chaos
war
disorder

 The word 'disorder' remains visible in the smoke as the live performers slowly retreat from the field into the darkness. A bright light flashes, and the image of a nuclear bomb blast is superimposed over the face of the woman. Then the woman's face and the blast slowly disappear, as do the first three letters of the word, disorder. What remains is the word 'order,' as the smoke shifts to a soft, pleasing, light-blue color.

 The word 'order' morphs into 'THE ORDER.' The crowd —which had succumbed to the dark, somber mood—suddenly explodes with joy. Spectators dance and hug each other. "THE ORDER" remains while new words appear in the smoke under it:

Clear Purpose
Value
Participation
Connection
Contributions
Collaboration
Togetherness
Support
Caring
Peace
Collective
Majority
Safety
Security
Technology
Health
Leading to...
Prosperity for All

'THE ORDER' is illuminated brightly again in the smoke. Ear-splitting cheers of the crowd echo through the stadium. The stage is illuminated as the smoke dissipates, and large groups of people—representing the four segments—file happily into the center of the stadium. Each group is dressed in their colors and follow a flag bearer carrying the national flag as well as their segment flag. Representatives of the four segments wave and smile at the crowd as they march around the stadium, before stopping in front of the main stage. The stadium lights dim again, leaving only soft white light bathing the stage, revealing the national orchestra sitting on the back half of the stage. The crowd quiets —waiting in anticipation for what might come next. With the wave of the director's baton, the orchestra begins to play the Anthem of The Order while the crowd sings along.

I wait anxiously next to the President and Mrs. Coldstone while the orchestra plays, and quickly wipe my sweaty hands on the back of my pantsuit. We're next. When the Anthem is complete, a narrow spotlight shines on the front of the stage, and we begin to rise on a mini elevator through an opening in the floor.

Initially, I'm disoriented—blinded by the spotlight as the crowd cheers madly at our arrival. Eventually my eyes adjust, and though I can't make out individual faces in the audience, I clearly see everything close to me. President Coldstone's face fills the huge screen above the stage. He raises his arms and addresses the crowd. "Citizens, welcome to The Order's platinum celebration!"

The crowd cheers with excitement. Eventually, President Coldstone raises his hand to silence the crowd, and then continues. "The key to the practical success of our nation is our focus on selflessness. Each of us has a strong sense of purpose and contributes to the collective in valuable ways. The Order provides a guiding framework that has led to astounding advances in technology and medicine, dramatically improving our quality of life. Citizens, together, our accomplishments have truly been remarkable!"

Shouts and whistles ring ecstatically through the stadium. President Coldstone allows the noise to die down before speaking again. "It is with great pleasure that Mrs. Coldstone and I introduce a very special person—one who embodies all that is good about The Order—Ms. Ren Sterling." With his introduction, my heart leaps into my throat. The noise from the crowd crescendos deafeningly.

President Coldstone waits a moment, and then continues. "Ren Sterling is a shining example of the power of resiliency and courage in the face of tragedy. You all know her story by now. Her father was taken from her—from all of us—by a selfish, misguided group of *individuals*. She has also recently endured the sudden and unexpected loss of her uncle to a rare heart condition. Yet, she carries on. She has bravely faced her losses and refocused her energies on a higher calling—contributing to the betterment of The Order. Ren Sterling is a role-model for all of us."

The President turns toward me and gestures for me to step forward. I'm so nervous, I'm shaking. The President pats me on the shoulder, and then retreats to where Mrs. Coldstone is standing. At the microphone, I turn toward to the Coldstones. "Thank you, Mr. President and Mrs. Coldstone, for your warm and caring support through this very difficult time. I'm both humbled and uplifted by your generosity and sincerity." My knees wobble as my voice rings throughout the stadium. It's so loud! At least my microphone is working.

I face the audience squarely and take a deep breath to steady my trembling voice. "One thing I've come to realize over the past few weeks is that we're very blessed to have such a kind, thoughtful President leading our nation. The support and love shown to me by our President and his wonderful wife have meant everything to me as I continue to grapple with the loss of my father and uncle."

My voice begins to break, and so I pause to collect myself. A hush falls over the crowd as they wait patiently for me to continue. I swallow and clear my throat. "The second thing I've realized is that having a deep sense of purpose is the most important aspect of healing from traumatic events. Redirecting my heartbreak into my work representing the youth of our nation these past few weeks has invigorated my downtrodden spirit. Despite my devastating losses, I now feel strong, happy, and at peace. So, if you find yourself questioning your life in any way, turn toward The Order for guidance and direction. I promise you, the wisdom of our Founding Fathers will show you the way." I raise my arm and gesture to the flag bearing the Emblem of The Order behind me. The crowd roars their approval.

I wait for the crowd to settle down before speaking again. "It is now my great honor to introduce the rest of our nation's leadership team—the four Central Advisors." Three men and Dr. Bagai, all impeccably dressed in their segment colors, walk onto the stage. They wave to the crowd and take their places to the right and left of the President and Mrs. Coldstone. I continue, "Representing the Financiers is Mr. John Wallace—a man who has provided immeasurable stability and guidance to our financial systems. Our economy has never been in better financial shape than it is today, thanks to the steady hand of his stewardship. Representing the Intelligencia is Dr. Das Bagai—the first women to be appointed as a Central Advisor. I can assure you, based on my personal experience with Dr. Bagai, that she truly embodies the practical and creative vision that drives our advances in technology, science, and medicine.

Representing the Providers is Mr. Charles Thomas—a man who supports the diversity of the Provider segment. He understands the vastly different needs and contributions of Providers, yet also understands what unifies them—pride in a job well-done for the betterment of The Order. Last, but certainly not least, is Mr. Juan Olivares, who represents the Producers—the segment which is truly the foundation of our nation. He integrates advances in agriculture and manufacturing, so that Producers contribute to The Order in a manner that is highly efficient and sustainable. We all know that we couldn't enjoy our prosperity if we didn't have healthy, affordable food to eat and products that support our lives. Thank you, Central Advisors, for your dedication and service."

The crowd cheers as I step back and stand next to the President and Mrs. Coldstone. I wave and the crowd goes wild. My knees are shaking, and everything is a blur, but I did it! I gave my speech without any mistakes or throwing up on my shoes. The ceremony continues as each Central Advisor steps forward and gives a short, inspirational speech. I try to pay attention, but all I can think about is what it felt like to speak to a crowd of 100,000 people—it was terrifying and amazing. I'd do it all over again, too. It might have just been the best moment of my life. I only wish Dad was alive to see it. He'd be so proud of me.

When the Central Advisors finish speaking, President Coldstone steps forward again. "We've reached the end of our opening ceremony. It is my great hope that each of you will participate in our platinum celebrations. I encourage you all to attend as many events in the next few days as possible. It is vital we rejoice in that which makes our nation thrive. Long live Cascadia! Long live The Order!" President Coldstone beams. He then steps back, and he and Mrs. Coldstone each grab one of my hands, and we lift our arms up in the air as fireworks erupt in the night sky. The crowd goes crazy. After a few moments of waving goodbye, the three of us walk off-stage, along with Abi and the Central Advisors.

CHAPTER TWENTY-THREE

I can't believe it. I've watched The Order Day Parade every single year of my life, and now I'm going to be in it! If I wasn't standing on a float next to Abi waiting for the parade to start—trying my best to appear patient and mature—I'd squeal with glee. Fortunately, Noelle sends a message to my neuroprocessor and distracts me.

"**From Noelle: You're famous!**"

"**Ha! Hardly,**" I reply.

"**From Noelle: You're all over social media. Pictures of you received the highest ratings this weekend and have been reposted more than the President!**"

"I heard! That's crazy. People have been taking pictures of me everywhere I go. It's fun but weird."

"**From Noelle: Enjoy it. You'll be back to your normal life soon enough. You** *are* **coming back—right?!**"

"Probably by next week."

"**From Noelle: Good—school's not the same without you! BTW, I went to the all-star soccer game today. Were you there?**"

"I couldn't go. I was getting ready for the parade. How was it?"

"**From Noelle: Amazing—decided by penalty kicks!**"

"Wow! I wish I could have seen it! What's been happening at school since I've been gone?"

"**From Noelle: Same old stuff. Tia is soaking up the

fame of being your sister. Prancing around and bragging. Very funny."

"Ugh. That's embarrassing."

"From Noelle: She's definitely enjoying the increased popularity. Are you gonna be in the parade?"

"Yes! I'm on the first float with Abi. The theme of our float is youth involvement in The Order. The President and Mrs. Coldstone are on the final float. Are you coming?"

"From Noelle: I'm already here, with the girls from soccer. We've got a great spot."

The float Abi and I are standing on jolts, and then begins to roll forward, starting right on-time as the sun goes down over the west hills of Capital City. My stomach flutters with excitement as we commence the slow trek from City Stadium through downtown, which is lit up with festive lights strung along the streetlamps. I can't wait to wave to all the people lining the streets! As is customary, everyone will be dressed in their segment colors and wearing masks of the Central Advisors or the President. This is going to be a blast!

"Nice! Gotta go, Noelle. The parade is starting. I'll look for you in the crowd. Pull up your mask so I can find you."

"From Noelle: Okay. I'm wearing a Central Advisor Bagai mask. Have fun!"

"You too!"

I quickly straighten the navy coat and orange scarf Ms. Elderberry dressed me in today, and try to smooth my hair, although the wind keeps blowing it around—so it doesn't stay in place for long. Abi's cheeks are rosy from the cold and match her red and pink coat.

As our float chugs forward, I gaze out into the raucous crowds feeling in awe that *I'm on a float in The Order Day Parade*. I wave continually and am received with cheers and applause. My heart soars when Noelle and my teammates lift their masks and scream my name. I jump up and down, waving and shouting to them. About halfway through the route, I see Tia and Mom standing next to Aunt Bliss, Uncle Ray, and Charlene. They all make exaggerated gestures of blowing kisses at me, and I blow kisses right back.

Several blocks later, when I turn to say something to Abi about wishing we had hot chocolate to keep us warm, a terrifyingly loud explosion rips through the night air. Our float rocks with the force of the blast, and abruptly comes to a complete stop. I fall to the floor—my heart pounding in my chest. The lights on our float and along the parade route go startlingly dark. Was there an accident? What's happening? Am I hurt? My ears are ringing and everything appears to be moving in slow motion as thick smoke fills the air.

I begin to choke and cough. Abi grabs my arm and pulls me to my feet. Peering over the railing of the float, I can make out spectators frantically running from the blast site. I hear screams but they sound far away. There's a large hole in the street between our float and the one behind us. Even though everything sounds muffled and weird, I can hear sirens in the distance. Abi says something, but I can't understand her.

"What?" I ask.

"We need to get off the float, now!" Abi yells. I nod, and taking her hand, we make our way cautiously through the smoke to the rear of the float, and down the stepladder. Plumes of smoke billow from a six-foot wide crater in the street. My eyes and throat burn. It's pitch black out and I can't see far.

"Follow me!" Abi shouts as she escorts me through the smoky darkness across the street and through the front door of an empty café. Our shoes crunch on shards of glass as we inch along—the café window must have shattered in the blast. We feel our way to the back of the dark restaurant, and then open a door into the café's kitchen. "I can't get my processor to turn the light on," Abi says as she gropes for the light switch. She flips it manually, but nothing happens.

In between coughing fits from the acrid smoke, I ask, "What happened?"

"I don't know," Abi replies, as she leans against the kitchen wall, trying to catch her breath. "My neuroprocessor isn't working at all now. You stay here. I'm going to see if I can get some information about what's happening. Don't move! You'll be safe here. I'll be right back, okay?" Abi gives me a quick hug, and then makes her way in the dark to the door leading back into the café.

"My processor isn't working either," I say. "Please hurry!"

Abi nods and closes the door behind her, leaving me alone. I lean against the wall in the dark room, dazed. Suddenly the back door of the kitchen swings open, and in walks a person carrying a flashlight and wearing a President Coldstone mask. Before I can say anything, he pulls the mask up from his face. It's Zian! His dark hair is curly from sweat, and his serious blue eyes meet mine.

Stunned, I stand up straight. "Zian?! What are you doing here?"

He shakes his head. "We don't have much time, Ren. Listen, there are several things I need to tell you. The most important thing is that you must go home. Leave the Presidential Compound and go home as soon as possible."

"*What?!* What are you talking about?" I ask, flabbergasted.

Zian nods his head. "Just do as I say. Please, Ren, you need to get out of there and go home. You're not safe," he pleads.

'Do as I say?' How dare he? Rage surges inside me. "Why should I listen to anything you say, Zian? WHY? You knew about the plot to kill my dad! Why didn't you tell me he was about to be murdered? I could have saved him! I hate you for what you've done to me and my family!" Zian reaches forward as if to take my hands, but I push him away. "DON'T TOUCH ME!" I shout.

Zian glances around the kitchen nervously. "Shhhh. Ren, lower your voice. You don't understand. They're lying to you. They're using you for their own agendas. *I* didn't have anything to do with your father's death. President Coldstone was the one who ordered his assassination. Your father was working on neuroprocessor technology that threatened The Order."

I back up against the wall, shaking my head. "What are

you saying? *You're lying!*"

Zian shakes his head. "No! I'm not! I'm sorry, Ren. The truth is that the SED uses our neuroprocessors to brainwash us. We've been programmed to respond to President Coldstone's face, voice, and smile—to trust and follow him. We've been brainwashed to be obedient followers, to never challenge The Order. Our processors interact directly with our brains, activating neurochemicals that soothe our fears and make us compliant. My father died trying to bring their lies and deception to light, and so did yours."

I recoil from Zian, horrified, but he gently takes my hands in his. He continues speaking quickly and quietly. "Hear me, please, Ren. Don't back away from the truth. Like my dad, your father was trying to free us. Your dad created a device that interrupts the government's manipulations of our neuroprocessor signals. He put the prototype device in a necklace he gave you. *That's* why your processor was flickering, and that's why you were having dreams—your mind was beginning to work on its own. The government found out about the device and had him killed. Then, they blamed it on Conation and labeled them as terrorists."

I shake my head, stunned. "I can't... I don't understand what you're saying," I stutter.

He gently squeezes my hand. "The device works best when you're sleeping—when you can forget who you *think you are*. You have to believe me."

Overwhelmed, I shake my head. He could be lying. How would I know? "President Coldstone and Central Advisor Bagai told me you've been manipulated by terrorists, and now you're trying to manipulate me," I retort.

"Not true. *They're* the ones manipulating *us*." Zian glances at the closed door to the café, and then gently squeezes my hand again. "I'm almost out of time. They'll be here soon. One more thing. Don't fight your dreams, Ren. Be open. Learn from them." Zian begins to back away, but I reach out and grab his forearm.

"Wait. What do you mean? Zian, I don't understand!" I exclaim.

Zian nods and steps closer to me. "I know. Listen. The dreams, the things you see, they're your *Real Self* trying to emerge. It's your intuition trying to guide you, to show you what's really happening, and what may happen in the future. You told me you know something isn't right—parts of your life don't feel *real*—that there's more going on, but you can't put your finger on it. You're right, Ren. Your intuition knows we're being deceived and manipulated to be compliant—that there's much more happening to us than the government wants us to know. We can all feel it a little, but you're special. You see it and feel it much more than most people do. It's a gift you have. After deep scanning you, the government knows you're special. That's why they've been keeping you so close—keeping you brainwashed—and having you do their dirty work for them."

Zian begins to step back, but I hold tight to his arm. "Don't go yet. Tell me more, please. I want to understand."

Zian glances worriedly at the closed door to the café, and then quickly nods. "Your father's device instigated your detachment from the government's control. Your intuition will continue to emerge and show you the way. You'll begin to see through the haze of deception that has been perpetrated on all of us. You're going to be the *One* to lead us through this, Ren."

I drop Zian's arm in astonishment and horror. "*What?!* What do you mean? Through what? I can't lead people, Zian, I'm only seventeen!"

Zian just smiles, slowly backing away. "There isn't time to tell you more. Besides, you aren't ready to hear it all. Soon, though, all be revealed, and you'll know what to do. Leave the Compound. Go home and don't tell anyone about seeing me." He turns and sprints toward the back door of the kitchen, and then stops suddenly. He glances back at me. "I care about you, Ren—more than you know. I'd never do anything to hurt you. Believe me." Zian pulls the President Coldstone mask back over his face, opens the door, and then disappears into the darkness.

"When will I see you again? Zian!" I call after him, but there's only silence as the door closes with a click. Alone, utterly confused, bewildered, and in darkness, I shrink against the kitchen wall, dropping my head in my hands. I forgot to tell Zian I lost my dad's necklace. Is it possible Zian is telling me the truth? Did President Coldstone order Dad's murder? I don't want to believe it. The Coldstones have meant everything to me the past few weeks. My chest aches and I feel like crying, but no tears come. Instead, I listen to sirens blaring in the distance.

Eventually I hear footsteps when someone enters the café and crunches on the broken glass. The door to the kitchen swings open. It's Abi, with two Presidential guards in tow. The guards do a sweep of the room with their flashlights, and then stand by the door leading back to the café. Abi rushes forward and hugs me. Peering into my face, she asks, "Are you okay, Ren? You're pale."

Part of me wants to blurt out everything that just happened with Zian, and ask a million questions about President Coldstone, the SED—not to mention my dad's murder—but I simply shake my head. "I was just scared. I'm fine now. What did you find out? What's going on?"

"It appears the explosion was a terrorist attack." Abi sighs, shaking her head. "The SED believes Conation was attempting to assassinate you--"

I gasp and recoil. I can't help myself. Abi gently squeezes my arm and continues, "--but the explosives went off a moment too late and just missed our float. It's remarkable no one was killed, though a few bystanders were injured by pieces of debris that landed in the crowd."

"Why...why would terrorists want to kill *me*?" I ask, incredulously as I shrink back against the wall and wrap my arms around myself.

Abi furrows her brow. "According to the SED, it's because you've been such an effective spokesperson for The Order."

I don't believe it. Shaking my head, I exclaim, "That doesn't make any sense, Abi!"

"I know! None of this does. Who can figure out the madness of these terrorists?" Abi sighs and shrugs her shoulders in bewilderment. "The good news is my neuroprocessor is working again. Somehow the terrorists blocked our processor communications for a short time. I don't know which is worse—almost dying in an explosion or not being able to use my neuroprocessor," she says with a half-laugh, half-sigh.

Hearing Abi laugh makes me laugh a little too, which helps relieve some of the tension, although I'm still reeling from seeing Zian and everything he just told me. My stomach feels like it's in knots. Abi gives my arm another gentle squeeze and wrinkles her brow with concern. "Ren, the situation is serious. President and Mrs. Coldstone want you to remain at the Presidential Compound indefinitely. It's the best way to keep you safe. You're too important to The Order to let anything happen to you."

Stunned, I stare down at my hands, shaking my head. Abi nudges me gently. "Hopefully, with all the amazing sleep and pampering from Suite A you've been receiving, you won't mind staying a little longer…?" she asks, with a wink.

My stomach hurts. I don't want to go back to the Compound. I want to go home. I shake my head. "Abi, I was hoping I could get back to my normal life at home and school. I miss my family and friends. I miss my dog." Mentioning Piper opens the floodgates, and I begin to cry.

Abi smooths my hair back from my face. "I know. I'm so sorry, but it's not possible—not right now, anyhow. I know it hurts to leave loved ones behind. Console yourself with the knowledge that you are part of a greater calling, Ren."

I wipe the tears from my cheeks and look up. "Are you saying I don't have a choice?"

Abi gently shakes her head. "No. You don't. We need to make sure you stay safe, Ren, for the sake of the nation. How would it look if something happened to The Order's favorite daughter? I'm sorry, Ren. There's nothing I can do, even if I wanted to. You must return with me to the Presidential Compound—on direct order of the President." Abi glances up at the guards and nods. One of them approaches me while the other opens the kitchen's back door.

"Ms. Sterling, please come with us." The guard firmly takes my arm and leads me out the back door into the alley behind the café. I glance around quickly, hunting for any sign of Zian. I'm relieved when I don't see him. After a moment, a black government car pulls up alongside us. Abi, one of the guards, and I climb into the back seat while the other guard slides into the front passenger seat.

Abi commands, "To the Presidential Compound, now!"

CHAPTER TWENTY-FOUR

I can't sleep. I've been pacing back and forth in Suite A for hours, but I can't seem to calm down from the chaos of the night. Over and over—like a loop in my mind—I hear the explosion, see Zian's face, and then hear him tell me President Coldstone ordered Dad's death. I wish I knew for certain that Zian is wrong—that he's being manipulated by Conation. It would make life easier and much less frightening. Yes, I'd lose Zian, but I'd be able to hold onto everything I've ever been taught and believe to be true about my life.

   I wish I could just go back in time to when life made sense, to when my dad was still alive. I stop pacing and flop backwards on the pillow laden bed. I wonder what Zian meant when he said I am "going to be the One to lead them through"? Lead whom? Through what? I don't know how I can possibly help anyone when I'm being held captive indefinitely at the Presidential Compound.

   Suddenly, my forehead begins to feel heavy and I can no longer raise my head up off the bed. The back of my neck tingles. A sound like wind whistles softly in my ears, and then it's followed by voices chanting and singing. By now, I know what's going to come next. Instead of fighting or fearing it, I close my eyes and surrender.

❖ ❖ ❖

When I open my eyes, I'm floating in the shadows above a room, witnessing a scene unfolding below me. The chanting in my ears has stopped. The room appears to be a large business office with a formal wood desk. The light in the office is dim, coming only from two small lamps on the desk. Despite the poor lighting, I can see that President Coldstone is sitting at the desk in a black leather, executive chair. Two SED agents, one of them Agent Rudy, are sitting in smaller leather chairs facing the President. Another man, who I can't make out, is sitting cloaked in darkness against the side wall, with only his expensive leather shoes visible in the light. The men are speaking excitedly, in hushed tones.

"I hope you have good news for us, Agent Rudy," President Coldstone begins.

"Mr. President, I'm afraid that the threat is very real," Agent Rudy responds. "We are in serious danger of losing control of the neuroprocessor technology."

"What do you mean?" the President asks.

"If this new technology gets further developed and somehow becomes available to the public, The Order as we know it may fall apart," Agent Rudy answers. "We must put a stop to it before it's too late."

President Coldstone leans back in his chair, shocked by what he's hearing. "What do you suggest?"

Agent Rudy crosses his arms and nervously raises one of his hands to his chin and mouth. "Well, I think we have to eliminate the source of the technology," he says.

The President quickly interjects, "And how do you propose that we do that, Special Agent Rudy?"

Before Agent Rudy can respond, the man sitting in darkness speaks up in a deep, authoritarian voice. "You eliminate Peter Sterling and wipe out all traces of his research, including any sympathizers."

After a short pause, President Coldstone leans forward and says, "Yes. The Order must be preserved. There is nothing more important. The platinum celebration is in less than a month. I want this resolved before then. Do whatever needs to be done, Agent Rudy. Just make sure that someone else takes the blame."

"Consider it done, Sir," responds Agent Rudy.

"Nooo!" I scream.

◆ ◆ ◆

I sit up in bed, soaked in sweat. My throat is raw from screaming, although I don't know if I made any sound. The heaviness in my forehead is gone, but the heaviness in my heart is unbearable. I know what I saw is true—President Coldstone ordered Dad's assassination.

"From Suite A: You're up early, Ms. Sterling. Would you like a vanilla latte and a shower?"

"No," I eventually respond. My heart is still racing.

"From Suite A: I have lowered the room and bed temperatures. You are overheating. Would you like me to notify the Compound doctor? You may be ill."

"No. I'm fine," I reply. **"Adjust the temperature back to normal."**

I lie back in the downy bed. I now know Zian is telling me the truth, but I have no idea what to do about it. I feel sick to my stomach. President Coldstone deceives and manipulates the innocent people of Cascadia through our neuroprocessors, and he is responsible for my dad's death. I don't know how I'm ever going to face him again. I *must* get away from the Compound. But how?

I do a quick neuroprocessor search to read about the terrorist attack on the parade. It's all over the news and social media because it's the first time The Order Day Parade has ever been interrupted. There's a lot of discussion about the "evil" terrorist organization, Conation. There's even speculation that I was killed in the attack.

My processor is full of hundreds of unread communications. Overwhelmed, I turn it off, change into a dry t-shirt, and then fall back onto the bed. My head is throbbing, and so I rub the back of my neck to release the tension from the muscles near my processor. Wait a minute. I sit up. I just had a nightmare—or daymare—or whatever, here, at the Presidential Compound. How is that possible if the neuroprocessor disrupter is in the shell necklace, which I lost? My dad's device couldn't possibly be in Suite A, and until now, my sleep has been dreamless since I arrived. How very strange.

CHAPTER TWENTY-FIVE

I'm still lying in bed when I receive a message from Ms. Parsons. **"Be ready in 90 minutes to meet with the President at Commitment Hall, Boardroom 127. Your breakfast will be delivered to you by the time you are out of the shower. I have sent an outfit to the suite that Ms. Elderberry has prepared for you. Please wear it to the meeting with the President. Ms. Torres will be doing your makeup this morning. She'll be arriving shortly."**

"Okay. Thank you," I reply.

Ms. Parson's communication is business-like, not as warm as usual. Perhaps she's just upset about what happened last night. I'm sure a lot of people are. I wonder why I have to wear a special outfit and makeup to the meeting with President Coldstone?

I send another message to Ms. Parsons: **"What's happening today?"**

"From Ms. Parsons: **You will be part of a special State of The Order address.**"

Great. Now I'm being told—not asked—what to do. Apparently, I don't have any say in the matter. Just thinking about seeing President Coldstone's face sends a shiver down my spine. I don't know how I'm going to look him in the eyes. Unfortunately, I don't think I have a choice but to play along, for now.

◆ ◆ ◆

Ms. Torres brings me a navy dress suit and high heels to wear. "I hate wearing heels," I mutter to her. She just smiles and hurriedly finishes my makeup. My heart is pounding, and my stomach is in knots by the time I arrive at Boardroom 127. 'Keep it together, Ren, just play along', I tell myself. The President and Abi stand to greet me as I enter. They're both wearing formal business attire, too.

"Ren, how are you?" President Coldstone asks, as he reaches out to give me a hug. I don't shirk from his touch, but I don't hug him back either. He notices, and then intentionally looks directly into my eyes and flashes one of his beaming smiles. Immediately, my anxiety and tension lessen. Feelings of warmth and security wash over me—but not completely. My disgust is giving me the strength to resist. This is the man who ordered Dad's death.

"I'm fine," I reply curtly.

"We're so grateful you weren't hurt last night. Horrible, horrible events," the President says, shaking his head sadly.

I nod, somberly. "Yes. What happened? Was it a bomb? How could this happen at the parade?"

Abi steps toward me and takes my hand comfortingly in hers as she replies, "Conation made an attempt on your life, Ren, and we're very lucky no one was killed. We don't know all the details of how it happened, but we're learning more every hour. The SED is quite embarrassed they allowed this to occur. They're taking it very personally."

President Coldstone nods in agreement. "I'm quite certain the SED will capture the terrorists, soon. There have been some very promising leads," he adds. My stomach tightens when I think about Zian. Wherever he is, I hope he's safe. "But the most important thing is that you and Abi are both unharmed," continues the President. "Ren, you're such a strong, resilient young woman. You've been through so much. Now, I must make another request of you."

He smiles broadly, shining all his radiance and warmth on

me. It's not working—I still feel icy toward him. "Many of our citizens are deeply worried about you. Rumors are running rampant about your well-being. I'm about to present a State of The Order speech and want you to be part of it. We need to reassure everyone that the beloved daughter of The Order is alive and well. Okay?"

Even while feeling the strong pull to be compliant, I continue to resist. I stare at him blankly, without saying a word. "Wonderful!" The President exclaims, as if I'd agreed. Then he glances at Abi, who releases my hand and motions for me to follow her—along with the President—down the hall to the Presidential Broadcast Studio. The room is staged with a large chair positioned next to a lit gas fireplace and a wooden mantle, adorned with the national flag. Beautiful artwork hangs from the walls on both sides of the fireplace, creating a calm and reassuring setting.

Abi rattles off instructions. "The President will be giving the State of The Order speech from this chair while you stand on his left, Ren. Mrs. Coldstone will be on his right. I'll be standing directly behind the President. Two of the Central Advisors will be standing behind you while the other two will be behind Mrs. Coldstone. We need to show the nation that our government leaders are unharmed and in-charge. At the end of the President's speech you'll read a few words that will appear in your neuroprocessor. Do you have any questions?"

I do, but I can't ask most of them. "Will it be live?" I manage to ask.

"Yes. It will. But don't worry, you'll do beautifully, Ren, you always do," Abi says, with a warm smile.

My heart thaws a smidge with Abi's warmth. I love Abi. It's not her fault she works for a monster—she's being manipulated, too. "When will the broadcast be, Abi?" I ask.

"Right now," Mrs. Coldstone replies, as she strides into the room, walking directly toward me. She wraps her soft, doughy arms around me, and gives me a long, comforting hug. Feelings of safety and love course through me, but once again, a part of me holds back. Her embrace feels fake, *unnatural* to me now.

"Thank you, Mrs. Coldstone," I say stiffly, as I try not to yield to her hug.

"For what?" she asks. "We're the ones who should be thanking you for your continued contributions to The Order, despite all the scary things that have happened! It's okay, sweetheart. You're safe now. We won't let anything happen to you. I promise."

The four Central Advisors enter. Each Advisor shakes my hand and expresses support.

"Ren, on behalf of the Central Advisors, I want to let you know how happy we are that you're safe!" exclaims Dr. Bagai. "I can only imagine how scary that must've been for you last night. I can't believe the depths of depravity that these terrorists will go to. Thank you for helping us reassure the public with this important State of The Order speech."

"Of course," I mutter, and then pretend to fidget with my dress suit.

"Hello everyone, may I have your attention?" Abi interrupts, clapping her hands together. "We're about to get started. Please take your places."

I stand to the left of President Coldstone. Abi directs me to place my hand on his shoulder, and it's all I can do not to walk out of the room, but I keep reminding myself that the only way for me to escape the situation safely is to play along. The last thing I want to do is to attract further ire from the SED. The stage lights brighten as several cameras move closer to us. A red light above the camera directly in front of us illuminates. A camera technician counts down: "Three, two, one," and then points to President Coldstone.

"Citizens of The Order, I, President Xavier Coldstone, am speaking to you today because of the profoundly unfortunate events that occurred last night. As most of you are aware, the terror organization, Conation, detonated an explosive device during The Order Day Parade. We believe they were attempting to assassinate Ren Sterling. Thankfully, they were unsuccessful, and no one was seriously injured in the attack. As you can see, Ren is alive and well." The President reaches up and touches my hand resting on his shoulder. It takes everything in me not to shudder.

The President gives his reassuring smile to the camera, and then continues his speech. "We believe Conation targeted Ren because she represents the true values of The Order—intelligence, hard work, commitment, loyalty, and resilience. I don't claim to understand the motivations of terrorists. Frankly, I don't care. What matters is that we find these criminals and put an end to their murderous ways. The threat posed by Conation is unprecedented and will be eliminated. I am confident that the Subversion Eradication Division will prevail in locating, arresting, and prosecuting the parties responsible for such villainous acts."

President Coldstone pauses, allowing his previous statement to land before continuing. "We have strong leads in the criminal investigation, which will soon result in arrests. Our primary suspect is Zian Reddington, an eighteen-year-old Intelligencia." Every muscle in my body tightens. I feel like I've been sucker-punched. I can't breathe. *Zian* is their main suspect?!

The President continues, "Although we have strong leads, we need your help. A special neuroprocessor hotline has been set-up to handle tips related to the identity and whereabouts of any suspected members of Conation. Please let us know if you have any information that can assist us in this vital investigation. The maintenance of our heritage and hopefulness for our future depend upon our collective success. Together, we will protect The Order and all it provides for us. We will return our nation to a place of absolute safety and security for all our citizens. Long live Cascadia. Long live The Order!" President Coldstone pauses, smiles warmly, and then says, "And now, at my request, Ren Sterling will share a few of her thoughts in this time of national crisis."

Words appear in my eyes. I take a deep breath and try to

compose myself, even though everything in me is screaming to run or yell or fight back in some way. There's no point in rebelling right now, though. "Thank you, Mr. President, for your inspirational words. Citizens of The Order, I am here to show my support for our President, --" my throat catches, and I have to swallow hard before continuing, "--the leadership team that you see here, and The Order. Our resolve is strong and unwavering. No terrorist bombs can change our cherished way of life. No cowardly acts of treason can dampen our spirit. More than ever, I am personally committed to the values of The Order and the need for all of us to do our part. Together, we are stronger than any radical group. Long live Cascadia. Long live The Order."

My voice sounds far away and flat. I wonder if anyone else can tell I don't mean a word I'm saying. The light atop the main camera extinguishes, and everyone relaxes, except for me. "Great job, Ren," says the President. "You're a *natural*." I stand stiffly while everyone else pats me on the back and assures me that I did well.

Abi gently pulls me aside and speaks quietly into my ear so the others can't hear. "Go ahead and take a break. I know it must have been hard to hear Zian's name. Get some lunch and walk the grounds. Maybe you could go back to Reception Hall. I know how much you enjoy it there. President Coldstone and I have a few other meetings we must attend, and then we'll meet with you later this afternoon to debrief everything." She gives me a quick squeeze, which I don't return. Instead, I just nod my head and then exit the Presidential Broadcast Studio. I can't wait to get away from these people.

CHAPTER TWENTY-SIX

My thoughts race as I pace the grounds beside the reflecting pool. Zian is in danger, and there's nothing I can do to help him. I can't believe *he's* the one being considered a threat. I see so clearly now—President Coldstone is the threat, not Zian. Staring at the reflecting pool, it no longer looks peaceful to me. It appears shallow, man-made, and fake.

Perturbed, I decide to follow Abi's advice and walk to Reception Hall so I can pace around the Event Ballroom instead. The open expanse of the large room and the beauty of the murals instantly helps me feel a little calmer and able to think more clearly. While I'm pacing around the Ballroom, an urgent neuroprocessor communication startles me out of my thoughts. It must be important, because it by-passes my screening function.

"**From Mom: Someone broke into our house. They turned your bedroom upside down. Do you know anything about this? Do you know why someone would search your room?**"

My heart starts pounding. Someone broke into our house? WHY? "**What?! Are you and Tia okay? When did this happen?**" I ask.

"**From Mom: It happened last evening while we were at the parade. We're so upset. Why would someone do such a thing?**"

"That's horrifying! I don't know anything about it. Was anything taken?"

"**From Mom: I can't tell. It's a real mess. Please see if you can find out some information and let me know?**"

"I'll ask Abi and let you know what she says. I'm so sorry. Please stay safe."

I'm in shock. Why would someone break into our home and search my room? There's nothing of value in there. Unless... I wonder if they were looking for Dad's neuroprocessor interrupting device? Perhaps it was the SED searching for it... or maybe Conation? Either way, I feel heavy with guilt. I need to go home and help Mom and Tia clean up the mess. I need to make sure they're safe, and then I'll feel better. I wish there was a way to sneak out of the Compound. If I did, maybe I could get Noelle to pick me up.

Suddenly, a new communication interrupts my thoughts. "**From Abi: No time for lunch. The President wants to meet with you now. Please rejoin us.**"

I hurriedly return to Commitment Hall, Boardroom 127. Abi and President Coldstone stand when I enter the room. The President smiles warmly as he gestures for me to sit.

"Well, I thought that went very well this morning, Ren," starts the President.

"Thanks," I say, quickly. "Before we continue, there's something I need to talk to you about. Someone broke into our house. Please, I must go home. My mother and sister need me."

The President cocks his head back. He's obviously receiving a neuroprocessor communication. He holds up a finger indicating I should wait while he takes the message. His facial expression changes noticeably, becoming more serious. He leans forward and clears his throat.

"Ren, some new information has just come in. The SED now believes the bombing last night was not an assassination attempt. They think it was a diversion—along with the neuroprocessor jamming—so that the terrorists could communicate with you. I need to ask you. Have you had any communication with the terrorists? Did anyone contact you in any way after the explosion?" He looks me straight in the eyes. I feel the power of his energy commanding me to tell him the truth.

I start to open my mouth to speak, but nothing comes out. Part of me wants to tell him everything I know, but another part wills me to resist. President Coldstone witnesses the struggle in my face. "Ren, you're hesitating. Tell me the truth. You won't be in trouble, but I need to know what happened."

I shake my head in silence for a few seconds, before calmly stating, "No. I didn't have contact with anyone. I was alone in the back of the café until Abi returned."

President Coldstone sighs. "Well, you see, that is a problem. Abi wasn't with you the entire time, so we can't verify that you're telling the truth. I wish I could believe you, Ren, but the SED will need to deep scan your neuroprocessor just to make sure. I don't want a black cloud of suspicion hanging over you. I have big plans for you, my dear," he says, with a warm smile.

I begin trembling at the thought of being deep scanned again. I'm suddenly having a hard time catching my breath. It feels like my ribcage is crushing my lungs. "Please, please don't make me go back to the SED. I've told you all I know. I promise," I say, breathlessly, placing a hand on my sternum.

"Now... there's no need to worry," the President remarks coolly. "The SED Director, Special Agent Rudy, will be there to personally conduct the scan. You'll be in very good hands." I recoil in horror, rasping for breath.

President Coldstone observes me panicking and furrows his brow. "Okay. This is what we'll do. Abi will accompany you —she'll oversee the interview and sit with you the entire time, Ren? You'll be fine, I promise, but you need to leave right now," he commands as he stands and directs me through the boardroom door.

◆ ◆ ◆

Two guards meet us as we exit Commitment Hall, and then escort Abi and me to an idling black car. As we drive downtown, I try taking long, slow, deep breaths to remain calm, resisting the urge to open the door, throw myself outside, and run away.

Soon, the SED will scan my neuroprocessor and see that I met with Zian. What will happen then? They'll find out that I know my dad's death was ordered by President Coldstone. Should I tell Abi the truth, right now?

Our vehicle stops abruptly in front of the Central Government Building. It's hard for me to breathe again—my lungs feel like they're collapsing. Witnessing my discomfort, Abi attempts to reassure me. "Don't worry, Ren. Just tell them the truth. I'll be with you every step of the way." To placate Abi, I nod my head. I'm not going to tell the SED the truth, but they're going to find it out anyway.

An SED agent meets us just inside the front door, and then escorts us down the hall to that horribly familiar room full of agents working at their desks. As Agent Rudy approaches us, I can feel panic rising inside me. My heart is beating hard against my ribcage, like a captive desperate to escape.

"Good afternoon, Ms. Zimmer," Agent Rudy begins. His breath reeks. Some things never change, I guess. "Thank you for bringing Ms. Sterling in today. The sooner we get this started, the sooner she can leave. Please have a seat over there." He gestures to the chairs lined up against the wall. "I'll bring her out once we're finished."

"Thank you, Agent Rudy, but I'll be joining Ren during the interview," Abi asserts.

Agent Rudy smirks. "Not today, Ms. Zimmer. I'll be speaking with Ren alone," he smugly replies.

Abi's pale cheeks flush angrily. "I'm under the direct order of the President to accompany Ren while she's here."

Agent Rudy grins wickedly, retorting, "The President may have ordered you, but he didn't order *me*. In this building, I'm the boss. Have a seat over there, Ms. Zimmer, or I'll have you removed from the building."

Abi's mouth drops open in shock, and her entire body flushes with fury. "I will be informing the President about this,

Agent Rudy. Your behavior will likely result in a review by the Central Advisor Oversight Committee," she threatens.

Agent Rudy shrugs again. "That's fine. Once we catch these terrorists, the Central Advisors will be the first ones to give me a medal. Ren, follow me," he orders. As I follow him to his office, I glance back, pleadingly, at Abi. She furrows her brow compassionately and mouths, "I'm sorry."

Once in Agent Rudy's office, he gestures for me to take a seat. "You may have fooled the President and everyone at the Compound, but you don't fool me, little lady," he says tersely, through lips curled in scorn. "I know you're involved with Conation. I know you have more information than you've been telling me. And right now, I will get the information I need."

Agent Rudy motions to the two other agents in the room. They grab my shoulders and force me to sit, and then strap my ankles and wrists to the chair. Agent Rudy removes a syringe and vial out of a black bag sitting on his desk. Filling the syringe, he barks, "I'm not messing around with you, Ren. I don't trust you to tell me the truth, so I'm not going to ask you any questions—I'm just going to take the truth from you."

Agent Rudy taps the syringe, squirts a little stream of fluid into the air, and then commands, "Stay still or I might just puncture your jugular vein. I'd hate to have to clean up the floor if it gets flooded with your blood." He chuckles sinisterly, and I shiver involuntarily. Maybe it's better if I just tell him the truth. "Wait. Please, Agent Rudy, I'll tell you whatever you want to know," I plead.

Sadistically, he smiles. "It's too late for that, Ms. Sterling." He nods to the other agents, who hold my head while Agent Rudy injects the serum into both sides of my neck, just below my skull. It burns, and the agents squeeze my head agonizingly tight. Tears well in my eyes, but I blink them back. I'm not going to give Agent Rudy the satisfaction of knowing he's hurting me.

"We were finally able to analyze that little blip we downloaded off your neuroprocessor," Agent Rudy says in an almost chipper tone. "It seems someone tampered with your processor and distorted your memories. Only the terrorists could have done this. You're either working with them, Ms. Sterling, or you're just a pawn caught in the middle of something much bigger than you understand."

As the agents release my head, the burning sensation in my neck is slowly replaced with a warm, fuzzy feeling, which courses through my body. I can't move. My energy to resist is gone.

Agent Rudy picks up the deep scanner from his desk, and the monitor on the wall illuminates. The familiar tingling in my head and spine begins as images appear on the monitor. Agent Rudy sounds almost gleeful as he speaks to other agents, "This will take a while. I want to see everything."

◆ ◆ ◆

After some time, I don't know how long, I'm suddenly lifted from the chair. Two agents drag me out of Agent Rudy's office and into the main room. I can hardly open my eyes, but I can hear commotion and voices.

"What have you done to her?!" I hear Abi's voice exclaim as we enter the room. "I will have your jobs for this! Agent Rudy, you WILL answer to the Central Advisors and the President for your behavior."

"You know where you can find me," Agent Rudy replies disdainfully. "Have your little talk with the President. We'll see how he responds after he reads my report. As for now, get your snobby little ass out of my building, Ms. Zimmer! I have a job to do." Agent Rudy crosses his arms and watches as one of his agents hoists me over his shoulder. I lift my head to get the last word.

"Your breath stinks," I say in a groggy slur of words.

Agent Rudy turns a furious purple. I flash my middle finger at him as the agent carries me out of the room. Abi follows us, barely suppressing a giggle. The agent and Abi slide me into the back of the government vehicle, and then we speed off to the Presidential Compound. The last thing I remember is being carried up to Suite A by Mr. Jacobs and Mr. Andrews.

CHAPTER TWENTY-SEVEN

I awaken on a deep blanket of pine needles, with my back against the base of a large, moss-covered tree. Startled, I glace around. I'm in a thick forest surrounded by evergreens. I have no idea how I got here. In a flash, I realize I'm dreaming. Strange—to know I'm dreaming while it's occurring. I take a deep breath and begin to relax. I'm safe. Whatever happens next is just happening in my mind.

The air is warm, and the trees are glistening with drops of dew. A stream trickles gently over rocks not far from my feet. The tree canopy blocks most of the sun's rays, but when the temperate wind blows, it causes the branches to sway slightly, allowing sunlight to peek through. I rest for a long time, taking in the tranquil scene—listening to the stream cascading, the birds chirping, and unseen animals rustling in the foliage. The forest may be peaceful, but it's teeming with life.

Finally, I stand and stretch my arms into the air. I'm not quite sure what to do next. I remind myself—if I'm dreaming then nothing bad can happen to me. Unlike my waking life, here I'm free. Anything is possible.

Alongside the stream, there's a trail worn into the pine needles. Worn by whom, I wonder? An urge to see where the path leads suddenly propels me forward. As I walk on the trail, with the sun on my face and the earth beneath my feet, I realize I'm a part of everything here. I'm one with the plants and trees, sharing energy and sharing the same air. When I breathe in, the forest exhales. When I exhale, the forest inhales my breath. It feels as if I am disintegrating, as if I'm being absorbed into the forest. It's a very peaceful feeling.

Eventually I encounter a large boulder, which blocks the path. A massive, fallen tree spans the width of the stream on my right. The stream has become much deeper, faster. The water rushes by, bouncing off rocks in the stream and lapping at the bottom of the fallen tree. On my left, there's a narrow trail heading up the side of a hill. I begin up the trail, but then stop. Something inside me urges me to cross the stream, rather than take the trail. I turn back, climb up the fallen tree, and then carefully cross the rushing waters to a slight clearing on the other side.

I hear a loud rustling in the brush in front of me. I startle, but then I remember I'm just dreaming. A raven pops out of a thicket of wild blackberries. Somehow, I know it's the same bird I've seen before in my dreams. The raven gazes into my eyes and cocks its head. I know it wants me to follow it. As the raven hops and flutters along, I stay close enough to keep it in sight. After about twenty yards, when the forest becomes very dense, I wonder if I'll have to turn around. I keep the raven in sight, though, until it disappears into a mass of foliage. After a few moments of groping through plants, I stumble into a clearing filled with sunlight.

In the clearing sits an earthen hut with a thatched and mossy roof, next to a still pool of water. The raven has disappeared, but a wrinkled, bronze-skinned woman in a long, woven dress and a hat made from plant fibers, steps out of the hut. She welcomes me without uttering a word—with just an inviting look in her eyes. I get goose bumps and an odd feeling of déjà—as if I've been here before. The woman smiles, as if she knows exactly what I'm thinking.

❖ ❖ ❖

I open my eyes and stretch out my arms and legs, reveling in the deep peace I feel. Wow! What an amazing dream! It wasn't at all like my nightmares—or daymares for that matter. It was so incredible to be aware I was dreaming while I was in a dream!

I lounge comfortably in bed for a few moments, until I receive a neuroprocessor communication.

"From Suite A: Are you ready for your latte, Ms. Sterling? You have visitors waiting for you in the main living area."

My calm is quickly replaced with concern. Who's here? Suddenly, I remember being at the SED office and having my memories deep scanned again. Agent Rudy's sneering face pops into my mind. Ugh. I shiver as I hurriedly get dressed.

Fully clothed, I rush into the main living area. President Coldstone, Mrs. Coldstone, and Abi are sitting around the dining room table, drinking coffee. They stand when I enter the room.

"Good afternoon, Ren," the President says calmly.

Mrs. Coldstone walks over and gives me a gentle hug. "Hi, sweetie. How are you?"

"Okay. Thanks," I reply, cautiously.

Abi nods hello to me as our eyes meet for a moment. She seems distant, cold, which is strange for Abi. She's nervously chewing gum.

"Please sit. Suite A has made a latte for you," Mrs. Coldstone says soothingly, as she hands me the steaming cup. "I assume it's your favorite flavor? Suite A is so smart."

"Yes. Thank you," I reply, and sit at the dining room table. I cradle the cup with both hands, absorbing its comforting warmth.

"Ren, let me begin by saying how sorry I am about what happened at the SED office yesterday," the President says, shaking his head. "Their methods and attitude have gotten out-of-hand. I've already discussed this with the Chair of the SED Oversight Committee, John Wallace. He was equally disturbed by Special Agent Rudy's behavior, and assured me there will be changes in procedures. I do hope you're feeling better. You slept for almost a full day."

I stare blankly at President Coldstone—I know I can't

trust anything he says.

"But there's a matter we need to discuss with you," he continues. "You see, I received a report from Agent Rudy which is rather disturbing. It seems you weren't truthful with me when I asked if you had been in contact with the terrorists. The deep scan of your neuroprocessor revealed that you met with Zian Reddington after the explosion at the parade." President Coldstone gazes at me with disappointment in his eyes. "But what bothers me most is how easily you lied to me. I thought we had trust between us," he says, sounding hurt.

"Now dear," Mrs. Coldstone chimes in, gently addressing her husband, "we shouldn't be too hard on Ren. It's true—this is a moral failing on her part. However, evil, cunning forces manipulated Ren. They went right for a teenage girl's soft spot—love. She probably didn't even realize she was being used."

"Yes, I agree. But unfortunately, there's more, Delores. The manipulation goes much deeper than teenage romance." The President turns to face me again. "Along with not telling us about seeing Zian, we know the terrorists have been using a device that interferes with your neuroprocessor. It's the reason your neuroprocessor has been flickering, and why you've had nightmares. They're communicating with you and manipulating you while you sleep. They've had the nerve to blame the device on your father—which we know is not true. Your father was a loyal and valued member of The Order. They've even blamed his death on me—which is an outrageous lie!"

Appearing angry and grief-stricken, President Coldstone stops to compose himself for a moment. He's an incredible actor. I almost believe him. "We also know—thanks to Suite A —that you've been having nightmares the last few nights here at the Compound, where we're certain there are no neuroprocessor-jamming devices. Our only conclusion is that the device they used to manipulate you while you slept has significantly, and seemingly permanently, corrupted your processor. They're able to continue to manipulate you even without the device being in your presence."

President Coldstone stands, walks over to the window, and stares outside. The gravity of his words hang in the air. "There's one more insidious part of this," he says sadly, as he pivots back to face me at the table, with his jaw clenched. "The SED has determined that the terrorists altered your neuroprocessor and replaced your actual memories with planted ones. The SED hasn't been able to recover the lost memories yet, but they're sure that false memories have been planted into your processor."

My jaw drops open in shock. Is he telling me the truth?! My head is spinning. "So, what does that mean? Are my memories false? How could this happen--?"

Abi interrupts me. "It means you've lost your way, Ren. You no longer have clear purpose. You're questioning The Order and your place in it, which means we can no longer trust you —even after all we've done for you. You've become a pawn for Conation, whether you know it or not." I stare at Abi aghast, shocked by how angry she sounds. "I've arranged for you to enter a specialized treatment facility," Abi continues. "This facility has neurologists and neuroprocessor specialists who study the interface of processors with the brain. They'll attempt to do a more complete deep scan to recover your memories—which will hopefully tell us who is responsible for these crimes. They'll also clean and adjust your processor to return you to your old self. Wouldn't you like to get back to your old life, before all this started?"

"What do you mean they'll *clean and adjust my processor*?" Alarm bells are clanging in my head.

"I don't know all the details of the technology they use but I trust you'll be in great hands. Certainly, you can't continue living like this," Abi adds, folding her hands together.

I set down my coffee and jump up from my seat. "I'm not going to some facility! I need to go home. My mother needs me. I want to go home, *now*," I demand.

Abi slowly shakes her head. "That's not possible, Ren," she replies coldly. "This isn't something that can wait. You're going to the facility today. We have a vehicle ready to take you there right now. The specialists are awaiting your arrival."

"It sounds like that's for the best, dear," chimes in Mrs. Coldstone. "I promise I'll come visit you. I can visit her, right?" she asks Abi.

"Of course," Abi replies.

"I thought you were my friend," I plead with Abi.

"I *am* your friend," she retorts. "I'm trying to help you. This is what needs to happen for you to get your old life back— to get your old self back."

I glance over at the President. We make brief eye contact, and then he turns away and gazes out the window. Panic sweeps over me. In a split second, I decide to run. I dash across the room and out the door of Suite A. As soon as I enter the hall, two men block my path—Mr. Jacobs and Mr. Andrews.

"This will be a lot easier if you don't resist, Ms. Sterling," Mr. Jacobs says. "Please, calmly come with us." I glance around wildly, to see how I can get away.

"There's no way to escape, Ms. Sterling. Come with us now," he commands. Suddenly, all in one motion, Mr. Andrews grabs me by the shoulders and pushes my face and body against the wall. He yanks my arms behind my back and zip-ties my wrists.

"Ouch," I yell, shocked by the aggressive way I'm being handled. They grab my upper arms and drag me down the hall while I kick and struggle to get away.

CHAPTER TWENTY-EIGHT

"Let go of me! I can walk!" I yell as the guards pull me out of the Presidential Residence by force. "Mr. Jacobs, please! You're hurting my arm." They don't respond and don't let go. If anything, they tighten their grip. They steer me past Ms. Parsons, who looks away as we pass by, and then drag me through the Compound. None of the staff members we pass say a word, or even look at me—it's as if I don't exist anymore.

Finally, we reach the front gate of the Compound. Two other guards are standing by a black car. One hurriedly opens the back door as Mr. Jacobs and Mr. Andrews push me into the back seat. Then, the two guards slide into the front seats and slam their doors shut. Mr. Jacobs and Mr. Andrews return to the Compound.

"Okay, listen up," the guard in the passenger seat growls as he turns to face me. "Our job is to take you to a treatment facility. Your job is to stay quiet and not cause any problems. If you say one word, we'll stop this vehicle and secure your arms in such a fashion that you'll be *truly* uncomfortable. Do we understand each other?"

I nod. I'm not going to challenge the guards' authority—for now. Maybe there'll be a chance at some point for me to escape. I dearly hope so. I sit silently and try to shift my body weight to get as comfortable as possible, which isn't easy because my wrists are still zip-tied behind my back and the muscles in my neck and shoulders are being pulled tight. The car jerks forward as it speeds out of the Presidential Compound, and I flop against the back seat like a fish.

Staring out the window as we drive, I can't stop thinking about what the President said to me. Could it be true that Conation has altered my neuroprocessor and planted false memories? Is my processor permanently corrupted? Have I been nothing more than a pawn for terrorists? Or have I been a pawn for the President and The Order? I trusted everyone—Zian, President Coldstone, Mrs. Coldstone, Central Advisor Bagai. I even believed Abi was my friend, but now she's sending me off to some facility where scientists are going to mess around with my brain.

We zip through the city streets, and when we pass the turn-off for my school, I'm struck with a pang of intense longing. I wish I were in school right now, seeing my friends, hanging out with Noelle, and playing soccer. I wish I could have my old life back. Everything was so much simpler. I regret complaining and yearning for more in life when I had so much that was good. If I could just go back in time, I never would have left with Zian during Dad's memorial. None of this would have happened if I'd just stayed home.

Staring out the window, it appears as if we're heading in the direction of Gladstone Farms. I wonder where the treatment facility is located. I imagine it being a secret installation surrounded by barbed wired fences and guards carrying weapons. It suddenly occurs to me that I should let my Mom know what's happening. Maybe she can help me get out of this mess.

"**Mom, I'm being taken to a treatment facility. I need your help. Are you there? Please respond,**" I send.

"**From Mom: I know. I received a communication from President Coldstone. Can you believe it? He contacted me personally!**"

"**You don't understand. I don't want to go. They're forcing me. Please find out where they're taking me and bring me home!**"

"**From Mom: You're just overreacting. You'll be fine! The**

President explained it's for the best. He said your neuroprocessor has malfunctioned, so they're going to fix it. It'll stop your nightmares from happening again."

Frustrated, I clench my jaw. Just as I'm about to send a response, my processor flickers, and then freezes. NO! Not now! I drop the back of my head against the seat and tears of frustration drip down my cheeks.

The car slows. Looking out the window, I can see we've pulled behind a slow-moving black van with tinted windows riding the middle of the road. The guard driving our vehicle honks and shouts, "Can you believe this guy? Move over!"

"Go around him," replies the other guard. "I'll run the license plate so we can send him a big, fat traffic ticket for crappy driving. Wait a second... my neuroprocessor isn't working. What in The Order is going on?"

"I don't know. Mine isn't working either," replies the driver.

"Just go around the van," commands the guard in the passenger seat. "We need to get this little package delivered to her special doctor's appointment." They both chuckle flippantly. Suddenly, the black van ahead of us abruptly stops. Our driver slams on the breaks and our tires screech as we skid to a halt and narrowly miss the van's bumper.

"What in The Order...? Now I'm really gonna have to hurt this guy!" exclaims our driver as he reaches for the car door handle. Suddenly, a powerful jolt rocks our car. I fall forward and my forehead bounces off the seat in front of me, hard. Something must have struck us from behind. "Are you kidding me!?" Our driver shouts, "This can't be happening!"

Both guards open their doors and race toward the back of our car. I turn to look out the back window just as middle-aged Financier woman emerges from her luxury vehicle, which has just crashed into the back of ours. She's carrying a bright pink, expensive handbag and wearing very high heels. Her clothes are bright colors of pink and violet. Her hair is multicolored and on top of her head in a giant bun. "Oh, I'm *so sorry*," the Financier woman says sweetly to the guards. "You stopped so suddenly that I didn't have time to avoid you. I'm usually such a safe driver."

"It's not your fault, lady. The guilty party is this jerk," one of the guards says. He turns and points back at the van. Out of the corner of my eye I can see a tall, broad-shouldered man dressed in all black creeping alongside our car. He must have come from the van in front of us. He's wearing a face mask and is carrying some sort of weapon, which he points at the guard on the driver's side of our vehicle. Without a sound, the driver suddenly falls in a heap to the pavement, clearly dead or unconscious.

I gasp for air and duck. The other guard reaches for his weapon, but before he can fire, the Financier woman pulls a strange-looking handgun from her purse and aims it at the back of his head. He immediately drops to the ground. A scream involuntarily leaves my mouth as I instinctively dive across the black leather seat, hoping I'm not next.

Laying here trembling, I expect bullets to rip through the vehicle, and me, at any moment. After several seconds, the door by my head swings open, and when I look up I see the man from the van staring down at me. "Ren, come with me," he urges. He has an unusual accent. "I'm not going to hurt you. I'm here to rescue you."

I'm paralyzed with shock and can't seem to move a muscle. Sighing, the masked man reaches into the back seat, grabs me under my arms, and yanks me out onto the pavement. With my wrists zip-tied behind my back, I fall flat on my face, hitting the ground hard.

"Hurry! We have to go now," the man orders urgently, as he brushes me off and pulls me to my feet. My head is throbbing and blood drips down my face from a gash on my forehead. When I glance around, I see that the Financier woman is already in her car. She puts it in reverse, dislodging it from the government car, and then speeds away.

"Let's go," the tall man says as he lifts me off the ground

and hoists me over his shoulder. He carries me to the van and tosses me into the back. As soon as I land on the hard floor of the van, several people wearing masks grasp my arms and legs, and then hold me face down on the floor. One of them rests something cold on the back of my neck.

After a few seconds, the man next to me says, "There, her locator function is disabled. Let's get out of here." They then force a cloth bag over my head.

"Who are you? Why are you doing this to me?" I ask, panicked, through the bag.

"We're saving you," a woman answers. Her accent is like the tall man's. "We're helping you become free."

"I don't understand!" I exclaim.

"Shhh. You need to trust us, Ren," she replies, soothingly.

"Why in the world should I trust you when you're kidnapping me?!" The bag is hot, and I feel short of breath.

The woman answers me calmly, "Everything will be explained once we're safe. For now, be as quiet as you can be, especially if we're stopped."

CHAPTER TWENTY-NINE

We travel in silence for a long time. Are these people part of Conation, I wonder? What do they want from me? What did the woman mean when she said they're helping me "become free"? I feel like I'm being kidnapped rather than saved. The cut on my forehead stings, and my head is throbbing. Lying face down on the hard floor with my arms in zip-ties behind my back makes me feel claustrophobic. My heart starts racing and my breathing becomes shallow. I feel as if I'm about to pass out.

"I can't breathe, please take off the bag! I can't breathe!" I say between gasps. Finally, someone reaches down, pulls the cloth bag off my head, and I inhale deeply.

"Okay, I'm going to let you sit up, but you must stay quiet," the woman commands, "or we'll put the bag back over your head. Do you understand?"

I nod and feel myself start to calm down. The people in the back of the van lift me into a sitting position, and then lean me against the wall. There are three of them, two men and a woman, all dressed in black with black masks concealing their faces. A fourth person, a stocky man with receding hair, is driving the van.

"That's quite a cut on your head," the woman says. She pulls out a first-aid kit. "May I clean and dress your wound?" I nod. With more tenderness than I expect, she gently cleans the blood off my face and applies antiseptic to my wound, which stings for a few moments. Then she places a bandage on the cut.

"That'll do for now. When we reach our destination, we'll tend to your wound more closely," she adds.

"Thank you. Where are we going?" I ask.

The two men glance at the woman, who appears to be the leader. She says, "You'll know soon enough. Right now, just be patient."

Gazing out the back window, I can see we've been traveling along a winding road. Just as we round a sharp bed, the tall man exclaims, "There's the check point!" The other man nods. "Activating the destabilizer now."

"Okay, here we go," says the woman as she closes a thick, black curtain between the front cab and the back of the van. "You know what to do. Follow the plan, stun weapons only." She pulls two odd-looking handguns out of a large duffle bag. They look like a blend between a weapon and a neuroprocessor scanner. She hands one to the tall man and keeps one for herself.

The van slows to a stop at the guardhouse, which has two guards inside. One of the guards stands and sticks his head out the guardhouse window. "What are you doing out here? This is a restricted area," the guard says gruffly, frowning.

Our van driver replies, "I have a delivery for the electronics factory."

"I'm not aware of any deliveries scheduled for that factory today," counters the guard suspiciously.

Our driver casually shrugs. "It was a late addition to my route this morning."

A confused look crosses the guard's face. "For some reason my neuroprocessor won't let me pull up the delivery schedule." The guard turns and asks the second guard something I can't hear. The second guard shakes his head, confused that his processor isn't working either. "Since I can't seem to verify the delivery, I'll need to scan your processor for identification," the first guard announces. He steps out of the guardhouse, carrying a scanner, and starts slowly walking over to the driver's window.

The woman man in the back of the van begins whispering

directions to the others. To the tall man, she says, "We move simultaneously. You take the guard by the vehicle and I'll take the one in the guardhouse." She turns to the man next to me and commands, "You stay with Ren. Use this weapon only if absolutely necessary." She hands one of the odd guns to the man, who turns to me and whispers, "Ren, you need to keep your head down and be very quiet." I nod and crouch down but continue to peek out the side window as the guard strolls up to the driver's side of the vehicle. The tall masked man quietly opens the back of the van, and then he and the woman silently climb out—without being seen by the guards.

It happens so fast. The tall man quickly sidles up to the guard by the driver and raises his weapon. The guard instantly drops his scanner and collapses to the ground. At the same time, the woman stealthily moves to the door of the guardhouse. Just as the guard begins to rise from his seat, the woman uses her weapon, and the guard falls limply back into his chair.

"What just happened?" I ask incredulously.

The man next to me in the van replies excitedly, "They're using the latest stun technology! The weapons send out a brainwave frequency that disrupts and disables neuroprocessors, and then temporarily produces unconsciousness. It's the same technology as the destabilizer, but at a higher level."

Curious, I ask, "What's a destabilizer?"

"A destabilizer interrupts and freezes neuroprocessors, crippling all communications, functions, and applications," he proudly replies.

The tall man pockets his stun weapon before picking up the guard's scanner in one hand and scooping up the fallen guard in the other. He carries the guard back to the guardhouse and deposits him in the other chair. The man and the woman turn a dial on the top of their stun devices and point them again at the unconscious guards—holding their aim for about a minute.

"Shouldn't we get out of here?" I ask, feeling panicky.

The man guarding me nods and replies, "Just a few moments longer. They're neutralizing the guards' recent memories. They'll wake up with a bad headache, but no memory of any of this. They'll feel stupid for falling asleep on the job, but otherwise be unhurt, and completely unaware. This new memory technology is so cool, isn't it?!"

The man and woman climb into the back of our van and our driver speeds forward. After a few miles, we turn off onto another winding road, and then begin to drive toward the mountain. I think we're heading east, but because my neuroprocessor is still jammed, I have no way of knowing for sure or clearly identifying my location. After about ninety minutes of driving, we exit onto an unmarked, dirt road.

By now, my shoulders, arms, and wrists are burning, and the pain is agonizing. "Please, take these things off my wrists?" I ask. "They're hurting me."

The woman stares at me for a moment, before taking out a small bag. "If I take off the zip-ties, I can trust you won't run, right?" she asks.

"Of course!" I exclaim.

"Out here, it's not like you would get far without us, anyway." She shrugs and then motions for the two men to turn me around so she can cut off the cuffs. As soon as my wrists are free, I sigh with relief. It feels so good to be able to stretch my arms and rub my bruised wrists. After a moment, I look the woman in the eyes and say, "If I knew who you are and where we're going, perhaps I wouldn't want to run away."

The woman gazes at me for a moment, and then nods in agreement. "At this point, I think it's safe for us to show our faces," she announces. All three people in the back of the van remove their masks. Along with being very muscular, the woman and the tall man both have amber-brown skin, dark brown hair, dark brown eyes, and angular facial features—characteristics of the Indigenous people I learned about in social studies class. They live off the land in mountainous, remote regions. We're taught to feel sorry for them and their children because they live separately from The Order and all its advantages, including technology and medical care.

The woman smiles. "My name is Sora." Her voice is slightly husky, and her dark eyes seem to pierce right through me. "This is my brother, Bahlam." With a proud look on her face she adds, "My brother and I come from a long line of hunters and protectors."

"Nice to meet you, Ren. We've been waiting for you." Bahlam's voice is deep and resonant.

I stare at them, awestruck. I'm especially captivated by Sora. I think she's the most beautiful, powerful woman I've ever seen. I can't take my eyes off her. I immediately feel safe in her presence.

Seeing my stare, Sora asks, "Have you never met a real, live *Natural* before?"

"A what?" I ask.

"I forget that the government doesn't tell you the truth about us. You have so much to learn. My brother and I were born free, like our parents, and their parents before them." She smiles and adds, "Unlike Jason here." She teasingly points to the other man in the back of the van, who has reddish hair, a light skin complexion, and a slight build. "And Frank." She slides open the curtain and points to the balding driver, who waves his hand.

Jason clears his throat. "Uh hum, I'm free now," he announces, while chewing rapidly on a piece of gum. "I became *emancipated* about 6 months ago… although I still need to chew lots of yanavis."

I shake my head, not understanding what they're saying. "Natural? Free? Emancipated? yana-what?"

All four laugh. "Emancipates are what we call the non-Naturals who've gone through defusion in an attempt to become free," Sora replies. "Defusion is a relatively new technology, but the wisdom is ancient and sacred for our people. Becoming free requires much more than getting defused."

"I'm sorry, but I'm even more confused than before you began to explain," I reply, wrinkling my forehead.

Sora smiles broadly, but before she can continue speaking, the van suddenly jolts to the left and then bounces up and down, slowing considerably as Frank navigates large potholes in the dirt road. "The recent rains have washed out parts of this road," Bahlam explains. "It keeps the tourists out," he adds with a chuckle and shrug. Looking out the window, I notice the foliage has changed dramatically. We're in a dense forest now—thick layers of green surround us as the road narrows. Finally, we turn into a clearing.

"We're here," Sora announces.

I feel tingly with anticipation—excited and nervous, all at once. "Where are we?" I ask.

Sora smiles. "Caracol, our home."

CHAPTER THIRTY

We roll to a stop next to another parked van. I'm amazed to see what looks like sixty huts or so tucked into the woods around the clearing where the vans are parked. Smoke from a campfire in the center of the clearing drifts up into the sky. There are quite a few people milling about, working, and talking with one another. Most seem to be Indigenous.

"You're free to roam about as you wish, Ren," Sora says. "Just don't wander off into the forest alone."

"Yeah, we wouldn't want you to get lost or eaten," Bahlam teases.

As Bahlam opens the back door of our van to let us out, Sora touches my arm. "There's someone here who wants to see you, and I think you'll want to see him, too," she whispers, with a wink.

"Who?!" I ask, curiously.

"You'll see," Sora replies with a sly smile.

We climb out of the van while Jason, Frank, and Bahlam carry the weapons and other devices to a building close by. The air is cool, but the sun is just beginning to peek through the clouds. Voices of children playing ring in the air. Suddenly, about a dozen Indigenous children run up to greet Sora and me excitedly. They're smiling and laughing, and dressed in loose, handmade clothes. Sora picks up one of the little ones and carries him in her muscular arms. Two children place their hands in mine, and then lead me toward the center of the village. Chickens dart about our feet as we walk.

"Do you live here, too?" I ask Sora.

Proudly, she replies, "Yes, my whole life. I was born in

that hut right over there. My parents still live there, along with one of my aunts. My mother is one of the village Elders. You'll meet her very soon, as well as my whole family. My seventeen-year-old daughter, Maya, can't wait to meet you."

She motions to the huts to our left. "These huts, and the ones over there," she gestures to a cluster of huts to the right, "are where most of our people live. This is the center of the village, where we cook our meals and gather together as a community."

A group of about twenty women are sitting under a very large thatched-roof, wooden pavilion at long, wooden tables. Just outside the pavilion is the biggest cast iron pot I've ever seen. It's suspended above burning logs and has food simmering in it, which smells delicious.

"Yum. Caracol stew!" exclaims Sora, grinning. "There's a little bit of everything in it." One woman stirs the stew, while other women knead dough and stitch handmade clothing. They wave and smile at us as we approach.

Intrigued, I ask, "How many people live here?"

"About 250 Naturals and fifteen Emancipates. We're all very excited for your arrival." Sora turns to me. "Some say you are The One."

"The One? The One to do what, Sora?" I ask, bewildered.

"The One to lead the non-Naturals out of the darkness and into responsible freedom," Sora replies with a smile.

Overwhelmed, I shake my head. "I don't see how I can lead anyone. I'm too young... it's all so confusing." Sora just smiles knowingly, in reply. "What do you mean by 'responsible freedom'?" I ask, quickly changing the subject. I'm not ready to talk about leading anyone.

"You and all non-Naturals have been tricked into believing you're free, but you're blindly serving The Order—that's not true freedom," Sora replies, shaking her long, dark hair.

Something deep inside me knows what she's just said is true, but another part of me can't wrap my head around it. I stop in my tracks. The two children holding my hands gaze up at me expectantly.

Gently, I say, "Sora, I'm embarrassed to say this because I don't want to offend you, but we're taught that The Order has allowed our nation to emerge from the darkness and chaos. We don't learn much about Indigenous people, other than that many of them were killed during the Civil War II, and that the remaining tribes rallied together to reject technology. I was also taught that the Indigenous ultimately aren't free because of their superstitious beliefs and traditions."

Sora smiles once again. "We prefer the term, Naturals. It is true that many of our people who lived near cities perished in the great conflict between non-Naturals, and since that time we have gathered in our ancestral locations and have rejected most technology, especially neuroprocessors." She pauses to gaze at me compassionately. "I know it's hard to understand, Ren, but true freedom comes with awareness and connection to your Natural Self, your Real Self. This will all make much more sense after you stay here a while and experience the Natural Energy that pulses so abundantly here."

Natural Self? Real Self? Natural Energy? "It's as if some part of me, deep inside, understands what you're saying, Sora. But then I lose it and become confused again."

"You'll soon learn to get out of your mind and become present with your experience—to trust your intuition," Sora replies, gently placing her hand on my shoulder. Just then, five Natural adults stroll up and greet us—three women and two men. Sora sets the little boy down and speaks softly to the children, "Run along and play, I'll come find you later." She turns to me. "Ren, these are our village Elders."

An elderly woman steps forward and speaks with the same accent as Sora and Bahlam. "Welcome to Caracol, Ren. My name is Akna. I'm the village Leader. On behalf of the Elders, I wish to tell you how very pleased we are that you are here."

One by one each of the Elders cups my face in their hands and gently touch their foreheads to mine for a few seconds. The last of the Elders to greet me says, "My name is Chimalis. I'm

Sora's mother. We've been waiting to meet you for a long time." Her words echo in my head. How could she be waiting to meet me? What does that mean? I smile graciously.

"Please sit and have some water," Akna says. "You must be thirsty after your journey. The stew and bread will be ready soon." Another elder woman hands me a ceramic mug.

"Thank you so much," I say, and suddenly feeling my thirst, I guzzle the water. It's cold, crisp, and makes my body feel immediately stronger. Suddenly, I hear my name.

"Ren!" I spin around to see Zian walking briskly toward me, waving. A Natural teenage boy with long dark hair and warm eyes is walking beside him. Zian, *here*?! Am I dreaming? We run to each other and I throw myself into his arms. He lifts me off the ground, hugging me tight. I'm so happy the SED didn't capture him; I start crying with relief.

"Zian, what are you doing here?!" I exclaim. Zian squeezes me tight one last time and then sets me back down. I quickly wipe my eyes.

"I live here now," he replies with a grin. Flushing a bit, he steps back and gestures to the boy standing next to him. "Ren, this is my friend, Coyopa." Coyopa smiles and cups my head in his hands, then touches his forehead against mine. I blush, although I try to hide my reaction. I can't help it. We're about the same age and he's very attractive.

Sora comes to my rescue, saying "Ren, you and Zian should go for a walk. He will show you around and help you further understand what's happening here."

"Thank you, Sora," Zian nods. Sora smiles, and gives me a wink, before she and Coyopa head back to the village center.

Zian takes my hand and leads me toward the recesses of the village. He points out the hut where he's staying with Coyopa's family, a few other buildings, and several trails splintering off into destinations in the forest. I can barely hear him. I'm still in shock at seeing him, and all I want to do is hug him close and stare into his beautiful eyes.

Eventually, we stop to rest at a quiet spot close to the

forest. We sit on a bench-like log. "I'm so happy you're here and safe, Ren. I was so worried about you. If we hadn't rescued you, you would be undergoing brain reconditioning at a government treatment facility, and at the very least, they would have deleted many of your memories. If the government decided that they were unable to rehabilitate you, you would have been killed. It's what they do to subversives."

"KILLED?" I pull back, horrified. "I thought they would adjust my neuroprocessor, or give me a new one or something, not kill me!" I exclaim as my entire body shudders involuntarily at the thought.

"There's so much I need to tell you, Ren." Zian takes my hand in his.

"There's so much I need to understand," I reply, leaning into his touch. "Start by telling me where we are and why you're here."

Zian caresses my hand as he speaks. "We're in Caracol. The government knows about this place but ignores it. They see no threat. The only interactions Naturals have with those in The Order occur when they bring their small batches of organic nuts and handmade goods to sell in specialty stores."

"Oh," I reply. "I had no idea!"

Zian nods. "Very few people do, which is for the best. The last thing they need is for the government to take an interest in them. They live their lives and organize their villages based on traditional, ancestral values and wisdom. Some technology is embraced—but not neuroprocessors. When Naturals say that they've been born free, it means they've never had a processor implanted. Their brains have developed naturally rather than being fused with a processor."

Furrowing my brow, I ask, puzzled, "What do you mean, 'fused with a processor', Zian?"

Zian takes a deep breath before replying. "Because the processor chip is implanted in us as infants, our brains and the processors comingle, as our brains grow, interacting in some sort of neurochemical dance. Our identities and consciousness are formed in concert with the processor. Our brains are literally fused with our processors."

Stunned, I recoil, shaking my head. "That's... terrible!"

Zian gently squeezes my hand, letting the full magnitude of what he just said sink in, and then continues. "What's worse is the government manipulates us through our neuroprocessors—influencing us to be obedient, compliant, and accepting of The Order. Like I told you at the parade, we are programmed to obey the President and respond positively to his face and eyes. They even program us to believe we're free—to believe we're freely choosing our own lives, but it's a big lie. Ultimately, we have no choice at all, only an illusion of choice."

I shake my head slowly, attempting to digest what Zian is saying. "We have no choice?" I ask, stunned.

Zian shakes his head. "I'm sure you've noticed your anxiety come and go," he continues. "Neuroprocessors are designed to sense your anxiety and to calm you down. The government knows anxiety can be a sign of your intuition warning you that something isn't right—that you're becoming conscious of their big lie. As soon as your mind starts to be aware that you have choices, you begin to feel anxiety. Your processor then stimulates neurochemicals to soothe you and remind you of the clear purpose that has been proscribed for you."

He reaches up to caress my cheek. "Ren, because your intuition is very strong you have experienced more anxiety than most. Several times you've told me that you know there's more to life. You were sensing the contrived and limited nature of life in The Order. You sensed the big lie. In the past, when your processor detected your anxiety increasing, it flooded your brain with feel good neurochemicals. You'd become distracted from your intuition, and once again complacent. Then your father gave you the disrupter, and everything began to change. The numbness eventually wore off."

My eyes widen, as I inhale sharply. That's exactly what has happened to me the past few months. Zian caresses my hand as he continues. "I can see it in your eyes, Ren. I can tell that you know what I'm talking about—what I'm saying matches your experience."

I nod. "Yes. You're right, Zian, it does," I reply, as my eyes fill up with tears. "I tried to talk to Noelle about it, but it was too much for her." My heart aches when I mention Noelle's name. I look up into Zian's eyes, which are tearing up as well. "You and my dad are the only people in my life who ever encouraged my intuition. But I don't understand. Why can't we just remove the neuroprocessor?"

"Like I said, it's complicated because the neuroprocessor has fused with your brain. If you remove the chip, you lose the obvious processor functions and applications, but the parts of your brain that define your identity and regulate anxiety continue to remain receptive to governmental programming. So, the government would continue to have you under their control. They're also alerted when processors are removed. The SED will swoop in and send you off to a treatment facility. That's what happened to my father." Anger flashes across Zian's face. He looks away.

"I'm so sorry, Zian," I say, squeezing his hand gently. "I thought he died in a boating accident."

"That was a false story created by the SED—a total lie! A few years ago, I learned the truth. My father was one of the founding members of Conation, which was started by a small group of Intelligencia scientists who were researching neuroprocessor technology. He was the first to have his chip removed in an attempt to regain freedom, but then the SED arrested him. He died in one of their treatment facilities. The SED made up the story of a boating accident. It makes me so angry. They murdered my father, just like they murdered yours."

Zian and I reach for each other and hug, holding each other tight for a long time. We've both lost so much. Eventually, we hear a chime in the distance. "Dinner time!" Zian exclaims. He stands and gently pulls me to my feet. "Let's go get some stew, Ren. I'm starving and you must be too. We can talk more after dinner, or tomorrow. Lots of people want to meet you at dinner."

CHAPTER THIRTY-ONE

By the time Zian and I reach the center of the village, the pavilion is packed full of people. A few Emancipates, but mostly Naturals, are seated at long wooden tables, and many are speaking a language I've never heard before. Coyopa greets us. A teenage Natural girl is at his side.

"Ren, this is Maya," says Coyopa. "Sora's daughter."

Maya looks just like a younger version of Sora. We touch foreheads, and then she hugs me. I feel instantly at ease with her. "Welcome to Caracol, Ren," Maya says, with a warm smile. "I'm so glad you're here. Come, sit with me and my family."

"Thank you so much, Maya!" I reply. Zian and I follow Maya and Coyopa to a table near the back of the pavilion. One after another, about fifteen of Maya's family members welcome me warmly.

Maya hands me a wooden bowl. "Let's get some food," she says. I nod, and follow her to the front of the pavilion, where we stand in line before receiving a serving of stew and bread. Our return to the table is slowed because so many people offer me welcome. It's lovely, but also overwhelming. I'm not used to so much kindness and attention.

We sit back down, and each take a carved, wooden spoon from the center of the table. I immediately feel ravenous and want to dive right in but notice that no one at the table has begun to eat yet. Just then, Akna stands up at the font of the pavilion. She raises her arms in the air and in a booming voice says,

"Thank you, Great Spirit, for providing the sun, earth, plants, and water—which nourish us along with all the animals in the Natural World. Your Energy is the source of everything around us. May we continue to live in rhythm with your breath. Thank you also for bringing a new visitor to Caracol. We welcome her to our village." She sits, and then everyone begins to eat. Loud and happy conversations break out across all the tables.

After shoveling in a few spoonfuls of stew, I lean toward Zian and quietly ask, "What did Akna mean by, 'Great Spirit'?"

Zian replies in a hushed voice, "Naturals are very spiritual. They see and feel powerful energy in this forest—which they refer to as the Natural World. If you stay here, you'll learn a lot more about it. Their beliefs and practices are very different than what we were taught."

"Honestly, I don't know what spiritual even means," I say. "In school, we were taught religion is based on superstitions rather than science."

Zian nods. "I don't know if I would call what the Naturals believe 'religion', it's more of a way of life. I'm just starting to learn about it in more depth. I've been mostly involved in the Conation cell in Capitol City, but I'm curious to learn more, now that I'm living here."

I nod my head, digesting what Zian just said, and then turn to Maya with a smile. "I love the stew, Maya. What's in it?"

Before Maya can answer, Zian interjects, "I've learned it's often better to not know." Everyone at the table laughs.

Coyopa replies, still chuckling, "Yes. We should let you stay here for a while before scaring you with all the ingredients."

From what I can discern, the stew consists of beans, potatoes, vegetables, peanuts, and some sort of meat in a spicy sauce. I guess I don't really care what's in it—all I care is that it's warm, delicious, and filling. I didn't' realize how hungry I was until I began to eat.

The conversation is light and easy amongst Zian and my new friends. I'm amazed by how familiar and comfortable it is to be with Maya and Coyopa. It feels like we could be seated at the senior Intelligencia table in the Pittock High School lunchroom. When I look up, though, I'm reminded we're deep in the forest.

My whole body feels abuzz with the excitement and newness of it all. I can't believe what's happened today. Just few hours ago I was at the Presidential Compound with my hands zip-tied behind me, being sent away to a treatment facility. I shudder at the thought of what could have happened to me if I hadn't been rescued.

The sun has slipped below the horizon and darkness is quickly descending. Lights from generators and kerosene lamps pop on sporadically throughout the village. Now that my belly is full, I'm suddenly overcome with exhaustion. Sensing my weariness, Maya invites me to return to her family hut to get ready for sleep. Coyopa and Zian remain behind to help with clean-up duties.

Maya sleeps in a three-room hut with Sora and two of her uncles. The hut has a thatched roof, wood frame, and wood floor. It is lit with kerosene lamps, which sit atop hand-crafted pieces of furniture made of pine. As we enter, Maya says softly, "My father died seven years ago—from a sudden illness."

"I'm so sorry, Maya," I reply.

"Sometimes I have a hard time remembering what he looked like," she confesses. I nod as an image of my dad's face pops into my mind. I wonder if I'll eventually forget what he looked like. Grief suddenly grips my heart. I'm determined to never forget anything about him.

Maya directs me to where I'll sleep—which is in one of the rooms with her and Sora. She removes some hand-sewn cushions from a large wooden storage box and arranges them on the floor. "I hope you will find these comfortable to sleep on—they're filled with dried moss." She then hands me a thick, hand-made wool blanket. "This will keep you warm," she says.

"Thank you," I reply, yawning.

As I lie down, I wonder if I'll be able to fall asleep—or if the excitement of the day and the unfamiliar sights and sounds will keep me up. There was no need to worry. I immediately fall into a deep sleep as soon as my body hits the soft cushions.

Next thing I know, I'm standing on the roof of my house in my Intelligencia neighborhood. I look at the familiar scene of large, expensive houses, which are built into the surrounding hills. I feel dizzy as I gaze at the pavement below and begin swaying precariously with the wind. Suddenly, a strong gust blows me off the roof. I scream as I fall in slow motion, waving my arms wildly. Before I hit the ground, though, I realize I'm dreaming. Telling myself I can't get hurt in a dream, I decide to fly. My body instantly feels light and I swoop up, flying above the trees and houses.

Suddenly, I'm no longer in my neighborhood. I'm soaring above the canopy in the forest. The sun is shining and there's a cool, comfortable breeze—which keeps me aloft. The world is quiet as I effortlessly swoop down to the tops of the trees and then back up again. I love this feeling of freedom! It's what I've been longing for.

Eventually, I can see the huts and buildings of Caracol in a clearing. In the distance, cascading down a cliff, is a waterfall. I sigh with contentment—filled with feelings of both peace and power. At this moment, I feel as if I could do anything.

I awaken to the loud chirping of birds in the trees welcoming the sunrise. Maya and Sora are still asleep, so I snuggle under my blanket, feeling wonder at where I am. I can't believe Zian is here, too.

◆ ◆ ◆

When Sora and Maya awaken, they show me where to wash up. Maya offers me some of her clothes, which I gladly accept. After a scrumptious breakfast of potatoes, beans, and eggs in the pavilion, Zian and I take a walk together while Maya and Coyopa help their families with some chores. I feel rested and ready to learn more about Caracol as well as how Zian happened to arrive here.

Zian and I stroll to the log-bench we shared yesterday, hand-in-hand. Once seated, Zian reaches into his pocket. "Before I tell you my story, Ren, I have something to give you." I glance up into Zian's bright blue eyes, questioningly. He smiles. "Hold out your hands." I reach out my hands, and into them, Zian drops a gold necklace with a shell pendant.

"My necklace!" I exclaim. "How... when...?" I sputter, shaking my head in wonder.

"Conation had to protect your father's technology, which was hidden in the shell. Once they removed the disruptor, I convinced them to let me return the chain and pendant to you."

Holding the golden spiral in my hands, I feel any residual armor I'd built up around my heart toward Zian these past few weeks melt away. Tears well up in my eyes, but they're from joy. Now, I'll have a piece of my dad with me always, even here in Caracol.

Zian lifts the necklace to my neck and fastens it. I clutch the pendant. "Thank you," I say. "Thank you." Zian wraps his arm around me, and I bury my face in his chest, letting the tears fall. After a few moments, Zian begins speaking softly.

"When I discovered the truth about my father's death, I had so many conflicting emotions. At first, I couldn't believe it. I wanted to trust the government and trust The Order. How could the government even perpetrate such a huge lie? Then, as I learned about the manipulation through our neuroprocessors, it made more sense—and I became angry. That's when I officially joined Conation and found out about your father's research."

"Was my dad part of Conation, too?" I ask, leaning into Zian.

"Yes. The government killed him because they found out he was researching how to interrupt government programming and manipulation. Your father was primarily responsible for developing the neuroprocessor destabilizer, which has led to many advances in the defusion process."

"Wow... I had no idea!"

Zian nods. "Once in Conation, I learned as much as I could about your father's research, and then decided to get defused. It was much harder than I expected—not the actual procedure—but the anxiety afterward. Eventually I returned to school while I was part of the Conation cell in Capital City. Your dad... became a role model for me, sort of like a father figure. Just before your dad's death, it was decided I would reach out to you—to see if you were ready to learn the truth. Once the SED deep scanned your memories, though, it was no longer safe for me to be at school or anywhere in the city, so I came here."

"You and my dad were close?!" I ask, again feeling shocked.

"Yes," Zian replies, and gives my hand a gentle squeeze. "I even visited Caracol a few times with your father when he began to study Natural brains compared to brains with neuroprocessors. He found some remarkable differences. Eventually, Conation scientists came to believe that defusion and emancipation would be helped by being with Naturals and learning about their ancestral wisdom. Even though the government has all but outlawed spirituality, it continues to thrive here and in other small pockets where Naturals live. As more and more Conation members have gotten defused, they've moved here and to other Natural villages to learn their spiritual beliefs and practices."

"Wow." I shake my head, astonished, and a little sad. "I... I can't believe you and Dad kept all this from me."

"We *had* to." Zian replies, gently squeezing my hand again. "After your experiences with the SED, you must understand why we had to keep it secret."

I nod my head, and then pull my hand away. "I know. It's just weird for me that you knew so much more about his life than I did." I'm feeling a little betrayed by how close Dad was to Zian. Why couldn't he have trusted me more?

"The secrecy was for your protection, Ren, only for your protection. Your father was afraid the government would go after you, and we wanted the timing to be right for you to decide about defusion."

"What exactly *is* defusion?" I ask.

"Honestly, I don't understand all the technical details. You can discuss the specifics with Harper, one of the scientists here. What I can tell you is how it affected me. I went through defusion almost two years ago, when I was out of school for three months—under the guise of having mono. Defusion neutralizes the neuroprocessor and the fused parts of the brain without removing the processor or affecting the applications. Your brain is *de-fused* from the processor, but you keep your processor, so the government doesn't know it's been removed. That way, you can operate in The Order without being detected as a subversive, although that just became a whole lot harder with the SED's new ability to deep scan memories. But you know all about that, don't you?"

"Yes, I do," I reply, shuddering.

"The bad news is that defusion neutralizes the parts of your brain which manage anxiety. No more feel-good neurochemicals are produced. Emancipates must learn how to control the anxiety and identity crisis which occur after being defused. It can be overwhelming—at least at first. Thankfully, yanavis helps quite a bit."

"What's yan-a-vis?" I ask curiously. Zian laughs.

"*Yanavis* is a plant which naturally occurs in the forest—it's easily found here. The Naturals have used it for centuries in some of their ceremonies. They chew on the leaves and drink it as tea. If you take too much, it produces a dream-like state. But in moderate amounts, it eases the effects of government manipulation by helping you manage anxiety. It also helps you connect to your intuition and your Natural Self—which is why it's used in certain rituals. Conation scientists have made a form of chewing gum out of it. That's why I'm always chewing gum. I'm chewing yanavis—just like every other Emancipate. It helps calm the nerves as we learn to become free."

Chewing gum yanavis? I've never heard of that. "Okay. I'm going to ask a stupid question," I confess. "If it's so hard to deal with what happens after defusion, then why do it?"

"Because it's the first step to becoming free," Zian replies without hesitation. "We've all been taught that The Order is responsible for providing our clear purpose and the dramatic shifts in how our society functions. Although the four segments benefit some people, especially those in power, in reality, it's the government's manipulation of our neuroprocessors which actually keeps us in-line and obedient—while giving an illusionary sense of freedom. Without awareness and choice, we are not free."

"Yes," I nod, "I get it."

"After being defused, we must figure out our own purpose, without governmental manipulation."

"Okay. But are you sure we're better off with our freedom?" I ask. "I don't want to defend the government, but maybe most people can't handle their freedom. Look what happened to the former United States when individuals had too much free will. As you know, there was a lot of crime and self-centered behaviors and problems. We ended up with societal breakdown, civil war, and the detonation of nuclear bombs. Maybe people need the structure of The Order and governmental intervention. Maybe what you call neuroprocessor manipulation is really necessary assistance."

"Wow! Ren, you're such an Intelligencia! I hear you, but do you think that before the Civil War II—when there was so much chaos and disorder—people were truly free? Most people had no idea about how to handle freedom, so they gave it away all the time."

"Yes, I get what you are saying. But I can't see how everyone will suddenly be able to handle their freedom now," I retort.

"I don't know if it can happen. But I know I had to find out for myself. Ultimately, it comes down to individual choice. People need to know they have a choice. We would be no better than the government if we forced everyone to go through defusion."

"Yes. I agree with that," I reply, nodding my head.

"All I know is that *I* want to learn how to live free," he says. "It may not be for everyone. It may even not be for you, Ren. It's your choice. You could go through defusion and learn to live with your eyes wide open and to handle your freedom. Or not, and..." Suddenly Zian's voice trails off and his face changes as he gazes over my shoulder at something in the distance. I turn my head to see what he's looking at.

CHAPTER THIRTY-TWO

A short, wrinkled, bronze-skinned woman with long grey braids enters the clearing where Zian and I are seated. I recognize her immediately—she's the old woman by the hut I saw in my dream. "It's you!" I say, astonished.

Zian stands respectfully. "Ren, this is Itzamna. She lives deep in the forest. She's the spiritual teacher for Caracol. Itzamna, this is Ren."

Saying nothing, Itzamna just smiles, leans forward to cup my cheeks in her weathered hands, and then rests her forehead against mine. Closing my eyes, I hear wind whistling softly and voices chanting, singing. Itzamna chuckles and pats my cheek. "Welcome young One. I've waited a long time to meet you in person." She tightens the woolen wrap around her shoulders and slightly bows her head.

Zian clears his throat and smiles. "Uh... I should let you two get better acquainted. Ren, Itzamna was close with your father. She'll be able to give you some important details about him and his work. Find me later today, at dinner." He gives me a quick hug, gently kisses me on the forehead, and then hurries off toward the center of the village.

"You knew my dad?" I ask.

She nods and smiles. "Come, Ren. Let's walk." She takes my hand in her small, warm, calloused hand. As we stroll slowly through the forest, I suddenly feel like I've known Itzamna my whole life. "Your father came to me for guidance. But long before I met him, the Ancestors spoke, and I saw you. I was there at your birth."

"Saw me... in a dream?"

She shrugs. "I was *awake*... not sleeping." After a brief pause, she continues, "I know who you are, Ren. I know what you see. I know you have been having dreams and visions, even without your father's device. Some of your dreams have been lucid—where you know you are dreaming while it is occurring. This is a sign that your inner, natural wisdom is freeing itself and beginning to emerge into your consciousness."

Itzamna peers deeply into my eyes. "You are like me, Ren—you have the gift of *visioning*. Had you been born free, your visions would never be clouded." There is sadness in her voice.

"Is what I've seen... dreamt about... real?" I ask.

Itzamna considers this thoughtfully for a moment. "Mostly, yes, but you remain clouded."

"Zian was explaining defusion to me. If I become defused, will I see clearly?"

She again pauses. "If you can control your fear after, yes," she eventually replies. "But there is much more to be learned, to truly become free and use your gifts."

"Will you help me?" I ask.

Itzamna stops in her tracks and looks up at me. "Yes," she says simply.

"Then, I want to see clearly and learn to be free. I want to get defused." I declare.

As Itzamna smiles, the wrinkles deepen in her wizened cheeks. "Follow me," she replies.

◆ ◆ ◆

As we pass through Caracol, I see a gathering of children clustered around Sora in an open field. Her muscular shoulders and arms are bulging out of her shirt. It looks like she's teaching something that's a cross between dancing and fighting. As the children run toward her and try to strike, she uses their momentum to flip them over or redirect them.

Itzamna notices my interest in Sora and nods. "The path of peace is not always peaceful. We teach our children how to defend themselves."

We reach a thatched, large, round building—the biggest building in Caracol. The sounds of a generator rumbles in the background. As we enter, I can see that the room is full of computers and lab equipment and is illuminated by electrical lamps strung along the ceiling. A thirty-something year old woman with bushy blond hair and glasses glances up from her work, and then hustles over to us. "Itzamna! You're in Caracol! What a pleasure to see you!" she exclaims.

Itzamna nods. "Harper, this is Ren. Harper is a scientist. She used to work with your father. Now she is the Director of the Conation Lab at Caracol."

She reaches out and we shake hands. "Welcome," Harper says. "I'm continuing your father's research on interrupting neuroprocessors. His work was so innovative. We miss him terribly."

Tears sting my eyes, and I reply softly, "Me too, Harper."

"So, what brings the two of you here today?" Harper asks, quickly changing the subject.

"Freedom," Itzamna states. "Ren is ready to be defused and to continue the process of reclaiming her Natural Self."

"Oh, wow! That's fantastic!" Harper nods respectfully at Itzamna, before looking intently back at me. "Do you have any questions about the procedure, Ren? I want to give you as much information as I can so you can make an informed choice."

"Uh, I'm not sure. Not really…?" I want to ask Harper if I'll be a wreck after, but I don't want to seem cowardly in front of Itzamna.

"Well, let me tell you a few things about it. Most people are quite distressed after the procedure, which I assume you have heard?" I nod, nervously. "There is no going back, once you get defused. So, you must be sure this is really what you want.

I know your father would want me to tell you that I could put you back into your old life. Think about it. We have the technology to replace your memories. I could replace your memory of everything that has happened, since right before you were rescued by Sora and Bahlam. You would have no memory of what you have seen and learned here at Caracol. I could adjust your neuroprocessor so that your time at the treatment facility would go very smoothly and raise no red flags. Conation would leave you alone, so you could go back to your normal life—at school, with your mom and Tia, with your friends, everything."

"Wow," I mutter. It's tempting.

"Life could go back to normal. You could finish high school, go to college, and do everything you had planned to do in life. As much as it pains me to say it, we could even adjust your neuroprocessor to dampen down your intuition—so that you wouldn't be as bothered by those feelings that there is more going on under the surface. You could blissfully carry on with your life." The weight of Harper's words hangs heavily in the air. "It's completely your choice, Ren, and your choice alone."

Wrinkling my forehead, I glance over at Itzamna. She nods reassuringly. "Yes. It is your choice, Ren."

Suddenly, without hesitation and with total clarity, I know. "I'm completely sure. I want to learn how to live free. I can't go back to a life based on a lie. It may not be for everyone, but I know I must try. The most important thing I've learned from all I've been through is that I need to trust myself. I can't rely on others to tell me what's best for me. I want my intuition to become stronger—and my Natural Self to come out. I can't do that unless I'm defused." In this moment, I realize that some part of me has been waiting for this my whole life.

"Okay! You seem very certain!" Harper exclaims.

"I am," I say confidently.

Itzamna gently pats my cheek. "Find me after." She opens the door of the Lab and slips outside.

Harper leads me to a long wooden table with hand-sewn cushions on top. I lie down while Harper wheels over some computer equipment and a medical tray. She places a paddle on the back of my neck and secures it in place with an elastic strap around my forehead. Then, Harper opens a sterile needle and begins to draw some liquid from a vile.

"Okay, Ren," she says. "This procedure takes about an hour. I'll be giving you two injections of a sedative—which we sometimes refer to as the neurochemical destabilizer. It's a formula your father created, and we've been perfecting for a few years."

"I received injections from the SED when they deep scanned my processor. Unfortunately, I'm an old pro, Harper."

"Oh no! Well, while there are some similarities to the substance the SED uses, this one produces a shorter-acting but deeper sedation, and actually begins the process of destabilizing the parts of the brain most affected by neuroprocessor manipulation—your identity and your ability to manage anxiety." I take a deep breath. I know this is what I want, but I'm scared. What will I be like when this is all over?

Harper continues, "After you're sedated, I'll send short, controlled bursts into your neuroprocessor. Essentially, we use the processor to lead us to the parts of your brain that need to be defused. I think it's both brilliant and ironic that we use the processor to defeat itself," she states, with pride. "Do you have any questions, Ren?"

"Will it hurt?"

"No, not at all. Are you ready?" I nod nervously. Harper injects the liquid into both sides of my neck and immediately a warm, hazy feeling courses through my body. The last thing I remember before falling asleep is seeing a reassuring look on Harper's face.

◆ ◆ ◆

Images race through my mind one after another—as if I'm watching a disjointed movie. I can see the streets and houses in my neighborhood. Then the word CONATION along with an open eye on the piece of paper in my locker at school appears. I observe Zian's face in the back window of my house, beckoning me to join him, which then morphs into Agent Rudy's angry face while I'm being strapped to a chair in his office, and he's holding a syringe. I can see the SED agents removing me from Aunt Bliss' vehicle and the fear in Charlene's eyes. Principal Chapman is now telling me about Uncle Patterson's death.

Next, Abi is standing over me, convincing me to go with her to the Presidential Compound. I witness images of President and Mrs. Coldstone's smiling faces, urging me to be a spokesperson for The Order. Dr. Bagai's face appears next, followed by the Presidential guards forcibly carrying me across the compound and tossing me into the back of a government car.

I can see the sneering faces of the guards driving me to the treatment facility. A masked Bahlam then pulls me from the government car and hoists me over his shoulder before setting me down in the back of the van. A hood is forced over my head and I lay powerless, struggling to breathe.

The movie in my head now shifts to a Natural village, but it's not Caracol. I'm walking toward the center of the village when I'm suddenly surrounded by three SED agents. One of them grabs my arm and says, "You need to come with us, Ms. Sterling." I spin out of his grip and dislocate his elbow in one fluid motion. He screams in pain and drops to his knees. I then kick another agent in the stomach. As he leans forward and grasps his midsection with both hands, I elbow him across the side of his face, breaking his jaw. The third agent grabs me around the neck and tries to wrestle me to the ground. I slip from his grasp and strike him in the throat. He falls in a heap alongside the other two. The first agent then pulls out a weapon, but before he can fire it, I kick him in the side of the head, knocking him unconscious.

I look up into the sky and feel my body being lifted into the air. Suddenly, black wings burst out of my back. I begin pumping them harder and harder until I'm high in the air. A raven appears in the sky ahead me and gestures for me to follow. We fly past Capital City and toward the mountains. As we begin to descend into the forest, I suddenly realize my wings have vanished, but I'm still flying with complete control. We approach a sunlit clearing in the trees, and the raven lands next to a familiar figure.

"DAD!" I scream and run into his arms the moment my feet touch the earth. He scoops me up and squeezes me tight. "You are the One, Ren. Resist The Order and lead the non-Naturals to freedom. Trust yourself. Trust your intuition," he whispers into my ear.

He releases me from his embrace, and I turn my head to look at the raven, but a smiling Itzamna is standing in its place. I turn my head back to Dad again, but his body has vanished, though his voice rings out, "I'll always be with you, Ren."

◆ ◆ ◆

"Ren." I open my eyes to see Harper staring down at me. "The procedure went perfectly. It couldn't have gone better," she says. I blink, disoriented and groggy.

My dad—he felt so close, so real. I wish I could hug him again. I reach for my shell necklace, and then my stomach twists. Gut-wrenching anxiety grips every inch of my body. I start shaking—I can't help myself.

"Here. Drink some yanavis tea," Harper offers. "It will help. Sit up."

I nod my head while she gently guides me, trembling, to a sitting position. Grasping the mug in my shaking hands, I take a few sips. It has an earthy, nutty flavor. I sip some more and feel myself begin to calm down. I can't get the images of all the times I've been manipulated and manhandled out of my mind. My Dad was right—I must resist.

"I'm done with being manipulated," I state forcefully. "And I don't ever want to be overpowered by anyone again. I need to learn how to fight and to resist The Order," I say as I hand the mug back to Harper and begin to slide off the table.

"Whoa... take it easy, Ren," Harper says, reaching out her hand to slow me down.

I gently push away her hand and stand. "I'm okay, Harper. This can't wait. Thank you so much for your help." I walk through the lab on wobbly legs, step outside, and then glance over to where Sora is taking a break from the class she's been teaching. Itzamna is standing by her side.

I stride purposely towards them. "Sora. Itzamna." They both look up at me, expectantly. "Will you help me? I need to learn how to fight," I declare, trembling.

Sora looks me up and down. "Yes... I will teach you how to defend yourself... to be a fighter."

Itzamna nods slowly, thoughtfully. "And I will teach you how to live free and to embrace your Natural Self... so you can be a teacher, and a leader of your people."

"When can I begin?" I ask eagerly.

Itzamna's eyes twinkle and her wrinkles deepen as she smiles. "You just did."

DISCUSSION TOPICS

NOTE: The Naturals do not represent any specific group. Although there are similarities with some Native American ideas/practices, the Naturals are intended to portray a non-specific Indigenous population as compared to dominant culture in this post-apocalyptic fantasy.

Sociocultural/Sociopolitical

1. To what extent do the four segments of The Order resemble people in your life? What segment would you and your family be placed in? What segment would you most and least want to be in? Why?

2. If you are in school, are the students in your school socio-economically diverse or do they mostly represent just a few segments?

3. The structure of The Order has contributed to a sharp reduction in crime and an improvement in the quality of life for most of the citizens, except for the Producers. How do you feel about the sacrifice of one segment for the betterment of the majority? How important is social and economic equality to you? How would you restructure The Order to incorporate social justice and equality?

4. Do you think that the government should have the right to download someone's memories if it helps solve crimes or stop terrorists? Ren wonders if trampling on individual freedoms and privacy undermines the shared values and trust of the citi-

zens. What do you think?

5. Dr. Bagai proposes that "while individual rights matter, they must be weighed against the need to maintain the system that works for everyone." She goes on to say that excessive focus on individual rights was a big part of the problem that led to the chaos and societal breakdown before The Order was instituted. What do you think is the proper balance between individual rights and sacrifice for the whole? When does an individual's rights become selfish and based on personal entitlement?

6. Individuals in The Order, especially women and people of color, are given the illusion of freedom while keeping them subservient to an oppressive system. What do you see as the differences between women's roles in The Order versus women in the Natural society?

Dreams
7. Do you tend to remember your dreams? What do you think is happening when you dream? What is the purpose of dreams?

8. Do you ever have lucid dreams, where you know you are dreaming while it is occurring? What is that like? What do you think lucid dreams could mean?

9. Have you ever had prophetic dreams? How have they affected your life? Have you been able to utilize this emerging intuition?

Philosophical/Psychological
10. Why does Ren feel simultaneously safe and anxious in her neighborhood? Do you ever have these seemingly contradictory feelings? When? What could the anxiety be trying to tell you? What does Ren mean when she says that her neighborhood doesn't feel *real*?

11. Consider the meaning of the word, Conation: an inclination

or impulse to act purposefully and intentionally; volition. Why does Ren feel anxious when she first learns the definition after seeing it in her locker? How often do you experience conation?

12. How often do you reflect on meaning in your life? Do these thoughts make you nervous and/or bring feelings of clarity?

13. Ren has a strong feeling that there is something more just under the surface of her life. What is she sensing? Do you sense this at times too?

14. Many people say that they can't live without their smart devices. Imagine what it would be like to have your smart device implanted in your body since birth and directed by your thoughts and eye movements. How do you think it would affect your day-to-day life as well as your sense of self in the world?

15. Zian asks Ren to turn off her neuroprocessor when they drive around to see new places. He says that he wants her to focus on her intuition, without distractions. How often do you listen to your intuition? How often is your phone or smart device a distraction that interferes with a connection to your intuition?

16. Ren tends to play the responsible role in her family while her sister is more self-focused. What roles do Ren's mother and Aunt Bliss play? What roles do you and other members of your family typically play?

17. Ren feels a great sense of purpose and contentment when she is planning the bicentennial celebration with Abi. Clear purpose and structure are often associated with positive feelings for many people. How and when do you feel purposeful in your life? How do you balance meaningful focus for a cause (e.g., school, sports, volunteering, work) with maintaining your individualistic sense of self and free time?

18. Zian says that Ren spends most of her time in her *zones of comfort.* What does he mean by this? What are your zones of comfort? How do you know when staying in the zones are helpful rather than restrictive in your life?

19. Throughout the book, the topics of choice and freedom come up. To what extent are any of us free? How much of your daily life do you intentionally choose? Conversely, how much of your life are you on autopilot, thinking and acting without conscious intention?

20. At several points in the story Ren is given the choice to return to her old life or take the uncertain and difficult path of learning more and striving for freedom. What would you have done if you were in her shoes?

21. In the last chapter Ren says that the most important thing she has learned is she needs to trust herself and not rely on others to tell her what is best for her. She also says she is done being manipulated and overpowered by others. How might the idea of self-empowerment be important in your life? How do you balance being open to others' ideas while staying true to yourself?

ACKNOWLEDGEMENT

I want to thank my wife, Joellyn, and our two amazing daughters, Madelyn and Mia. Thank you for your editorial guidance and for being the inspiration for Ren.

Thanks also to Bernie Johnson, Robin Bagai, Melissa Chernaik, and Emily Fagan for providing editorial and content feedback.

A special thanks to Jennifer Skyler for your invaluable support in developing the characters and building the dystopian world in Conation.

BOOKS BY THIS AUTHOR

Reclaiming Your Real Self: A Psychological And Spiritual Integration

Many of us struggle periodically with feelings of disconnection and meaninglessness in our lives. A life journey with sustainable meaning must include a connection with the essence of who we are, our Real Self. Our Real Self contains our inner wisdom and discernment as well as impulses for growth and creativity. This self-help book presents an integration of psychological concepts and spiritual themes in inclusive and engaging ways that invite readers to embrace a process of discovery and health.

Spirituality In Counseling And Psychotherapy

Although many clients want spiritual and philosophical issues to be addressed in therapy, many mental health professionals report that they are ill-equipped to meet clients' needs in this area. Providing a model that is approachable from a variety of theoretical orientations, this book supports therapists in becoming open to the unique ways that clients define, experience, and access life-affirming spiritual beliefs and practices. It also provides practical steps for integrating spirituality into psychotherapeutic process.

ABOUT THE AUTHOR

Rick Johnson

Rick Johnson, Ph.D., is a licensed Psychologist in private practice and a professor at Portland State University. His scholarly interests include the psychosocial development of young adults and the integration of psychological and philosophical/spiritual health. In his various roles as a teacher, psychotherapist, consultant, and author, Rick enjoys empowering others to connect with their own inner wisdom and intuition as a guide in their lives. He is married with two young adult daughters, who have inspired the writing of this book.

To connect with Rick, visit his website at RickJohnsonPhD.com.

Made in the USA
San Bernardino, CA
26 February 2020